"Your men are watching us."

Brett angled himself to shield Ginny from his crew's prying eyes. "Maybe we'd better kiss instead. Make this charade look real."

"No."

"No? We're supposed to seal an engagement, not a traffic citation."

Her deep, fortifying breath matched his own. "I hate it when you're right."

She pressed her lips together, zeroing in on his mouth.

Brett caught her chin in his palm and stroked his thumb across her lips. "Relax. I'll meet you halfway."

Ginny sank back as he lowered his head and re-placed his thumb with his mouth. The lower arc of her sweet lips trembled. Drawn to the tiny flutter of movement, Brett pressed the generous curve between his own lips.

Her lips barely moved.

Her hands were another story altogether.

Her fingers dug into his chest, then crept up to his shoulders, holding herself steady or holding him close, Brett couldn't tell. He wondered if she even knew.

Dear Harlequin Intrigue Reader,

Yet again we have a power-packed lineup of fantastic books for you this month, starting with the second story in the new Harlequin continuity series TRUEBLOOD, TEXAS. *Secret Bodyguard* by B.J. Daniels brings together an undercover cop and a mobster's daughter in a wary alliance in order to find her baby. But will they find a family together before all is said and done?

Ann Voss Peterson contributes another outstanding legal thriller to Harlequin Intrigue with *His Witness, Her Child*. Trust me, there's nothing sexier than a cowboy D.A. who's as tough as nails on criminals, yet is as tender as lamb's wool with women and children. Except…

One of Julie Miller's Taylor men! This month read about brother Brett Taylor in *Sudden Engagement*. Mystery, matchmaking—it's all part and parcel for any member of THE TAYLOR CLAN.

Finally, I'm thrilled to introduce you to Mallory Kane, who debuts at Harlequin Intrigue with *The Lawman Who Loved Her*. Hang on to your hat—and your heart. This story—and this hunky hero—will blow you away.

Round up all four! And be on the lookout next month for a *new* Harlequin Intrigue trilogy by Amanda Stevens called EDEN'S CHILDREN.

Happy reading,

Denise O'Sullivan
Associate Senior Editor
Harlequin Intrigue

SUDDEN ENGAGEMENT
JULIE MILLER

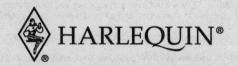

HARLEQUIN®

TORONTO • NEW YORK • LONDON
AMSTERDAM • PARIS • SYDNEY • HAMBURG
STOCKHOLM • ATHENS • TOKYO • MILAN • MADRID
PRAGUE • WARSAW • BUDAPEST • AUCKLAND

ISBN 0-373-22619-5

SUDDEN ENGAGEMENT

Copyright © 2001 by Julie Miller

Visit us at www.eHarlequin.com

Printed in U.S.A.

ABOUT THE AUTHOR

Julie Miller attributed her passion for writing romance to all those fairy tales she read growing up, and to shyness. Encouragement from her family to write down all those feelings she couldn't express became a love for the written word. She gets continued support from her fellow members of the Prairieland Romance Writers, where she serves as the resident "grammar goddess." This award-winning author and teacher has published several paranormal romances. Inspired by the likes of Agatha Christie and Encyclopedia Brown, Ms. Miller believes the only thing better than a good mystery is a good romance.

Born and raised in Missouri, she now lives in Nebraska with her husband, son and smiling guard dog, Maxie. Write to Julie at P.O. Box 5162, Grand Island, NE 68802-5162.

Books by Julie Miller

HARLEQUIN INTRIGUE
588—ONE GOOD MAN
613—SUDDEN ENGAGEMENT

THE TAYLOR CLAN

**Sid and Martha
Taylor:**   butcher and homemaker
ages 63 and 62 respectively

Brett Taylor: contractor
age 38
the protector

Mac Taylor: forensic specialist
age 37
the professor

Gideon Taylor: firefighter/arson investigator
age 35
the crusader

Cole Taylor: the mysterious brother (the
family's not quite sure what
kind of work he does—
undercover)
age 30
the lost soul

Jessie Taylor: the lone daughter
antiques dealer/buyer/restorer
age 29
the survivor

Josh Taylor: police officer
age 27
at 6'3", he's still the baby of the
family
the charmer

Mitch Taylor: Sid's nephew—raised like a son
police captain
age 39
the chief

CAST OF CHARACTERS

Detective Ginny Rafferty—As a rule, this headstrong cop works alone. So temporarily joining forces with her potently sexy "fiancé" is bound to wreak havoc on her steely self-control—and on her heart.

Brett Taylor—This neighborhood hero would do anything to protect his family or a friend. And he never forgets a promise, especially when it is made in the heat of passion to the woman he can't resist.

Sophie Bishop—She survived a treacherous past. But will she survive her future?

Eric Chamberlain—Attorney-at-law. Brett's high-school rival still wants to be #1.

Pearl and Ruby Jenkins—This mother and daughter have their sights set on Brett.

Dennis Fitzgerald—Ginny's attentive neighbor knows a lot more about her murder investigation than he's letting on.

Detective Merle Banning—Is Ginny's true-blue partner jealous of the new man in her life?

Zeke—Just another homeless guy. Or does his occasionally lucid mind hold a decade-old secret?

Amy Rafferty and Mark Bishop—These star-crossed lovers paid dearly for their dreams.

Alvin Bishop—The neighborhood bully finally got what he deserved. But who put him out of his misery?

Acknowledgments

I'd like to thank my two ace research assistants, who possess a lifetime of expertise on Kansas City, Missouri, and its history—aka Mom and Dad!

Dedication

This book is for the Mom's Group, especially my friends Linda Whitely and Lee Carter—because I promised.

Chapter One

"Brett. Over here."

Brett Taylor ducked beneath the yellow tape that marked off the condemned building as a crime scene. He took the concrete steps two at a time and joined his younger brother at the top.

Mac Taylor adjusted the wire-rimmed frames of his glasses, pulled off his plastic gloves and extended his hand to greet him. "I said I'd call you when I knew something. What are you doing here?"

Brett shook hands, then splayed his fingers on either side of his denim-clad hips. He looked down a couple of inches at his tall, fair-haired brother. "I'm saving the world. What does it look like?" He surveyed the team of men and women in black Kansas City Police Department jackets, who were swarming in and out of crumbling doorways and kicking up dust from the disintegrating brickwork. The old Ludlow Arms apartment building was an accident waiting to happen. Apparently one already had. "Your people know to watch their step, don't they?"

He crossed the entryway to a hole in the plaster. He glanced at the connecting struts within the wall, then reached inside and pried loose a rotting two-by-four. He turned and displayed the evidence of age and neglect for his brother. "This is one gal I can't fix."

"We understand 'structurally unsafe.'" Mac shook his head. "Though I still don't get the concept of buying this old place if all you're going to do is tear it down."

Brett wasn't sure he could explain the tricky combination of memories and guilt and dreams that had prompted him to take out a loan against his business to buy a block of dead buildings in his old neighborhood. "This old Victorian lady—" he said, giving the structure a feminine appellation like any devoted captain. He tilted his chin and cataloged the remains of the intricate molding that outlined the ceiling, appreciating their elegant curves the way he'd appreciate any woman's figure "—is beyond help. But I can turn the acreage into a pocket park to add value to the other sites I'm remodeling."

"You sure you can afford a project this size?"

"I have investors." Brett tossed aside the beam—and Mac's concern—and got down to business. "Now show me this dead body you found."

"Not me. A couple of homeless guys tried to camp out in the basement." He checked the notepad he carried. "A Zeke and a Charlie. No last names. Heard sounds in the walls. Thought the place was haunted. Went to check it out."

Brett laughed. "Yeah. Old Zeke's a war vet. The only enemy he's afraid of is the real world."

Mac nodded and led the way downstairs to the basement. "I guess. He called 911 and said he'd pulled a buddy from a foxhole."

Brett's admiration for the seventy-eight-year-old gave way to habitual worry. "I'm hoping to turn the old Walton Building into a shelter. Put in office space upstairs. Maybe we can get the therapists and clients in the same building and save a few bucks."

"You really are out to save the world," Mac teased.

"Just my corner of it."

Maybe this time he'd get it right.

The Ludlow Arms hadn't seen electricity for years, but the path was lit by a series of battery-powered lanterns, spaced evenly between puddles where the steady drizzle of rain leaked in. Even inside his red-and-white flannel shirt and thermal top, Brett felt the drop in temperature as they descended into the unheated darkness.

"You know this place has a subbasement?" asked Mac.

Brett trailed his hand along the cool concrete walls. The drowsy sunshine of early April would never penetrate this far. Layers of plaster dust and ancient dirt and moldy slime came away on his fingertips. He curled his fingers into his palm and crushed the sensation in his fist. This place was as dark and unwelcoming as it had been fifteen years ago when Mark Bishop had first brought him down here.

The best place to hide from my dad, he'd said with a laugh that hissed through his broken tooth and bloody lip. *Right beneath the old man's nose.* Brett had suggested the hospital emergency room as a better place to go after that fight. Mark had been little more than a kid then, an honorary little brother. But with no money and no insurance, with nothing but a young man's pride to sustain him, Mark had wanted to hide out down here. Brett had brought him ice, peroxide and some food for the night. Mark took strength from their friendship, and from the idea that his dad, Alvin Bishop, would never be smart enough or sober enough to find his way down to the basement.

If only he'd known.

"Brett?" Mac was staring at him in that quizzical way of his that questioned everything but revealed nothing.

He quickly pulled himself back to the present and processed Mac's question. "Yeah. It's on the old blueprints. This is one crazy lady," he added. "I wish I had more time to check out all the nooks and crannies. Abandoned dumbwaiter shafts, stairwells boarded over for remodeling."

Mac had stopped them at a trapdoor in the floor. His grim sigh put Brett on guard. ''I don't think this particular nook shows up on your blueprints.''

Wary, but equally intrigued, Brett climbed down the ladder after Mac. As his work boots hit the dirt floor, he inhaled sharply and winced. The air smelled stale. Cold and damp like a cave, with no circulating breeze to cleanse the heavy air.

The basement had been chilly. The subbasement raised goose bumps along his forearms. He adjusted his yellow hard hat on top of his head and gazed into the darkness made dim by Mac's flashlight and a lone stationary lantern. He followed him over to the collapsed section of bricks built up around the iron infrastructure of the building. Mac stepped aside and shined his flashlight into the closet-size hole.

The smell of rust and rot hit him a split second before he looked inside. He pulled his head back and spun around, cutting across the room with the calculated prowl of a caged animal. He swore low and viciously.

Mac remained cool and detached. A prerequisite for the kind of job he did, Brett knew, but still... He stopped in the center of the room and pointed toward the manmade hell-hole. ''Doesn't that make you sick? We grew up in this neighborhood. Stuff like that...''

Hell. He wasn't the eloquent one. He had no words for the gruesome sight, for the personal violation he felt at seeing a corpse like that in *his* building, in *his* community, in the place *his* friend had considered a haven.

''Stuff like that makes me angry, too,'' Mac conceded. But unlike Brett, he kept his emotions firmly in check. ''I have to ask you to delay demolition of the building until we're satisfied with the crime scene.''

Brett returned his hands to his hips and nodded. ''Any idea who? Or why? Or even how long he's been in there?''

"Obviously, we're beyond the fingerprint stage, so I won't have any ID for a while. I'm not even up to motive yet. And as far as time, the dampness down here accelerates decomposition. But, nobody's lived in this building for five years or so, right?"

"Eight years." Brett breathed in, needing fresh air. "Do you think he was alive?"

Mac's uncharacteristic hesitation snagged his full attention. "Yeah. I do."

Brett cursed the cruel inhumanity of the crime. He went to Mac and squeezed his shoulder, offering a degree of comfort he'd yet to find for himself. He'd been half joking about saving the world. He'd like to reclaim at least a part of it for his mother and father and younger siblings.

But maybe he was already too late.

"I'll hold the crews as long as you need me to." Taking charge came easily to him. And even though Mac was the expert here, he couldn't help but offer, "Anything else you need from me?"

Mac shook his head. "I know where to find you."

A reviving breath of fresh air soothed Brett's frustrated sense of justice. He turned to the creak of footsteps on the ladder, seeking the source of the delicate, flowery scent that drifted past his nose. It wasn't a specific perfume, but a clean fragrance, faintly scented like the purplish freesia plants his mother had cultivated to add color and freshness to the drab, overcrowded apartment where he'd grown up.

Mac moved into the light while Brett savored the memory. "Mac, have you figured out any details for us?" Brett snapped to attention at the familiar female voice sparkling with intelligence and clipped with professional patience. He remembered that voice. "What's this unauthorized civilian doing here?"

He smiled, knowing he was the cause of her accusatory tone. Mac urged him forward, out of the shadows. "Let me introduce you to the lead investigator on the case. Detective..."

"Ginny Rafferty."

Mac and the second man down the ladder looked at Brett, surprised by the recognition. But he had eyes only for the petite woman standing in the muted light of the lantern and flashlights.

Angelic wisps of white-gold hair, damp with rain, curled and clung to her jawline. Dark blue eyes, wide and clear as a cobalt pane in a stained-glass window, studied him without expression. She was a pint-size package of beautiful woman that didn't even reach his shoulders.

He remembered her.

Proper and preachy and stubborn enough to get under his skin like an itch he couldn't reach, Ginny Rafferty unsnapped the front of her jacket and fisted her hands on her slim hips, exposing the holster and badge clipped to her belt. Her proud, wary stance dared him to question her authority.

Oh yeah. He definitely remembered her.

His smile broadened a notch. "We've met."

"Yes. We shared guard duty of your cousin Mitch's wife before they were married. My boss called in all his favors to protect her from the man who assaulted her." She let the front of her jacket slide back into place, but her tiny body retained its stern posture. "As I recall, you cheat at Scrabble."

"Being a bad speller doesn't make me a cheater."

"No, but doing anything necessary to ensure a victory does make you annoying."

She walked past him, directing the beam of her flashlight into the hidden corners of the room. Mac laughed at the clear brush-off. "Yep, big brother. She knows you, all right."

She put on a pair of plastic gloves and knelt beside a dust-filled footprint. She measured it with her hand and made a notation in her notepad. "Anybody been down here today but the two of you?"

Mac, too, slipped into his professional mode. "The two men who found the body. The preliminary scan team. We've taken photos. Marked samples. It's slow going, though. This place is falling down around us and won't withstand a lot of traffic."

Ginny stood and flashed her light onto Brett. "So why don't we clear the crime scene before we disturb any more evidence."

"Brett knows the building inside and out. He can tell us where it's safe, and where it isn't. Besides, he knows more history about this neighborhood than city hall. I thought he'd be a good source of information. And, he can tell us about the construction of this wall."

Her blue eyes flashed with the same intensity as the powerful beam. "Nice defense, Mr. Taylor. I suppose you can stay."

Brett couldn't resist the challenge thrown up by her all-too-serious concession. "You missed me, didn't you?"

But she didn't rise to the taunt. Instead, she flashed her light past him to the second detective. "That's my partner, Merle Banning."

The trim, six-foot package of suspicion eyeballed him before shaking his hand. "Mr. Taylor."

"Everybody calls me Brett."

"I'll remember that, Mr. Taylor."

He wondered what he had said or done to earn the younger man's disapproval. This guy didn't look too far past the rookie stage. Maybe he was working on his tough-guy routine. He had the master champ to learn from in his partner. Brett backed off a step. "You do that."

"Is the body still here?" Ginny asked. Apparently, what passed for pleasantries had ended.

Mac swung his light around to the hole in the wall. "In there."

Ginny nodded, taking charge of the scene. Brett noted that his brother and her partner responded to her commands without hesitation. "Merle, you get Mac's report. Then see if you can track down the two gentlemen who found the body. I want their statements ASAP."

"Right."

A split second passed before Brett understood that the others were leaving. And Ginny was heading toward the corpse. An instinct to protect, a need to shield shot through him. His property, his emotional territory had already been violated by the gruesome scene behind that wall. No one else should have to see it. Especially not a lady. With a lineman's quick agility, he moved his big frame and blocked the opening. "Wait a minute. You can't go in there."

Ginny stopped at the broad expanse of red-and-white flannel. Damn the man! Couldn't he put his flirting on hold for two minutes?

"Mr. Taylor, let me pass." She looked up to add a practiced glare to the authoritative pitch of her voice. She gripped her toes inside her shoes to conquer the urge to take a step back. The teasing light that danced with perpetual humor in his eyes had disappeared behind a mask, cold and clear like the sapphire gems they resembled. He was sending her a silent message, telling her, warning...oh hell. She didn't understand the silent message.

She never could read men. Not on a personal level, at any rate. And this smooth-talking con artist, with the old-fashioned chivalric edge she'd discovered the last time their paths had crossed, really perplexed her.

So she did what she had always done when she felt at a disadvantage. She buried her emotions, sucked in a deep breath and pretended she had everything under control.

"Mr. Taylor," she repeated, glossing over the husky

catch in her voice, "I am a detective, first-grade, KCPD, assigned to the Special Investigations Unit. I'm here to look into a possible homicide. Right now, you're obstructing justice. I can have you arrested."

"Then do it." A hard chill had seeped into his chest-deep bass voice. "I'm trying to spare you a nightmare tonight, Detective."

He propped his hands at the waistband of his jeans, an inherently masculine pose that accentuated the breadth of his shoulders and the imposing girth of his biceps and forearms.

He was such a big man. But then, next to her, most of them were. She'd fought the good fight her entire adult life. At five-three, she'd barely made the cut to enter law enforcement. But her determination had made the difference.

Too pretty, too petite to be taken seriously in a man's world, she was used to having to prove herself. She trained harder, worked longer, studied more carefully than most of her male counterparts. She'd earned her badge, earned her rank and earned some respect.

But all that meant nothing each time she came up against a Wyatt Earp wannabe like Brett Taylor. A man who imagined himself to be a larger-than-life folktale hero, who still believed it was his mission to protect the little woman from the big bad world.

Acutely aware that he made up two of her, Ginny pocketed her flashlight and pulled out the one symbol of authority that most men *did* respect.

Her badge.

She jabbed it right at his chin, forcing him to turn his face to the side. "Move it, Taylor."

He swept his gaze from the badge down to her upturned face. Considering the amount of time she spent on her feet in this job, it had always seemed impractical to wear high heels. But right now, she'd trade that badge for a pair of three-inch pumps.

Control, she reminded herself. If she didn't feel, she couldn't be hurt. It always came down to staying in control.

She refused to even blink.

Brute strength finally bowed down to sheer will. With a tired sigh, he relaxed his stance and moved aside. "Don't say I didn't warn you."

Not allowing herself time to savor the small victory, Ginny clipped her badge to her belt and stepped inside the brick alcove. Darkness rushed at her, making her head spin. She squeezed her eyes shut against the dizzying sensation and struggled for a clear thought. She breathed in deeply, gagged on the stale air.

And then it hit her. She'd turned off her flashlight to haggle with Brett. Plunging her fingers into her pocket, she curled them around the reassuring bulk of stainless steel, the one weapon to fight her phobia. She pulled it out, flipped the switch on and opened her eyes.

"Oh God." The scene before her wasn't much better than what her fears had conjured.

Steel rivets bolted into the wall. Attached chains showing signs of rust from years of disuse in the damp air. A tiny stainless-steel bell hanging around his neck. Bony fingers clasping a chipped cup in its lifeless grasp.

Ginny snapped a mental picture, then tucked it away in a hidden corner of her mind to deal with later. She turned off her emotions and tuned in to logic and the power of her five senses.

She noted the partial decomposition of the body. The stale smell resulted as much from the lack of fresh air in the chamber as from the death itself. Even now, the faint crumbling sounds, showers of brick dust and dry mortar, told her the wall had been sealed together by an amateur. She ran her fingers along the original bricks. Age had taken its toll on the wood-and-iron framing down here, but the old masonry had stayed intact.

Kneeling down, she reached inside the skeletal fist and touched the china cup. The victim wasn't inclined to release it. Ginny set her flashlight on the floor beside her and angled the beam at the milk-colored porcelain trimmed in blue and gold. Touching only the inside of the cup with her gloved fingers, she lifted it from the floor and turned it, along with the hand, to read the pattern name on the bottom. *Liberty.*

"What's with the good china?" She spoke her thoughts aloud, wondering at the scenario of a man left for dead, yet being given something to eat or drink.

While she pondered, the cup slipped from her grasp. Ginny snatched at the falling arm, but as she shifted, she kicked her flashlight, jarring the electrical connection and plunging the tiny alcove into absolute darkness. The skeleton toppled onto its side, leaving only the sounds of the ringing bell and her pounding heart to keep her company in the darkness.

She squelched the instant panic with a useless trick she'd taught herself long ago. She squeezed her eyes shut, pretended the light was still there, pretended there were no enemies lurking in the dark, then groped through the shadows for the missing flashlight.

She touched Liberty Man's arm instead.

Her breath whooshed out as fear and memories won out over logic. She pushed to her feet and whirled around, seeking light, needing light.

She shot through the opening, her fist pressed tightly to her mouth. She would not scream. She would not let this beat her.

Quick, purposeful strides took her to the ladder. There, she latched onto the fourth rung and tilted her face into the lantern light filtering down from the floor above. Her shoulders rose and fell in rapid gasps.

"Gin, are you all right?"

Five gentle fingertips touched her shoulder and she jerked

away as if they'd singed her. Damn. She'd forgotten anyone was here. So dark. She'd forgotten. He'd seen her.

She dredged up enough voice to answer Brett. "I'm fine."

It wasn't her best lie, but she didn't care. She didn't owe him any explanation. She began to climb, attacking the rungs of the ladder as if the darkness itself pursued her. In her haste, she misjudged a step and slipped.

Instead of falling, twin vises caught her thighs. Big hands. Brett's hands. Long, strong fingers and supple palms that nearly spanned the circumference of each leg. Supporting her weight with effortless ease, he guided her feet back to the second rung.

"Easy." He crooned the warning in that cavernous voice. The sound of it skittered along her spine, sending soothing tendrils of comfort along her sparking nerve relays. She cursed her body's foolish reaction to the sound.

Once on solid footing, he released her. Ginny clung to the ladder and quieted her pulse. The imprint of warmth from his hands stayed with her, mocking her attempts to ignore him and don her detective facade once more.

"Claustrophobic?" he asked.

"No." She spun around and looked straight into eyes of sapphire blue.

He stood a bit too close. Close enough to see the stubble of dark brown beard shadowing his jaw. Close enough to smell the honest scent of wood and work on him. Brett was clearly a man who built things with his hands. It was evident in the outdoorsy tan of his skin, the rough rasp of his fingertips, the minuscule bits of sawdust that clung to the coffee-brown twists of hair that brushed his collar.

Years of practice made it possible for Ginny to note her observations without attributing any emotional or physical response to them. She cataloged her reaction to Brett the same way she cataloged her observations of a crime scene. "It's the—"

Ginny snapped her mouth shut. She couldn't let this man know her weakness. Her fears were her own to handle. She would not be made vulnerable. One of the ugliest aspects of her job—of her life—was seeing how cruel the world could be to anyone who was vulnerable.

Let him think the close quarters had gotten to her. A white lie would be better than the truth.

"Maybe a little."

He backed off a step. "Sorry to crowd you."

The considerate move surprised her. Maybe there was a touch of real hero beneath his thick, flirtatious veneer, after all.

"You work in construction, right?" she asked.

"Contractor. Run my own business." If he thought anything strange or rude in her abrupt change in topic, he didn't comment.

She let her gaze move past his shoulder to that shadowy void that reminded her of more than she cared to remember. "Can you tell me anything about that new wall? The one built to seal him in?"

She averted her gaze from the dark chasm. Some memories refused to die.

"Yes." He lifted his left hand in a timeless gesture of "ladies first." "But let's talk outside. I could use some fresh air."

Ginny recognized the gallant gesture for the excuse it was, but appreciated it anyway. She gave him a curt nod and climbed the ladder. The basement brightened into artificial twilight. And when she emerged on the front steps of the concrete stoop, she breathed in the mist-filled air like sunshine.

With her phobia behind her, Ginny could think clearly again. She'd been shaken by the darkness, that was all. Any traitorous response her body had had to Brett Taylor had simply been the result of humiliating fear. She was too smart to be attracted to a charmer like him. Way too smart.

This time, she heard the weight of his tread on the threshold and knew he stood behind her. She pulled out her pen and notebook, and turned to meet him. "So, Mr. Taylor, do you think you can tell approximately when that alcove was built? And can you verify that it was built by a nonexpert? The mortar seemed to be inferior grade, falling apart. Maybe it wasn't mixed together properly."

He answered her questions with a laugh. "You are one tough cookie, aren't you."

Ginny lifted her gaze with a stern look that only seemed to fuel his good humor. "The term 'cookie' went out with girdles and seamed stockings. You can call me Ms. Rafferty or Detective."

He sputtered as he struggled to contain his laughter. "You can call me Brett."

"I don't have to call you at all."

He jabbed a finger in the air at her. "That's it. That's the voice."

"What are you talking about?"

His hands settled on his hips. "That tone of voice you get that says you are too tough to care. The one that could lay out a platoon of soldiers at fifty yards."

"If you're referring to the tone of authority…"

"I'm referring to the show you think you have to put on for people to take you seriously."

Ginny's confusion puffed out on an abrupt sigh. "Excuse me?"

"All you have to do is talk to me." He leaned toward her, his height putting him head and shoulders above her. She tilted her face to maintain eye contact. He never stepped closer, never touched her. Yet she felt the breadth and power of him surrounding her, as if he hovered above her, circled around her. A show of force? Or a shield of protection? "You don't have to talk down to me."

For a rare instant in time, she stood speechless. No clever zinger sprang to mind, no command seemed appropriate. No one had ever complained about her professional demeanor before. She never meant to be insulting. Damn him, anyway, for taking a criminal investigation and turning it into something personal.

With a surprising degree of decorum, Brett was the first to resume business as usual. He reached into the back pocket of his jeans and pulled out his wallet. He slid out a business card and pressed it into her hand.

"Here's my card. Call me if you need anything, or you find out something. I have a great deal of money and time and history invested in the Ludlow."

His odd statement triggered her curiosity, overrode her self-conscious habit of feigning emotional control. "History? What do you mean?"

The look that darkened his face revealed Brett Taylor wasn't all fun and games. But the grim expression was fleeting. He smiled once more, a handsome crease that formed dimples on either side of his mouth. Ginny wondered if, in her own hypercritical state, she had imagined his quick revelation of sorrow. But he gave no explanation.

"In answer to your questions about the wall, I'd say it was put up ten, twelve years ago. And yes, the mortar work was amateurish. Maybe done in haste, maybe done by someone who didn't know any better."

She jotted down the information, too dutiful a cop to do otherwise, but her attention remained focused on his previous cryptic words. "You didn't answer my question. What history are you talking about with the Ludlow? Is it related to the murder?"

"No. It's just that…" He stuffed his wallet into his back pocket. Ginny recognized the procrastination of buying time before an unpleasant task. But to his credit, he looked her straight in the eye before answering.

"That's not the first dead body I've seen at the Ludlow Arms."

Chapter Two

"Got a new case?"

Ginny Rafferty turned to the cemetery's caretaker and nodded. The chocolate-brown eyes set deep in the wrinkles of the African-American man's face looked as old as she felt. "It's that obvious, John?"

With his hands shoved deep into the pockets of his coveralls, he twisted his face into a sympathetic frown. "You make this pilgrimage out here every time you take on an unsolved murder."

She turned back to the pink granite headstone, with the name Rafferty engraved upon it. "Maybe once I can solve all the rest of them, I'll get a chance to finally solve hers."

More than a casual acquaintance, John McBride shared a sad, unique bond with Ginny. He might be one of the few people who understood her need to come to this remote haven nestled between busy Truman Road and Twenty-four Highway time and time again. He shrugged his shoulders and offered a fatherly smile. "It's gettin' dark. I'll have to close the gates soon."

"Give me a couple of minutes. Then I'll ride down with you."

"Sure."

She watched him walk down the hill to his truck, his dignity unbowed by age or sorrow. Everyone coped with loss in his or her own way. Maybe one day she'd move beyond hers and find the acceptance that John seemed to have found.

Until then, she'd maintain her solitary vigil. She'd hang on to the love and loyalty she'd once forsaken in the pursuit of her own misguided dreams. The chilly spring rain drizzled along her cheeks, side by side with the single tear that scorched her skin.

The trees that surrounded the hills of Mount Washington Cemetery muffled the sounds of Kansas City at twilight. The haunting silence wrapped her up in its lonely hug, a small comfort for all she had lost.

She understood that the rest of the world moved on, despite her grief. Despite her guilt. But part of her would never understand why.

Twelve years had passed. And she still didn't understand.

John had become the closest thing she had to a friend over the years. They'd first met the day of her sister's funeral. He'd been kind enough to let her stay, long after the funeral had ended, long after the guests had departed to a reception at her parents' Mission Hills home.

She'd been gone a year and a half before that, painting in Europe, losing her heart, learning some harsh truths about life, while Amy learned a harsh truth of her own on a deserted pier in downtown Kansas City.

Like this evening, John had waited with her until after dark the night of Amy's funeral. Then he called for a taxi and paid her fare, even though she had money of her own.

Six months later, she'd lost her mother to a bottleful of the sedatives that were meant to help her cope with the loss of a child. John had been a good friend that day, too. She had needed one. With her father steeped in grief, Ginny had withdrawn to the fringes of the ceremony. An easy enough task for a shy creature like herself. She took a vow that day, made a promise to her sister and her mother. Planned her own quiet rebellion.

John had found her then, much as she was today, standing in the rain, swearing all kinds of vengeance on the world. He'd told her of his son, an officer in the State Highway Patrol, who'd been slain in the line of duty. He shared his feelings of pride and mourning for his brave son. He truly understood her anger and her loss.

And he inspired her.

She'd met John again last year, finally losing her father to an overworked heart, though emotionally, she'd lost him years earlier. Her parents had never been the same after Amy's senseless murder. Ginny was a grown woman now— no grief-stricken teen, no rebellious coed—a mature career woman of thirty.

She'd willingly given up her scholarship to study art in Europe and enrolled in the justice studies program at Central Missouri State University in nearby Warrensburg. She'd taken care of her father, and now she took care of Kansas City, Missouri, too.

She sought justice for the innocent victims like her sister. Like her mother and father. And like that poor man this afternoon, buried alive and left to die.

Like a family reunion of battle-scarred survivors, she and John now met at the start of every new case. Each time, he waited patiently to drive her to her car at the front gates. And each time, she made the same promise to her sister and parents.

She spread her palm flat over the cold granite that bore her family's names and recited her vow. "I'll find out who did this to us. There will be justice for the Raffertys."

She curled her fingertips into the grooves cut deep into the stone.

"I promise."

Ginny headed down the hill toward the road. Her charcoal-gray chinos, damp from a day's worth of rain, stuck to her legs like a second skin and chilled her. The warmth of John's truck sounded pretty inviting right about now. She really ought to make an effort to cultivate his friendship. He'd always been so kind. But she'd never been very good at that sort of thing. Making friends had always been Amy's forte. Some day soon—tonight, maybe—she'd overlook her insecurities and take him out to dinner.

Well, maybe not tonight. A telltale chirping vibrated at her hip. Stopping beside the road, she pulled out her cell phone and flipped it open.

"Detective Rafferty."

"Yeah, Gin. It's Merle." She turned her face away from the phone to mask her weary sigh. She and her partner had been on the clock since eight that morning. How could he still sound energetic nearly eleven hours later?

"What's up?" she asked.

"I got a name on that murder at the Ludlow you asked about. Back in 1989. An eighteen-year-old kid named Mark Bishop."

That's not the first dead body I've seen at the Ludlow Arms.

Ginny's own energy kicked up a notch. "Was that case solved?"

Merle spoke as if he was reading the information straight off his computer screen. "History of family violence. Died from a blow to the head. The death was attributed to his father, Alvin Bishop. Neighborhood bully. He had a record of abuse and neglect with Social Services, and a string of minor convictions. Everything from drunk and disorderly to assault on the garbage collector."

"But no charges were filed?" She sensed more unfinished business.

"A warrant was issued for the father's arrest. But he disappeared before his arraignment. Listed as a missing person ever since.''

"So justice was never served." Either pieces of the puzzle were beginning to fall into place, or she'd opened a box with more pieces than she could count. That body at the morgue could be Alvin Bishop. "Get Mac Taylor at forensics on the line. Tell him to run Bishop's name through as a possible ID on our John Doe."

"Will do."

"Anything else?"

"Yeah." A twinge of frustration colored his voice. "The statements I took from those two homeless guys, Zeke Jones and Charlie Adkins, are useless."

His frustration just became hers, too. "They didn't see anything?"

"Who knows? Charlie said nothing, just sat there staring at me. Zeke kept spouting off his name, rank and serial number. I thought I was in the twilight zone."

Sometimes, witnesses saw a male detective as a threatening presence, and were more apt to open up to a female. She hoped that, and not one of the mental disorders that affected some homeless people, was the case with these guys. "I'll give it a shot tomorrow."

"Thanks. I'll get you the address for the shelter where I sent them." She was just about to hang up when she heard Merle call her name. "Hey, Gin?"

She put the phone back to her ear. "Yeah?"

"You have dinner plans?" Ginny rolled her eyes heavenward at the sincere catch in his voice.

She pictured his sweet, unlined face and the gradual aging she saw day by day in his dark green eyes. This wasn't the first time he'd asked her out. It wouldn't be the first time she said no, either. "You know how I feel about going out with the men I work with."

His voice rushed over the line. "Hey, no. I'm your partner, I'm just worried about you. We missed lunch, remember?''

"I remember." She forced a smile, as if he could see her relief. "I'll get something to eat, don't worry. You get out of that office, too, okay?"

"I will."

"Good night, Merle."

"'Night, Gin."

She hung up and dug inside another pocket for a specific slip of paper. A business card. Taylor Construction, Brett Taylor, Owner.

She looked at the card and pictured the man. Big. Rugged. Smart-mouthed. "Do you always show up when there's a dead body in the neighborhood?" she asked the image.

Memorizing the number, she hurried to John's truck and dialed before climbing in.

John spared her an indulgent smile before putting the truck in gear. "Duty calls, I take it."

She nodded through the unanswered rings. "I've got an opportunity to ask a few questions I shouldn't put off."

He wound through the hairpin turns toward the cemetery's front gates. "One of these days I want you to tell me you're in a hurry to meet a young man."

She smiled. "John, you sound just like my dad."

An answering machine picked up. Brett himself had left the recording. Even across transmitted miles of a recorded message, Brett's basso profundo voice reverberated through her like a mellow jazz tune, at once enervating and intriguing her.

She asked him to call her cell number and then hung up.

"Just like that." John's amused voice captured her attention.

"What?"

He shook a gentle finger at her. "The look on your face

when you talked to that man. That's the look that tells me you've got a social life.''

Ginny frowned. "I talked to his machine."

He pulled up behind her car and put the truck in Park. "But you're wishing it was the real thing."

"Please." Brett Taylor? Social life? Neither phrase was part of her regular vocabulary. "He's a possible material witness to a murder case, nothing more."

"If you say so."

"I say so." Her protest sounded vehement, even to her own ears. She tried to come up with a plausible explanation. For John. "Look, I don't really date much. I'm too caught up in my work."

"It's important work you do," he said in a voice of sage experience. "But it isn't everything."

For her, it had to be. Relationships were too awkward for her. Many men were threatened by the nature of her job, her devotion to duty. More men lacked the patience to work through her eccentricities, and she'd never developed those most feminine skills that could encourage a man to make the journey with her.

And if she should ever meet a man with the patience and fortitude and self-assurance to withstand a relationship with her, she'd run away as fast as she could. She would never put herself in the position of losing someone she cared about again.

Maybe John understood that, after all. His weary silence revealed a man who had lived more life than most people his age. He surprised her by reaching across the seat and squeezing her hand. "Don't take this the wrong way, but I hope I don't see you again very soon."

She squeezed back, understanding. "Me neither."

BRETT PACED the small confines of his office, turning the mouthpiece away from his impatient sigh while one of his investors grilled him for information about the story he'd seen on the local evening news.

"The Ludlow's still going to be renovated, right, Brett?"

Brett righted the phone. "No, Mr. Dennehy. That's the one we're tearing down, remember? The other buildings are structurally sound. But not the Ludlow Arms."

"It was home to a lot of people, you know."

The older man's wistful tone added another rock onto the load of responsibility Brett carried on his shoulders. "I know, sir. Hopefully the refurbished buildings will draw quality tenants like yourself."

Bill Dennehy perked up as a new thought hit him. "Do you think that body was in the basement when Alice and I were living there?"

"I don't think so." Bill had been lucky enough to live in the Ludlow Arms during the building's heyday. He knew these streets the way Brett's grandparents had known it. Thriving. Friendly. Safe. "Trust me. A little bad press isn't going to stop me from renovating the neighborhood."

"Alice won't come to that fund-raiser of yours if there's any more news like this."

"Of course not, but…"

He felt a tap at his shoulder and stopped midprotest. Five perfectly shaped, copper-tinted nails reached for the phone. His gaze dropped to the half-amused smile on the mouth of the tall brunette beside him.

"I'll handle this. You pace." She nudged Brett to one side and turned her attention to the caller. "Mr. Dennehy. Sophie Bishop. Yes, I remember you from the old neighborhood…"

Brett's frustration turned to admiration as he watched his old friend work Bill Dennehy through a trip down memory lane and onto the road toward a charitable donation. He sat back in the chair behind his desk and watched her do her thing.

He'd hired Sophie for her expertise in fund-raising and public relations. He could only afford to pay her peanuts, but she'd been quick to volunteer her time. She, too, came from the Market Street area of Kansas City, and seemed as eager to see a rebirth of the community as he was.

Things were a little awkward between them, but he hoped she'd moved past their broken relationship. No longer the adoring young college student he'd once dated as a favor to her brother, she'd matured into a powerful, successful woman of the world. And she put her money where her work was. Sophie had been the first to sign up for one of the luxury condos he planned to put in the Peabody Building. Surely that kind of support was proof that they could still work together as old friends.

"Mr. Dennehy, that's sweet." It wasn't as if Sophie had to be any man's charity date. With long, shapely legs that stopped somewhere just short of her neck, and the sleek, sculpted features of a fashion model, she'd draw any man's attention. But Brett looked at her and saw…Mark's sister.

His feelings for her weren't all that different from what he felt for his own sister, Jessie. Just as strong, just as protective, just as pure.

He rolled his chair up to the desk and leaned his elbows on top, watching with pride and gratitude as she smoothed over the investor's concern. "I'll be sure we have a corsage for her at the fund-raising ball. I look forward to seeing you and Mrs. Dennehy there. Bye now."

She pressed the off button and handed over the phone with a flourish that made Brett throw his hands up in surrender. "Okay, so you saved my butt. Go ahead and gloat."

"I'm just doing my job, big boy," she laughed. She perched on the corner of his desk and tugged the hem of her taupe silk suit down to within inches of her knees. Brett sat back and waited for the rebuke. "Next time there's a publicity glitch like this, call me. Don't wait for me to see it on the evening news.''

"He was my third call tonight."

Sophie shook her head, making light of his doubt. "We can use this in our favor. Murder's the kind of thing that *used* to happen in this neighborhood. But no more. Not with Brett Taylor on the job, transforming the dark alleys and dangerous streets into a place where families can work and kids can play."

Brett frowned and pushed to his feet, uncomfortable with the heroic status, even if it was said in a teasing vein. He walked around the desk and picked up her cashmere stole. "You'd better hit the road. I'm keeping you from your date."

Sophie grabbed her purse and joined him. She turned her back to him and let him wrap her shoulders in the oversize scarf. He closed his arms briefly in a friendly hug. "Thanks, kiddo. I owe you one."

"I know. I'm keeping tabs." A knock on the office door gave Brett the excuse to pull away. Sophie used the opportunity to pull on a pair of leather driving gloves. "Expecting any reporters?"

"No." Maybe he was looking forward to this next visitor just a little too much. Heedless that Sophie followed him, he hurried through the outer office and opened the trailer door.

Ginny Rafferty stood outside. The harsh glare of the porch light softened in the silver shimmer of her hair. He released his anxiety on a single breath and let his features relax into a genuine smile. Her crossed arms bespoke all business, but he appreciated her sunny beauty like a breath of fresh air. And the challenging glint in those cobalt eyes stirred his thoughts away from spooked investors and a budget that wouldn't balance.

"You said to meet you here," she said in greeting.

Those blue eyes shuttered and darted to the side before he heard the voice beside him. "Brett?"

He stepped back, feeling ridiculously jarred by Sophie's intrusion. The contrast between the two women rendered him silent for a moment. Tall and petite. Dark and fair. Smiling expectantly and expressionless.

Fortunately, Sophie had the sense to see him past the awkward moment. She extended her hand in polite greeting. "I'm Sophie Bishop, an old friend of Brett's."

Ginny shook hands. "I'm Ginny Rafferty. I'm a—"

"New friend," he interrupted before she could rattle off her official job and title. Sophie had done enough for one night. He didn't need her to run interference for a police investigation. He didn't want anyone to interfere with a chance to talk to Ginny. "Soph does public relations for me."

"I see," said Ginny.

"Well…" Sophie smiled and excused herself. "I'd best not keep Eric waiting. I'll call you in the morning to touch base." With a tilt of her chin, she leaned in and kissed Brett's cheek, then wiped the spot with her thumb as if she had left a mark of lipstick. "Good night."

"Good night." Brett squeezed her arm affectionately, and watched her until she climbed into her car and pulled away from the curb.

Only then did he realize that Ginny was still standing on the porch, waiting to be invited in. Brett wiped at his cheek, as if Sophie's kiss was still visible, and concentrated on the woman before him. He stepped aside and held the door open for her. "Ms. Rafferty."

He rolled her name around his tongue like a piece of candy. He ought to be on a first-name basis with this woman, call her Gin—or Angel, a compliment to her looks she wouldn't want to hear.

At least, not from him.

As she stepped over the threshold, he noted the trappings of her trade, a blue plaid blazer that masked the bulk of a gun and badge at her waist. When she walked past him, tantalizing as a breeze of fresh air, he noticed her stiff posture and the cool expression on her face.

He set aside the inexplicable desire to hear her loosen up and laugh just once, and followed her into his office. He hadn't worried about the mess before with Sophie. But when Ginny picked up an untouched sack of fast food off the chair, he wished he'd taken time to clean up the place.

She dangled the bag between her thumb and middle finger, eyeing the grease spot that had soaked through the brown paper. "Did I interrupt dinner?"

"That was lunch." He took the bag from her to throw away—once he located the trash can. He spotted it, supporting one corner of the scale model of the revamped city block where the Ludlow, Walton and Peabody Buildings sat. "Yesterday's."

She perched on the very edge of the chair once it had been cleared. He lifted a corner of plywood and ditched the day-old food.

"Do you spend a lot of time in your office?" she asked. He could almost read the phrase *bachelor pad* on her lips, and wished he could show her the clean, uncluttered space of his condo that he'd designed and remodeled himself in a nearby warehouse.

He pulled out his own chair and sat across the desk from her. So it was to be strictly business between them. Again. Thinking of the waste of those beautiful, expressive eyes of hers, when they could be sparkling with laughter or drowsy with passion instead of so cold with single-minded determination, he tried to accommodate. "I do the paperwork here. But mostly I'm out on the work sites. Lately, I've been conned into attending some fund-raising events. I'm working toward three million to rebuild the Ludlow block the way I want to."

"Three million, hmm?" Her ever-watchful eyes continued to scan the office. "I think you'd be a natural at schmoozing people for money."

Ouch. Though the comment was superficially complimentary, her tone of voice gave her words a condemning twist.

Feeling the unjust sting of failure, he pushed to his feet and circled the desk. He couldn't let her taunt—intentional or otherwise—go unchallenged. He shoved aside a stack of bills and sat on the edge, right in front of her. Close enough that his knee brushed hers when he crossed his legs at the ankle. He ignored the traitorous rush of heat that shot toward his toes at that slightest of contacts. He crossed his arms in front of his chest and flexed his muscles in his most intimidating display of force.

"I'm doing a good deed here, angel. At best, I'll break even. Any profit I might end up with will be reinvested in future projects to improve the neighborhood."

Undaunted by his face-saving attack, she tipped her chin and looked straight up into his eyes. "You seem to have several projects in mind, Mr. Taylor. You're quite the philanthropist. How much money have you raised so far?"

Damn, she was a cool customer. Instead of taking offense, the blood surged through Brett's veins at her show of strength. Why the hell did he have to get twisted up inside over this pint-size bundle of woman who was all backbone and beautiful eyes? He was a healthy male, more than decently attractive, according to the women he'd dated. He knew his manners and how to make a woman laugh.

And yet this one, Ginny Rafferty, with the Nordic looks and Arctic demeanor, got under his skin. The one woman whose only interest in him applied to whatever information he could give her in a murder investigation, fascinated the hell out of him.

He liked the challenge of sparring with her. He'd like it even better if he knew this battle of wills was leading someplace interesting. "We're halfway there. We've pledged about one million in donations. And I put up half a million of my own money."

"Really."

One elegant eyebrow, a darker shade of blond than her silvery hair, arched above her skeptical gaze. He felt her scrutiny from the shoulders of his worn flannel shirt to the toes of his scuffed work boots. He seemed to fall short, in her opinion, judging by the doubt etched on her face, an observation that rankled his male ego. He'd butted heads with beautiful women before, and had never failed to charm his way into their good graces.

But Ginny was different. She didn't play the game at which he excelled. With her, the battle of wills was for real.

Brett couldn't help but defend himself. "My business is successful."

"I wasn't accusing you of lying."

"Then what *are* you accusing me of?"

His taunt seemed to strike a nerve in her. She averted her face and blew out her breath on a long sigh. In the space of a heartbeat, Brett's adversarial instincts switched to an uncomfortable mix of guilt and concern. She rose to her feet, a coordinated series of movements blending grace and control.

Regretting his self-serving need to strike back, to assert himself, Brett chose to remain seated. She stood beside him, not quite face-to-face, and he could see the ultrafine spiderweb of bluish veins beneath the pale porcelain of her skin.

He curled his fingers into his palms, combatting the urge to touch her, to see if her cheek was as smooth and soft and fragile as it looked. He'd forgotten her job for the moment, given vent to his frustration. He'd simply reacted. Without much thought or consideration of the consequences.

"How much do you stand to lose if the Ludlow project fails?" She didn't look at him until she'd finished the question.

When he turned his face to her, he nearly sank to the floor. Eye-to-eye, mere inches away, he felt the gentle heat of her reaching out to him like a tentative caress.

He must be tired and imagining things, he thought. He'd seen those eyes cool and blank. He'd seen them wide and dark with fear.

But he'd never seen them as he did now. The tiniest of frowns made a shallow dent between her eyebrows, and her eyes gleamed with a warmth that reminded him of sunshine streaming in through a stained-glass window.

The uncustomary openness in her expression triggered an unexpected response inside him, a desire to be equally frank, without sugarcoating the truth with a smile or a clever joke.

"I could lose my shirt, if I'm not careful. If this project fails and I have to repay my investors on top of the accumulated debt, I'll go bankrupt. Taylor Construction would be no more."

"What about your personal assets?"

His family suspected he was in this building campaign up to his eyeballs, but he'd never shared the extent of what he had laid on the table to make this reclamation project happen. But alone in his office with the bright-eyed detective, the words spilled out. "I could lose everything."

She uttered a sound like a gasp of disbelief, then turned and paced to the far end of the room. When she spun around, Brett sat up straighter. That brief glimpse of compassion he'd imagined had vanished. She was primed for battle again.

"Then why do this? Why not take the renovation one building at a time?"

He took the offensive, standing and bracing his hands on his hips. "Are you investigating me or the murder?"

"This is personal for you, isn't it?" She walked closer, each step a brick of suspicion building against him on some unknown case. "Does this have anything to do with Mark Bishop's death?"

Brett turned his face to the ceiling and swore. When he looked at her again, he didn't bother softening the blow. She hadn't pulled any punches, and neither would he. "You got a lot of nerve, lady."

"I understand Mark Bishop was a friend of yours."

He shook his head, admiring her gall, if not her choice of topic. "That woman you just met was his sister. The Bishops were like family to me." A defensive edge slipped into his voice. He didn't try to mask it. "I met Mark through the Big Brother program. He was a good kid who needed a break. I tried to give him one."

"What can you tell me about his death?"

"Somebody beat the hell out of him, then left him without any medical attention. Why do you want to know?"

"That body in the basement could be Mark and Sophie's father, Alvin Bishop."

"Hell." He collapsed back onto the desk. "Are you sure?"

"I don't have the forensics yet, but the timeline fits. It's a possibility."

It seemed impossible. To hear that name again. Twelve years after the man got away with murder...or maybe he hadn't, after all. Brett looked Ginny square in the eye. Her phone message had said she wanted to discuss the case. But which one?

He schooled what was left of his patience and asked, "Just what is it you want from me?"

"Do you have any idea who'd want to kill Alvin Bishop?"

"Me, for one."

"Brett."

He liked the sound of his name in her crisp, clean voice, even if it was couched in a reprimand. But she'd made it more than clear that he was just a means to an end of a case for her. Keeping that sobering thought in mind, he answered, "Just about anybody in town back then. He wasn't a nice guy."

She moved a step closer, folding her hands together and beseeching him in an unconscious gesture that he found difficult to ignore. "Mac says you know more about the neighborhood's history than anyone. Records about the Ludlow tenants are sketchy and outdated. Do you think you could give me some specifics?"

The intelligent gleam in those dark blue eyes never wavered. "You're serious, aren't you?"

"I'm investigating a murder. I'm always serious."

He could see that. "All right, then. But not on an empty stomach." Her challenge galvanized him. Shoving himself to his feet, he grabbed his keys from the desk and strode toward the door. "I haven't eaten since breakfast, and it's past nine o'clock. I need to fuel up if I'm going to do this right."

Ginny hurried after him in quicker, shorter strides. "What do you mean?"

He shrugged his shoulders. "I mean I'm hungry. I'm going to go eat."

"Now?"

He pushed the door and held it open for her, amused by the incredulity of her question. Once she was outside, he closed and locked it behind him. "That's the general idea."

He heard a rapid rush of air behind him. "I'm just getting started. There's more I need to ask."

"I figured you'd come with me."

He swept his arm out, indicating she precede him down the stairs. Instead, she took a step back against the iron railing. Maybe it was a trick of the overhead light, but her already fair skin blanched to an unhealthy shade of pale.

Brett reached out and touched her shoulder. "You all right?"

For an instant, time suspended itself between them. But before he could question her jumpy reaction, Ginny shrugged away his fingers and bolted down the steps. He could tell by her hushed tones that she'd dropped him from the conversation. "I'll look up the names of some of the longtime residents of this part of the city. Maybe I can get them to talk. Forensics alone won't tell me why that man was buried alive."

"Time out." He caught up to her in three long strides, and coiled his hand around her upper arm, holding on when she would have pulled away again. "I didn't say anything about not talking. You stirred up some ghosts when you mentioned Mark and Alvin Bishop. I want to be sure I'm thinking clearly. I don't want to make a mistake about either death."

Beneath the coiled tension of sleek muscles, he felt…trembling. He glanced from his hand up into the smooth perfection of her face. Cool and rock-solid as always, she revealed no emotion. But the fine tremors didn't lie. Something made her nervous. Had he startled her? Or was it the fact that he refused to let go?

He was torn between putting her at ease and demanding to know why she'd so easily dismiss his help. Conscience beat curiosity.

"Look, my uncle was a cop. My cousin Mitch, your boss, is captain of the local precinct. I have three brothers who are in law enforcement or criminal investigation. A fourth who used to be. It'd be suicide at family reunions if I didn't help a cop when she asked me."

No laugh.

Shrugging off his inability to coax even a smile from her,

he released her. She backed off a step and buried her hands in the pockets of her blazer.

''The older a case is, the harder it is to solve,'' she said, as if explaining her aversion to his touch. ''If I don't have your full cooperation, then this is pointless.''

''We'll find out the truth. Together.''

With the challenge hanging in the air, he dared her to retreat a third time. Her gaze darted from the sidewalk to her car and back to the middle of his chest. ''All right. We'll eat.''

He rewarded her hard-won agreement with a smile, overlooking the bothersome observation that she hadn't looked him in the eye. ''There's a diner on the next block. Since the rain stopped, we can walk.'' Keeping a comfortable distance between them, Brett headed for the corner, shortening his stride so Ginny didn't have to pump her legs in double time to keep up.

''I suppose it makes good sense.'' She seemed intent on reasoning this out. ''I need background. You need to eat. We can combine both and save some time.''

''See? It's a good plan all round. Not bad for an arrogant bozo like me, huh?''

''I didn't say…''

He sensed the snap of her head as she looked up at him. He came to an abrupt stop and turned. Whatever she was about to say died on her lips when their gazes met. She didn't know he'd been teasing! She would have defended him against the self-mocking insult.

Big bad Brett Taylor, neighborhood hero and resident handyman, had always taken care of himself and those around him. To know this dainty bit of curves and confidence had been willing to do the same for him warmed a chilly place inside he hadn't acknowledged for a long time. Ginny Rafferty wasn't quite the all-business woman who fascinated him. She was human. The woman was as much of a mystery as the cases she worked to solve.

Reaching an unspoken truce of sorts, he checked for traffic, took her by the elbow and crossed the street with her. He released her as soon as they were safely across. "If we can prove that old man Bishop finally got what he deserved, I'll answer any question you have, as many times as you want to hear it. There are plenty of folks around here who would love to know the truth."

"One thing I've learned, working homicide..." He glanced down to see the wry wisdom in her voice reflected in the expression on her pretty face. "There's always one person who doesn't want you to find out the truth."

Chapter Three

Ginny halted, a French fry halfway to her mouth, as Brett launched into his second burger with the works. He hadn't been kidding when he said he needed to fuel up. She'd never seen a man pack away food the way he did, with such relish, such fulfillment.

For all his brawn, he had a connoisseur's palate, an artiste's demeanor, savoring the textures of meat and grain, appreciating the tastes both rich and mild. She likened the expression on his face to what she'd felt at the Jeu de Paume museum at the Louvre in Paris when she'd seen the perfection of color in Claude Monet's paintings with her own eyes.

The word *sensual* sprang to mind as she watched him. And just as quickly, she squashed it. She was here for necessary sustenance and to ask questions. Not to observe and evaluate the grace and gusto of Brett Taylor.

He towered over her by more than a foot, putting him at six-four or five, and maybe two-twenty, two hundred thirty pounds. As a big man, he had room to store all that food. Yet, with her eye for details, she couldn't help noticing the flatness of his stomach and the healthy ripple of bicep and forearm beneath his flannel shirt.

He must be pushing forty, too, though the mischief that danced in his eyes made him seem several years younger. He seemed to be able to shrug off the cares of the world.

While she…

She realized he was staring at her, watching her stare at him. She cast aside his amused curiosity by taking a vicious bite of her fry, then stuffing the whole thing into her mouth. She concentrated on chewing each and every bite.

"You sizing me up as a suspect?" he asked, dabbing at his mouth with his napkin.

"Maybe." Ooh. Clever comeback, she chided herself. She forced her distracted brain to concentrate on the reason she had agreed to join him for a late dinner. "Earlier, you said Alvin Bishop wasn't a nice guy. Can you be more specific?"

His dimples deepened briefly, then disappeared. "Do you always use work as an excuse to avoid having a real conversation?"

She raised an eyebrow, refusing to take the bait and launch into another verbal duel with him. "This isn't a date."

He pushed his plate aside, rested his elbows on the table and leaned toward her. "Would it be so bad if it was?"

Disaster was the answer that leaped to mind. Thank God she had intelligence and experience on her side, and didn't have to rely on her malformed relationship skills to conduct an investigation.

Ginny folded her napkin and matched his position, ignoring the obvious taunt. "Alvin Bishop?" she prodded.

He relented. "Let me demonstrate."

Brett snapped his fingers and waved Pearl, the owner and chief cook, over to the table. Pearl Jenkins was a plump, ageless woman with a musical laugh and knowing smile. She'd come out from the kitchen to greet him in person when they arrived and he'd swallowed her up in a hug that showed they'd been good friends for a long time. Now she hurried over with an enthusiasm that bordered on doting-aunt status.

Pearl beamed directly at Brett when she reached the table. "You ready for some pie?"

He smiled right back, and Ginny thought she detected a blush in the older woman's cheeks. "What do you have tonight?"

Pearl went through the list as if she was naming off her children. "Coconut cream, lemon meringue, peach cobbler, caramel apple..."

"Mmm." Brett winked, and Pearl's color deepened even further. "Say no more. Caramel apple it is."

Pearl turned to include Ginny with a fixed smile that lacked the welcome she'd shown Brett. "You, too?"

Ginny eyed the half-eaten sandwich on her plate. She'd been hungry enough to down the whole thing, garnish and all. But she'd been unable to relax enough to enjoy her food. Self-conscious about her inability to read Brett with much success, she wanted to keep her guard up.

But caramel?

Some things even her considerable will couldn't prevent her sweet tooth from passing up.

"Caramel apple sounds delicious."

"Pearl?" The woman stopped, mid-bustle, and latched her attention back onto Brett. "Tell Ginny what you remember about Alvin Bishop."

"That good-for-nothing devil?" The blush drained right out of the older woman's face. "Why does she want to know?"

Ginny straightened her spine at the suspicion that shadowed Pearl's voice. She pulled back the front of her jacket and flashed her badge. "I'm a detective with KCPD. I'm doing some background research on a case."

Pearl's eyes narrowed to tiny slits in her plump face. "You're not from around here, are you?"

Ginny sensed the information locking up tighter than a vault at the board of trade. She tried to find some way to connect with the woman. "I was born and raised in Kansas City. I've lived on both sides of the state line. I asked to be transferred here to the Fourth Precinct two years ago when a position opened up."

The dull look in Pearl's dark eyes told Ginny she hadn't scored any points. Kansas City was a big town. Living inside the city limits wasn't the same as living on Market Street. At least not to Pearl Jenkins.

While Ginny regrouped to think of another way to get Pearl to talk, Brett interceded. His face creased with a boyish grin and he nodded across the table. "Ginny's a friend of mine. She works with my cousin Mitch. You remember Mitch, don't you?"

"Mitch? Of course." Pearl warmed to the subject immediately. "He came in here not too long ago with that new bride of his. I hear she's from the ritzy part of town. But you know what? She's common as dirt. I liked her right away."

Ginny watched with grudging admiration as Brett tapped Pearl's hand and steered her eager tongue back to the original question. "Alvin Bishop?"

Just like that. With a smile and a touch from Brett, Pearl opened up. "He got my Freddie fired from the steel plant over by the river. He's broken things up in my diner more than once. Finally got to where I needed a restraining order to keep him out. I don't serve liquor here, but it didn't matter. He was always picking fights."

She paused only for a breath, and continued. "One time old Alvin climbed up the fire escape of our building and stole a set of wind chimes Freddie had made for me at the foundry. Five little steel bells, handmade and strung on a rope. I used to love the sound they made in the evening breeze. Old Alvin said they kept him awake at night." The cautious regard she had given Ginny earlier vanished beneath a curious frown. "What do you want to know about him for?"

Ginny tucked her envy and resentment of Brett's success behind the emotional armor she wore as conspicuously as her badge, and kept her answer brief and to the point. "I'm investigating a murder."

"Whose? Did old Alvin kill somebody else?"

She opened her mouth to answer, but Brett cut her off. "Better get that pie. You'll be closing soon."

Pearl perked up in an instant. "Coming right up."

Ginny attacked Brett the moment the other woman was out of earshot. "What did you do that for? That's the kind of motive I need to hear about."

He leaned back against the vinyl booth, ignoring her burst of temper. "You said you wanted my help. I'm helping. You gotta know these people like I do. If she thinks you're trying to help Alvin, she'll clam up again."

"I'm trying to find out the truth. I thought that's what you wanted, too."

"I do." He rubbed his hand across the scruff of his jaw in a weary gesture. "But these are my people. You're the outsider here. Trust me. Life hasn't been easy around the City Market for a long time. If you ask too many questions, word will get around, and then they'll circle the wagons and nobody will talk."

"How else will I find answers?"

"Just be patient. You're good at that, aren't you?"

"Patience is one thing. Wasting my time is another." She'd be better off at the office, scrolling through the police archives on her computer. She tossed her napkin on the table and scooted across the seat to leave.

Brett reached across the table and snagged her hand in his. She froze in shock at the rough rasp of his callused palm on her skin. His touch was light, gentle. Yet he trapped her there all the same, her small hand lost in his, an evocative contrast of male and female proportions.

"Stay." His deep voice was little more than a whispered plea that vibrated through her with deceptive power. She forced her gaze up from the spot where their hands were joined to the urgent request in his eyes. "If they think you're with me, they might be more apt to open up."

"You mean..." Surely he wasn't suggesting... "Pretend...?"

"Look, I know I'm not your type. I imagine you date yuppies in three-piece suits."

"I don't..." No. Her solitary existence was too much to admit to this man. Her inadequacies were difficult enough to bear without offering them up for him to make a joke. "You're suggesting I go undercover as your girlfriend?"

"Not exactly. They can still know you're a cop. But a connection to me might smooth things over a bit. Make you one of us, so to speak."

Ginny tugged at his grip, and he released her without protest. She pulled her hand into her lap and rubbed at it with her fingers, trying to dispel the electric aftershocks of his touch there. "I don't know. That seems like a drastic step. We don't even know for sure if that was Mr. Bishop chained in the subbasement. I think it's a little premature to start looking for suspects who wanted to avenge Mark's death or kill his father for some other imagined slight."

"Dating me is a drastic step?" A look of affront played over his features, just as it had back at his office when she'd questioned the amount of money he made. This time, though, he laughed. "Never mind. You run your investigation your own way. I'll do what I can to help, whether the body is Bishop or not."

"I don't mean to insult you."

"You didn't." He pulled his wallet from his pocket and plunked a couple of bills down on the table. "Look, I understand you're all work, and you think I'm all play. Believe me, I'm not. Especially when the people I'm responsible for get hurt.''

"Like Mark Bishop?''

"Yeah.'' Whatever smile had been left on his features vanished completely. "Trust me, angel, I can be as cold-blooded about this as you. We could be an item around here and it would be strictly business, if that's the way you want it.''

Strictly business. For some inexplicable reason, his explanation didn't give her the reassurance she'd expected. Of course, they could pretend to be a couple. She could move around the Market Street area without raising any suspicions because she'd be labeled something as old-fashioned as "Brett's girl.''

But it wouldn't be real.

He could blow her logical, self-sufficient train of thought to smithereens with the simple touch of his hand. No, she couldn't afford to have a relationship of any kind with Brett Taylor—real or pretend.

"I'll think about it.'' She made the hollow promise, saving face without really meaning it.

If Brett could see through her insincerity, he didn't get a chance to comment. A second waitress, twenty years younger and forty pounds lighter than Pearl, but with the same unmistakable flush in her cheeks and the same ample curves to her figure, set two slices of pie on the table.

"It's good to see you, Brett,'' she bubbled.

"Ruby,'' he greeted her.

She balanced her empty tray on her hip and turned to him, blocking Ginny from the conversation. "Say, we're about to close shop. I don't suppose I can talk a big bruiser like you into walking Mom and me home.'' Her round hip sashayed right on cue. "Maybe we can even ditch Mom and keep walking.''

Brett didn't laugh with her. He leaned to the side to see Ginny and introduced them. "Ruby Jenkins. This is Ginny Rafferty."

"Hi." Ruby turned and nodded, then sat on the bench beside Brett. He politely obliged and slid farther across the seat. "You're new around here, aren't you?"

"I work at the precinct office."

"You're a cop?" Ruby's eyes widened in surprise.

"She's a friend of mine," explained Brett.

"I see." Ruby's wide smile left her eyes, and Ginny was reminded again of a close-knit ganglike mentality to the residents of Market Street.

Ruby refocused her attention on Brett, and they caught up on local events from the past week while Ginny, virtually ignored, nibbled on her pie. She had to be borderline exhausted and uncharacteristically depressed to push around something loaded with so much sugar, instead of devouring it.

The curly-haired blonde must be an old friend, Ginny speculated. A very good friend, judging by the way she flicked a stray lock of hair from Brett's forehead as if she had done so many times before.

Maybe that's what Brett had meant when he said he could have a strictly business relationship with her. He flirted with every woman. And every woman flirted with him.

Except one.

Ginny's fork clattered to her plate, stopping the conversation across the table and earning two curious stares. She'd forgotten her job and gotten caught up in some silly battle-of-wills game with Brett.

He'd lured her so far from her usual routine that she'd stopped asking questions. A resentful anger gave her new energy. "Ruby, do you remember Alvin Bishop?"

Ruby's eyes widened in surprise. "Mark's dad? Sure." She turned and offered the rest of her answer to Brett. "I used to date Mark in high school, remember? Old man Bishop tried to break us up. Said he needed Mark at home all the time. Mark would sneak up to our apartment sometimes. Even stayed the night once or twice. Until my dad found out."

Ruby's soap-opera tale went from proud to wistful to angry.

But Ginny tuned in to something else altogether. "You lived at the Ludlow Arms?"

"Yeah. We even talked about gettin' married one day. That is, until he met that uptown girl, Amy what's-her-face, and decided she was the end-all of the world. Once he set his mind to runnin' off with her..."

The sensation of darkness rushed in, spiraling to a pinpoint of acute awareness that left Ginny shaking. "Did you say Amy?"

Oh God, no. No, no, no.

"When? What year?" She snapped the questions.

"Gin, what's wrong?" She heard Brett's deep voice through a thick fog of memories and fear and injustice. A heartbeat later, a warm hand touched hers, making her realize how icy cold she had become. "Ginny?"

She cleared her head and looked at Brett. His mouth had thinned into a grim line. She pulled her hand away, detaching herself from her emotions and him at the same time.

"I need to go home now."

"I'll walk you to your car." He started to rise, but the table and Ruby blocked his path.

Ginny had no such hindrances. She slipped from the booth and pushed through the door. The entrance bell pierced her eardrum like a siren. It jangled again and she ran from the sound. She had rounded the corner before Brett caught up with her.

"What the hell's going on?"

She slowed to a walk but didn't stop.

"Dammit, Gin." Brett grabbed her and whirled her around. She twisted away from him, but his quick reflexes snared her again. This time he wrapped his arms around her back so he couldn't lose his grip. Her elbows bent and caught between them as he pulled her up against his chest and lifted her right off the ground.

She knew how to disentangle herself from an assailant. But the steel-hard warmth of his body pressed beneath her hands and along her stomach and thighs and shocked her into stillness. Eye level with his chin, she dangled there, mesmerized by the blunt strength of his jawline. Inch by tantalizing inch, his warmth seeped into her, clearing her mind to the textures of soft cotton at her fingertips, worn denim against her legs and solid man beneath it all.

Suspended in time and space, she clutched at him, seeking his strength and shelter. His broad hands imprinted themselves at her back and waist, thawing the chill within her from inside and out.

"You with me?" he asked. She watched the play of his lips, felt the deep rumble in his chest within her own.

All male. Too male.

Like the stinging pain that follows the thaw from frostbite, she realized she had her legs wrapped around his. She clung to him in a most intimate way, on a sidewalk beneath a streetlight in the middle of downtown Kansas City.

The humiliation felt all too familiar. The heat in her cheeks was sudden and deep.

"Put me down."

His laughter shook her as he bent and lowered her feet to earth. "Now you're back." He released her and retreated a step, as if respecting her discomfort with the situation. "You want to tell me what just happened?"

She straightened her blazer, checked her holster and bought herself time to collect herself. "I'm sorry I was rude."

''Don't sweat it. Something got to you. I'm just hoping you're going to explain.''

Apparently, she couldn't erase the hard imprint of his body on hers. The April night had been cool, but now every part of her seemed to be on fire. ''If I promise to slow down, you won't pick me up again, will you?''

''Deal.'' She noted the way he shortened his stride to match her pace. Maybe there were a few pluses to being an old-fashioned male, she conceded.

She had parked on the street just outside the trailer that housed his office near the Ludlow Arms building. She didn't speak, and he didn't press her until they stopped on the sidewalk beside her dark blue Taurus.

She unlocked the passenger-side door and retrieved her purse from the glove compartment. She wondered if he would have said anything more if she hadn't broken the silence first. ''Your young friend, Mark Bishop. Did he ever say who he was running away to meet the night he was killed?''

He stood beside her, his hands splayed at his waist in that self-assured, macho pose. But she could read the caution in his expression. She hadn't been able to understand much about him as a man, but she knew the distress and distrust of a witness who had to recall an unpleasant scene from his life.

''Just Amy,'' he said finally. ''He never told me her last name, didn't want to get her in trouble. He was afraid his dad would go after her. He showed me a picture once.''

Ginny unsnapped her purse and pulled out her wallet. With the most reverent of care, she slipped a frayed photograph from its plastic sheath. A family portrait taken the year she graduated from high school. She and her sister wore their hair long, in fluffy curls. Her parents looked so proud.

She passed the picture to Brett and pointed at the girl on the left. ''Did she look like this?''

The streetlight cast shadows across his downturned face, but there was no mistaking the shock of recognition when he glanced up at Ginny. "Yeah. That's her." He pointed to the other girl in the picture. "Is that you?"

Ginny nodded and returned the treasured photo to its place of safekeeping. "Her name's Amy Suzanne Rafferty. My sister." She caught her breath and asked one more question. "Do you remember the date Mark died?"

Something like guilt or regret tightened the set of his mouth. "October seventeenth. The Chiefs were playing a football game. I went down to a bar to watch it. Got caught up in the game and friends and beer, and was running late to meet him. I wanted to talk him out of eloping. Tell him he had his whole life ahead of him." His powerful shrug sent ripples through the air around him. "Empty promise, right?"

She watched the connection hit him. The same discovery that had rendered her mute prompted Brett into a surprising fury. "Your sister was the girl? Did she talk to Mark that night? Did she know he'd been hurt?"

"I don't know." The familiar emptiness welled inside her, nearly swallowing her whole. The hollowness echoed in her voice. "My sister died that night, too."

BRETT SAT at the bar, rolling the warm beer bottle back and forth between his palms. What the hell was he supposed to do? He'd always been a man of action, at times to his parents' chagrin, at times with a note of pride. He made things happen.

But how could he make this right?

He'd not only failed Mark Bishop, but he'd failed to protect Ginny's sister as well.

So much for his big-brother instincts. So much for making the world a better place.

He could build buildings, give good workers steady jobs.

But he couldn't come through when it really counted.

He watched the golden liquid swirl in the neck of the bottle. The rich amber color paled in comparison to Ginny's silvery-blond hair.

He'd held her in his arms tonight. She'd been soft and sweet and full of fire. Not so fragile as he first thought. She'd fought like a frightened animal, acting on instinct alone, without the filter of that quick-thinking mind of hers. She'd wrapped herself around him, holding on as tightly as she'd first tried to escape. Did she know how much passion lay dormant and untapped inside of her? Did she have any idea how badly he wanted to find the extent of it for himself?

At least she had the ability to maintain some good sense, and avoid depending on him.

He was stewing deep in his bottle of untouched beer when he heard the vinyl stools creak on either side of him.

"This doesn't look good."

From the corner of his eye, he glanced to the brother on his right, then to the brother on his left.

"You gonna drink that or just play with it?"

He turned first to Mac on his right. "Are you guys the search party?" he asked.

"Should we be looking for you?" asked Mac. Brett couldn't tell if he heard concern or mockery in his brother's voice.

Gideon, his second eldest brother, ordered two beers. With short, dark hair, and equally dark eyes, he was the spitting image of their father. He pulled a ten-dollar bill from the pocket of his fire department uniform and handed it to the bartender. "Mac called me at the station house with an interesting question. Wanted to know the last time the Ludlow Arms had had a fire inspection. I said, 'Isn't the place condemned?' and he…"

Brett knew a taunt when he heard one. He took the bait anyway. "Is there a point to this story?"

"No." Gideon grinned. "But the glare in your eye tells me you're still alive and kickin'."

Ever the voice of reason, Mac pried the bottle from Brett's fingers. "How many of these have you had?"

"None." Brett scowled at both siblings. "I'm a lousy drunk these days. I sit down and buy one, but I never drink it."

Mac and Gideon exchanged knowing looks across Brett's shoulders. They knew he hadn't touched an alcoholic drink since the night of Mark's death, when he'd been too plastered to keep track of the time.

"Good." Mac set the bottle on the bar. Brett sensed the subtle change in his demeanor, and suddenly knew this visit wasn't accidental, and that it had more to do with familial support than with camaraderie.

Brett sat up straight. "What?"

"I got a positive ID on the body in the subbasement of your building." Brett had a sickening idea that he already knew the answer. "It's Alvin Bishop."

The accuracy of Ginny's suspicions didn't make the fact any easier to swallow.

"Old man Bishop didn't run off?" Gideon asked. "You mean somebody killed him?"

"Somebody he knew, judging by the elaborate setup," answered Mac.

"Wait a minute." Brett hushed them both. He had a more important question to ask. "Have you told Ginny yet?"

"I left a message on her machine."

"Damn." Brett stood and headed toward the exit.

"Where are you going?" Gideon asked. "It's almost midnight. Stay and I'll buy you a soda."

Mac added, "It's not like the two of you are friends. This is her work, big brother. Ginny can take care of herself."

Yeah. A lot better than he could.

Brett stopped in his tracks. Man, he hated when those little weasels were right.

He raked all ten fingers through his hair as if he could sweep away his troubling thoughts as easily. Surrendering to practicality for the moment, he stalked back to his stool and ordered a ginger ale.

Who was he to ride off in his pickup truck to rescue the damsel in distress from bad news? He had no business rescuing anybody.

"MR. RASCONE." Ginny bit her tongue to control the frustrated scream that threatened to erupt from her throat.

"Excuse me, my dear." The balding jeweler moved to the far end of the counter and asked the lady who had told him she was just looking whether he could help her.

Again.

Her fingers itched to snatch one of the long strands of silver hair that he combed over the top of his head and yank him back to the conversation she had started nearly ten minutes ago.

The corpse recently discovered down the block has been identified as Alvin Bishop, a one-time resident of the area. You've been in business here nearly fifty years. Did you know the victim? Were you ever at the Ludlow Arms where the body was found?

Can you hear me talking? she wanted to shout.

Apparently Mr. Rascone hadn't heard the third-time's-a-charm cliché. Neither the elderly Bert Hampstead at the shoe repair shop, whose hearing aid was suddenly on the fritz, nor the hide-behind-his-paper Dizzy from the barbershop next door, would answer any of her questions about Alvin Bishop.

Oh, they'd been friendly enough when she walked into their shops. But once she showed them her badge, they suddenly had very little to say.

Ginny eyed the elderly woman and the rest of the empty shop. Retreat seemed the best answer for the moment. She straightened her navy blazer and headed back into the April sunshine, scanning the streets for Merle, and wondering if her partner was having any better luck piecing together Alvin Bishop's story.

A halfhearted bustle of indigents looking for a handout scattered before a trio of suit-and-tie executives hurrying down the sidewalk.

At first glance, Ginny thought the neighborhood was dying. But a closer inspection revealed a few healthy businesses with newly painted storefronts and bright-striped awnings. Pearl's Diner, for one, nestled at the base of a four-story brick building, survived with a retro type of charm. Farther down the block, a giant metal archway spanned the entrance to the Historic City Market, a revamped circle of tents and brick stalls that sold everything from spices to T-shirts to sides of beef.

But the Ludlow Arms, Peabody and Walton Buildings towered over them all like menacing tombs rife with secrets. Ginny tilted her chin and studied their decaying silhouettes. If she had a canvas, she'd paint them in hues of gray and black. Shadows and death.

Despite the sunny warmth soaking into her shoulders, she felt a chill. Alvin Bishop wasn't the only corpse to turn up in those buildings. Mark Bishop had died there, too.

And just five blocks away, beneath a dock on the Missouri River, her sister's battered body had floated to shore.

Had Amy suffered at Alvin Bishop's hands? If Amy and Mark had been killed by the same man, why weren't their bodies found together? Had Amy gone for help after finding Mark's body and met with a horrible coincidence of fate? Or had she died first, and Mark, in some twisted mix of heartbreak and vengeance, confronted his father with fatal results?

Twelve years in the past, on the night of October seventeenth, two people died. Now a third body had turned up.

And no one wanted to talk about it.

''Gin!'' She turned to the summons, filing away her speculation to be analyzed later. Merle Banning dashed across the street. A wave of his blond-brown hair caught in the noontime breeze and fell across his forehead, drawing her attention to the frustration in his eyes. ''You getting anywhere with this crowd?'' he asked, his tone revealing he'd had little success himself.

She shook her head and fell into step beside him as they walked to his car. ''Are you kidding? If I tattooed *leper* on my forehead, I couldn't feel any less welcome.''

''So what do we report to the old man?'' he asked, using the ironic nickname the detectives had dubbed their forty-year-old precinct captain.

''I don't know yet. Supposedly, nobody liked Alvin Bishop. You'd think they'd be relieved to hear he was dead, and eager to talk about why he deserved it.''

''Could they be protecting the killer?''

She'd thought of that already. ''If the murderer did them a favor, they might be rewarding him by not turning him in.''

''We could go back to Zeke and Charlie.'' Merle laughed at Ginny's grimace. Her interview with the two homeless men had been an exasperating comedy of errors. ''They think you're an enemy spy. Maybe if you threaten to torture them, they'll spill the beans.''

''I doubt testimony like that would stand up in court.''

''Probably not, but it'd make a great story to tell your grandkids.'' She matched his smile for a moment. But her mouth straightened when he added, ''We need to find another way to attack this case. Except for the forensics report, we're at a dead end.''

No, a dead end was the lives of two innocent young people snuffed out before their time.

At Merle's Buick, he unlocked his door and climbed in to open the passenger side for Ginny. As she waited for him, a battered white pickup truck with the Taylor Construction logo drove past. The driver, with short hair and a full beard, clearly wasn't Brett. But by the time he turned the corner into the fenced-in construction site, Ginny had made a decision.

"Can you cover for me this afternoon?" she asked, pulling her focus away from the disappearing truck.

"You got an idea?"

"A half-baked one, maybe." Finding Alvin Bishop's body had provided the first possible lead in years to discovering her sister's killer. She wasn't about to let a neighborhood full of closemouthed homebodies keep her from finding the truth. No matter what the personal or professional risk might be. "I think I know how we can get some answers."

"Need some help?"

"No." She closed the car door and offered a reassurance she didn't quite feel herself. "I'll check in this afternoon and let you know if it works."

"You be careful, partner," he warned in that half brotherly, half boyfriend way of his.

"I will."

After he'd gone, Ginny took a deep breath and hurried to the construction site. With the Ludlow Arms temporarily off-limits, Brett had moved his entire crew over to the Peabody. Inside the gate, she scanned the people and machinery scurrying about with the diligent purpose of worker ants.

Seconds later she spotted a shock of shoulder-length hair as dark as the Vandyke brown oils she painted with. Ignoring the dust she kicked up onto her khaki slacks, she skirted a gravel pile and crossed to the two men standing beside a stack of lumber.

Working undercover had never been her strong suit. She was all about details and observation and insight.

But for Amy and the truth, she could do this.

The other man spotted her first and stopped talking. Brett turned before she could call to him. She'd forgotten how big he was up close. How unforgiving the line of his jaw could be.

She'd forgotten how he liked to stand with his hands splayed on his hips. The direction his fingers pointed when he stood that way. Emphasizing that most masculine part of him without meaning to.

I can't do this. Determination deserted her for an instant. She prayed the rush of heat she felt in her cheeks didn't show.

"Ginny?" He said her name in that dark fog of a voice, scattering her thoughts. The contours of his face narrowed into a frown. He touched her elbow and turned her, guiding her back the way she had come. "This is a hard-hat area. Until we shore up the infrastructure of the top floors, nobody walks around here unprotected. Not even a stubborn detective like you."

Taking advantage of the time to reaffirm her strategy, Ginny allowed him to lead her outside the gate. But once they cleared the danger of falling debris, she planted her feet and refused to go any farther. She had to do this fast. Before she changed her mind. "We need to talk."

Brett removed his hat and ran his fingers through his hair. "So I gathered." When he faced her, that proprietary frown had been replaced with a curious smile. "What's up?"

Ginny didn't believe in soft words or seductive smiles or playing hard to get. She simply asked.

"Will you marry me?"

Chapter Four

Brett pushed Ginny inside the trailer and locked the door behind him before she could bolt away. Hauling her up the steps to his office in front of his crew wasn't the most gallant thing he'd ever done, but she hadn't left him much choice. She had a tendency to run away when things got personal or a little interesting.

And Ginny's blunt proposal sounded *really* interesting.

Even now, like a cornered animal, she paced to the far side of the room and hovered there, putting the desk, two chairs and a tight-lipped expression between them. Damn, but she reacted to things quickly. Almost as quickly as she squelched those very same reactions.

Why didn't the good detective allow herself to express her emotions? Like that anger shimmering in her bright blue eyes. Or maybe what he glimpsed was fear. Down in the Ludlow basement, she'd had a similar surge of panic before retreating and regrouping the way she was doing right now. Claustrophobia, she'd said then. And now he'd locked her in his office.

Sid and Martha Taylor hadn't raised their firstborn to be a bully. He tossed his hard hat onto a chair and leaned back against the doorjamb, allowing Ginny the width of the room to feel safe.

Sid and Martha hadn't raised their sons and daughter to back away from a challenge, either.

"You just proposed marriage to me, right?"

Ginny's heart-shaped face flushed with color, but her expression never changed. "Put your testosterone back in your pants, Taylor. What I suggested was merely a business proposition."

He laughed at her wry choice of words, relieved to see she wasn't truly frightened of him or the enclosed space. "None of the clients I put up buildings for ever included a wedding ring in the deal."

"None of your clients are trying to solve a triple murder."

His amusement ended at the sobering reminder. Brett folded his arms across his chest and straightened, suddenly as serious as Ginny ever could be. "Maybe you'd better explain."

"I don't really want to marry you. I just want to pretend." He ignored the insult and watched her smooth a lock of hair behind her ear. The gentle curl of it hugged her jawline, drawing his attention to the faint quiver there. She might be talking business, but something about this unusual proposition made Ginny uncomfortable.

A desire to understand and protect her from that inner torment simmered in his veins. But he didn't know what he could say or do to put her at ease, so he remained silent. He tucked his thumbs into the front pockets of his jeans, assuming a more relaxed pose, and waited for her to continue.

"I want to use an engagement to you as a cover to help me with the investigation." She ventured out of the corner to his desk, where she idly began to straighten the chaos. Her small, supple hands worked with unconscious efficiency. "I haven't found anyone who's mourning Alvin Bishop's death. Yet nobody wants to talk to me about it." She paused. "But they'll talk to you."

Brett remained silent.

She folded the sports section back into the newspaper and matched the creases before answering. "Ruby Jenkins fell all over herself trying to talk to you last night. Her mother was no different."

Brett began to wonder if Ginny's manic housecleaning had less to do with perfection and more to do with nervous energy. Did she really think she was asking such a huge favor of him? Or did it gall her independent attitude that she had to ask for any help at all?

He called her on it. "Last night, you thought dating me was a drastic step. This morning you want to get married."

"Just pretend…"

He nodded, showing what he considered an amazing degree of patience at her adamant insistence that she had no real interest in him. "You want to *pretend* we're getting married. What changed between now and then?"

A stack of bills slipped into a neat pile beneath her hands before she stopped. Her shoulders rose and fell with a sigh. When she finally tilted her chin, he caught a glimpse of the same raw vulnerability he'd seen the night before. Those clear cobalt eyes, brimming with emotions she hadn't wanted him to see, sucker punched him in the gut. His instinct to wrap her up in his arms propelled him forward. But he halted at her next words.

"You're a real hero around here," Ginny said. "From what I've seen and heard, you'd think you're transforming this neighborhood single-handedly by tearing down the dead parts and bringing in new business. Saving old buildings like Pearl's Diner. Turning broken sidewalks into historic walkways. You practically walk on water around here, Taylor."

He flinched at the undeserved compliments. He turned his face to the side and breathed out a silent curse. "Gin…"

"You know people of every generation, every walk of life in the Market Street area. I want to know what happened inside that basement twelve years ago, and the chance to find the truth is slipping right through my fingers.'' He looked to see her fingers cup the air and curl into graceful fists. ''I don't have time to wait until everyone decides I'm not the enemy here. I need an ally they trust already. I need...'' Her fingers uncurled and beseeched him. ''...you.''

Her hands returned to the desktop, where the loose pencils and paper clips fell prey to her relentless fingers. The resignation that made her last word sound like a last chance should have rankled his ego. Instead, it blew a spark into the long-buried embers of guilt that had plagued him without redemption for twelve long years. He snagged her by the wrist across the top of the desk, scattering the supplies that had been clenched in her hand.

''You're doing this for your sister, aren't you?'' he challenged.

Their eyes locked.

Brett became aware of the fragile bone structure and sinewed strength of her delicate arm closed inside his large, work-roughened hand. So small, and yet so strong. Stronger in will and spirit than any woman he'd ever met.

Ginny swallowed, drawing his gaze to the pale skin of her throat. His mouth went dry at the distracting thought of putting his mouth there. Of tasting the creamy perfection with the tip of his tongue.

The wide curve of her mouth articulating her words to exacting specification proved an equally fascinating distraction.

''My sister and your friend Mark were running away together to get married. Someone stopped them both. You assume it was Alvin Bishop. But we don't know that for a fact. Unless we can prove he murdered them both, justice will never be served.''

Her gaze settled to where he still held her. Her eyes widened as if she, too, had just made note of the blatant differences, male and female, between them.

"Screw justice." Her gaze snapped back to his. "This is personal for you. Otherwise, you wouldn't stoop so low to make a deal like this with me."

"Stoop so low?"

Arctic ice worked its way past the confusion in her features. Brett willingly released her. He turned his back and sat on the front edge of the desk. He had to clear his mind, fight his way through an unexpected mix of anger and guilt, admiration, and even a lingering frisson of lust. But turning away from those cool eyes couldn't dampen the clarity of her voice that hit his conscience like a bull's-eye.

"I want the truth, Brett. I'm putting my job on the line for this. For Amy. For Mark. Will you help me or not?"

Why me? Brett squeezed his eyes shut, torturing himself with the question.

Circumstances might make him the right man for the job at hand. But fate made him the wrong one.

People he cared about had counted on him once before. They'd paid for his failure with their lives. Would granting Ginny's request be the penance he owed the past? Or would he reward her faith in him with another unforgivable screwup on the larger-than-life Brett Taylor scale?

She offered him a chance to reveal the truth and find peace for his battered soul. Or to dredge up enough old ghosts to ruin a hundred other lives.

She offered him a chance to get to know the real Ginny Rafferty. And to prove there could never be anything but fiery words and cool mistrust between them.

"Brett?" The gentlest of touches singed his thigh through worn denim. "I know I'm not the type of woman you usually date."

Was this why she hesitated to ask for his help? Something cold and calculating slowed the blood in his veins until he could count each pulse beat. It was an old self-defense trait that had grown rusty but had never been forgotten.

He opened his eyes and turned to her. She jerked her hand away, drawing herself up like a bantam hen. Small, but poised and ready to fight. He took her up on it. "Just what kind of woman do you think I *usually* date?"

He braced for the crack about working class. Something about hookers with hearts of gold. Trailer trash. Project primas. He had a hundred jokes to tell her how wrong she was. Poor didn't mean stupid or unloved. Low rent didn't mean low-class. A man's background didn't define his character. Or his taste in women.

Ginny thought he was a full-time flirt. A man who couldn't possibly be involved with a professional, high-class, delicate piece of work like herself. He had one hell of a comeback for her snobby—

"I see you with someone more spontaneous, more passionate."

Spontaneous? Passionate?

Where was the insult?

He had no comeback for this one. Maybe he'd misunderstood. Did she think *she* was the unsuitable partner in this proposed charade?

Her steely mask eroded at his silence. "That sort of thing doesn't come naturally for me. But I've done a bit of undercover work. The only murder in my career I haven't solved is the one that counts the most. I have to know what happened to my sister. For her sake, I can be whatever you need me to be to pull this off."

The desperation in her words shamed him. This had never been about him or where he came from. No passion? Couldn't she hear the pain and determination in her own voice?

Her energy spent, her guard down, she offered up one last word. "Please."

The hesitation in that whispered plea wound into his big heart, nudging open a corner and making room for one more try. The war between his conscience and his doubts was ultimately short-lived.

He caught her hand and squeezed it tight. In reassurance or apology, he wasn't sure.

"Okay. Here's my proposition to you." Brett straightened, standing head and shoulders taller than Ginny, giving at least a physical impression of the hero he was supposed to be. Hell. The last thing he'd call himself was a hero. But if she needed him to become one…

He crossed to the scale model of the Ludlow Arms, visualizing the building as it had existed twelve years ago, formulating his own plan of action.

"I'll pose as your fiancé. I'll do everything I can to make it look real, everything I can to help you fit in around here." He turned and held up two fingers. "But you have to do two things for me."

"This is a police investigation, Brett. I don't make deals."

"Two things," he repeated. She crossed her arms, standing closed and defiant. But willing to listen. He hoped. "I get to be your full partner in this investigation. Anything you find out about Amy, Mark or Alvin will be shared with me."

"I can't guarantee that." She shook her head at the very idea. "There are rules I have to obey. An investigation is not public record…"

He planted his hands on his hips and leaned toward her. Just far enough to make her tilt her chin and pierce him with the defensive daggers glaring from her eyes. "Maybe you need to break the rules. Maybe that's why you've never solved this case."

Her chin plunged as if he'd punched her. He, too, looked away, scanning the room for the common sense that eluded him whenever Ginny pushed his buttons. He turned back, ready to apologize for going too far. But she tipped her face up, her usual mask of control betrayed by the tight set of her mouth.

"What's your second condition?" she asked, without actually saying yes to the first.

"That you shut off your professional armor when you're with me."

"What are you talking about?" True to a nature he was just beginning to understand, she tucked that jaw-hugging curl of hair behind her ear.

He reached out and traced the same curl with his fingertips, learning the sensations of feather-soft hair and taut, smooth skin before she flinched away.

"That's what I'm talking about," he answered, his hand still hovering in the air beside her face. "You're going to have to at least *act* like you like me."

"I like you just fine."

"No. You *like* shades of blue. You like sweets." With just his index finger he pulled aside the front of her jacket and dropped his gaze to the polished brass shield hooked to her belt. "But you never turn off the badge, angel. Even when you're angry. Even when you're afraid."

"That's not true." She snatched the material and retreated a step, straightening the lapels and placket as if she was suiting up in a bullet-proof vest. "I'm just…reserved."

Brett shrugged, allowing her that concession. "Maybe you *are* shy. Maybe you're the consummate professional. But if you're in love with a man—even if it is just pretend— you have to show it. Drop that guard of yours. Don't be afraid of me touching you. Don't be afraid to show your emotions."

"What makes you think you're an expert at undercover work?"

"I don't have to be a detective to know how to be in love.

If you want anyone to believe this charade, you have to show some of that vulnerability. Show some heart.''

''Vulnerability?'' She snapped to attention, little more than five feet of steel-boned cop, just the opposite of what he had suggested. ''I can be very convincing, I assure you. I'll hold up my end of the bargain, Taylor. Just make sure you hold up yours.''

Properly chastised, yet gloriously challenged, Brett watched her storm to the door. She slipped the dead bolt and was down the stairs before he reacted to the dare she had thrown at his feet.

He stopped in the open doorway as she sped toward the gate, admiring the symmetrical flare of shoulders and hips from her tiny waist. Her silver-blond hair caught in the breeze, exposing the graceful column of her neck above the trim fit of her blouse and blazer. A soft, feminine contrast to the tailored work clothes she wore.

Something male, something primal inside him responded to the glimpse of softness beneath her hard exterior.

''You're not so tough,'' he called after her. Ginny halted in her tracks at his soft-spoken taunt.

He took the steps in one bound, and closed in behind her before she could tuck her hair and armor back into place.

''What the hell do...?'' She whirled around, her open mouth rendered speechless with surprise. She hadn't heard him coming.

Enjoying the advantage for a change, Brett smiled. ''We didn't shake on our proposition.''

''What?'' Unable to find the precise word to put him off, Ginny relented by lifting her hand.

Brett swallowed it up in his. Soft skin and sleek muscles held their own inside his big, callused grasp. ''Partners?'' he whispered.

''Part...'' Her gaze darted from their hands up to a point past his shoulder, then zipped straight to her right. Like curious wild creatures peeking out from their dens to see the unexpected predator stalk past, Brett's crew, one by one, stopped their hauling, planning, drilling, chatting, and watched their boss chase after the pretty lady. "Your men are watching us."

His amusement at their interest in his business faded when the fearful note in her voice prompted him to look down at her. Rosy heat filled her cheeks. She blushed so easily, another feminine attribute that mocked her all-business facade.

Brett angled himself to shield Ginny from his crew's prying eyes. "Maybe we'd better kiss instead. Make this charade look real."

"No." Ginny's hand went suddenly cold within his.

"No?" He questioned her vehement refusal. "We're supposed to seal an engagement, not a traffic citation."

Her deep, fortifying breath matched his own. "I hate it when you're right."

He felt a tug round his neck as she latched onto his collar and pulled herself onto her toes. She pressed her lips together and puffed them out, zeroing in on his mouth.

Brett caught her chin in his palm and stroked his thumb across her lips, softening the unnatural pout. "Relax. I'll meet you halfway."

Ginny sank back onto her heels as he lowered his head and replaced his thumb with his mouth. At first, he simply touched her there, learning the contours and taste of her. Suddenly, the lower arc of her sweet lips trembled. Drawn to the tiny flutter of movement, Brett pressed the generous curve between his own lips. She snatched in a quick breath and Brett took advantage by covering her open mouth with his own.

Her lips barely moved, as if the sensation of a man's gentle possession was a new experience to be studied. It seemed as if Ginny concentrated solely on keeping her mouth aligned with his, without enjoying the pleasure it could offer her.

Her hands were another story altogether.

Those strong, articulate fingers clutched handfuls of flannel and thermal cotton and man. As his own fingers tunneled into her angel-fine hair to tilt her head and position her mouth more fully beneath his, her fingers dug into his chest, then crept up to his shoulders, holding herself steady or holding him close, Brett couldn't tell. He wondered if she even knew.

The rigid passivity of her lips made him want to teach her about kissing and loving. The needy snatch of her fingers made him think that somewhere inside, Ginny already knew.

"Way to go, boss!"

The whistles and catcalls registered a split second after that first discovery.

By will alone, Brett pulled his mouth from Ginny's and rested his forehead against hers, his gaze catching on the quick rise and fall of her breasts.

"I have a couple of things to finish up here," he whispered, struggling, like Ginny, to regain his ability to breathe. "I'll meet you at Pearl's at one o'clock, take you to lunch. We should establish our cover before we start asking questions, right?"

"Of course." Her fingers curled into fists between them and she pushed him back a step. A loud wolf whistle from behind rang harsh against his ears. Ginny's cheeks flushed with color. "Looks like we're off to a good start."

She broke contact entirely, leaving a chill where she had touched him. Steel crept into her jaw as she finger-combed her hair into place. The shy, passionate woman who had shown herself for one brief moment disappeared behind the detective's facade. "I'll meet you at one o'clock."

Brett didn't move while she turned and walked away.

Only when she had disappeared around the corner did the quaver in her clipped dismissal register.

A frown tightened the muscles in his face. Ginny Rafferty wasn't a prude. She wasn't a snob or a cold fish.

She was frightened of something. And fighting with every bit of her composure to hide the fact.

That kiss might have been for show, but it had scared the hell out of her. Brett spread the flat of his hand up across his chest where she had touched him. His insistence had reminded her of something. Or someone.

But what? Who?

What could possibly make the confident cop tremble with fear?

And what had *he* done to trigger it?

He decided to allow her this one retreat.

Brett turned at the friendly slap on his shoulder. A beaming grin cut across the beard of his project foreman, Clay Fensom. "Anything you want to tell us?"

Now was as good a time as any to put the charade into motion. "Congratulate me, Clay." Brett smiled past the lie. "The little lady just said yes."

Amidst the whoops and hollers and congratulatory handshakes, Brett pondered one inescapable truth.

Ginny wasn't the only one who had been rattled by that kiss.

"YOU WANT some more coffee, hon?"

Pearl Jenkins's rote request held all the warmth of the tepid liquid sitting in Ginny's cup.

Ginny glanced around at the empty restaurant. If, at 1:30 p.m., there'd been a rush of business, she could understand Pearl's attempts to move her along and free up a table. As the lone customer, though, she certainly wasn't being given any preferential treatment. "I told you I was waiting for someone. I'd like to give him a few more minutes."

I'd like to give him a swift kick in the...

The bell above the door jingled and Ginny never got to finish her condemning thought.

"Brett!" Pearl brightened as if Santa Claus himself had come down the chimney. The plump hostess waddled to the door to greet him. "You missed lunch. But I can rustle up something in five minutes."

Brett dropped a kiss on the woman's weathered cheek and smiled. "Maybe later, Pearl. I'm here to pick up Ginny."

He extricated himself from her one-armed hug, dodged the coffeepot, and strode over to Ginny's booth.

Ginny sat up straight, girding herself for his approach. A yellow tie and tan corduroy blazer had done little to tame his earthy vitality. The same faded jeans he had worn earlier draped like a careless caress down his long legs, hugging a bit tighter around his thighs with each easy, endless stride.

She never thought of a man having sexy legs before. But Brett's were a testament of strength and proportion. A length of calf and foot balanced the symmetry of his narrow hips and muscular thighs. Her fingers burned at the memory of touching the solid strength of one of those thighs in a misguided attempt to drag him back from the dark thoughts that had clouded his face at his office.

She shoved the traitorous thought away, reminding herself of the need to stay cool, calm and collected. Sexy legs or not, Brett was merely her cover to find answers on a case. One of them had to stay in control. She decided, on the spot, it would have to be her.

"Sorry I'm late." Stopping beside the table, he hesitated long enough for Ginny to look up. She zeroed in on his mouth descending toward her. The firm lips smiled easily. They'd been more dangerous to her self-control than she'd expected that morning. The twin bands of seduction had intrigued her with their gentle warmth, robbed her of reason with their sheer male potency.

Even his lips could act the part well.

At the last second she turned and offered her cheek for him to kiss. She sensed his widening grin before she felt the brush of moist warmth at her temple. Fine. A simple peck like that she could handle and still keep her mind on business.

A silent breath tickled the shell of her ear an instant before Brett nipped at the lobe. Her hand and a zillion pinpricks of sensation rushed to the spot. Remembering her part, and their one-woman audience, she pulled her hand back to her lap and forced a smile.

"It's one-thirty." Okay, so it wasn't the most romantic greeting she could come up with. But she'd never taken the time to cultivate her romantic side. Not since that summer in Europe. Not since the phone call that had summoned her home for Amy's funeral.

It was the first of three phone calls in her life that had taught her not to waste her time on tragic setups like love and romance.

Brett slid into the seat across the table, a teasing light evident in his expression. "I got held up at the bank." He laughed at his own joke, a rich, warm sound that rumbled deep in his chest. The deep pitch of it resonated inside her, but she didn't join him. She had a job to do, after all. "Don't you want to file a report?" he asked.

"For criminal lack of punctuality, maybe."

Brett propped his elbows on the table and leaned toward her. "Why, Detective Rafferty, you made a joke."

"I didn't mean to, I assure you." He fell back in his seat, laughing again. Ginny felt a betraying quiver tease her own lips.

But Pearl's hovering intrusion kept her from laughing. "Brett, honey, what are you doin' all dressed up? Did somebody die?"

"Not at all, Pearl. I put on a tie because I'm celebrating."

He stood and reached for Ginny. The extra squeeze in his grip sent a quick warning and gave her time to prepare for being pulled up snug against his side. She fit beneath his shoulder, and his arm spanned her back at a diagonal. His hand skimmed the left side of her waist, bumped into her holster, then settled on her hip. She slipped her arm beneath his jacket, holding on to his belt and completing the picture before he made the announcement.

"We're getting married."

"Oh, my." Pearl's hand shook, sloshing coffee over the rim. She reacted quickly, grabbing a napkin and mopping up the spill on the floor. She set the pot on the table and smoothed the front of her dress. Then she reached for Ginny's free hand and squeezed it tight between her own pudgy paws. "Why didn't you say something, dear? Congratulations. But this is all rather sudden, isn't it?"

Brett's electric smile worked its magic on the older woman, dispelling her doubts. "You know how impulsive I can be."

"That's true. Our Brett has charmed a lot of pretty ladies through the years. I just never knew he was serious about any of them."

Ginny laughed right along with Pearl. But the joking observation threw up a familiar red flag inside her head. If Brett truly was the playboy Pearl described, then she'd do well to remember his charm and humor were all just part of the game.

She'd carefully cultivated her studious, professional facade. Her job demanded it. Her personal life had never called on her to be any other way. She was smart enough to play the charm game with Brett without forming any emotional attachments.

"Ginny's different, Pearl." She cringed at the accuracy of Brett's statement. "I've never met anyone like her before."

"Well, I'm happy for you both."

Ginny summoned an appropriate response. "Thank you."

Pearl latched onto Ginny's fingers, spreading them wide for inspection. "But, my dear, you don't have a ring yet." She released Ginny and shook her own finger at Brett. "What are you thinking? Every girl wants to show off her engagement ring."

"We're off to fix that right now, Pearl."

"We are?" Ginny craned her neck to look up into Brett's face.

The possessive expression on his features as he smiled down at her looked serious enough. "Surprise."

Brett's arm tightened around her, leaving Ginny no choice but to turn and walk with him to the door. Pearl hustled along behind, shooing them out. "You hurry right over to Frank Rascone's jewelry shop. I'll want to see the ring when you're done."

Brett pushed open the door and let Ginny precede him. "We'll be back. I promise."

Out on the sidewalk, beyond sight of Pearl's animated wave, Ginny stepped away from the broad hand at the small of her back. "If you didn't want to eat, what was the purpose of that meeting?"

A startled couple who had meant to pass on the right excused themselves and walked between them. Brett took a step to counter them, avoiding a collision. He quickly fell back into step beside her. "Simple. If Pearl Jenkins knows we're getting married, everyone will. She gets news out faster than the *Kansas City Star.*" His mouth twisted into a frown. "Didn't you eat?"

Ginny hurried her pace. "No, I was waiting for you."

Brett easily stayed beside her. "Sorry. Ring first, then food."

"I have to report in to the office sometime this afternoon."

"Okay. Ring, report, then dinner." He reached for her hand. "Isn't it time we started asking some questions?"

The instant she felt his touch, Ginny halted. She turned on him, pointing to her own chest. "I'm the one who asks questions." She pointed to Brett. "You're the cover. Remember?"

He caught her hand as she pulled away. His grim expression showed none of his trademark humor. "Equal partners. Remember?"

When he released her, Ginny retreated a step, surprised by the show of temper. With his charm turned off, Brett's overwhelming size and deep voice made him an intimidating force to be reckoned with.

"I did go to the bank." He continued in that grim, humorless voice. "I wanted to make sure I had enough money to do this right."

"You don't have to buy me a ring."

"An engagement without an engagement ring?"

Damn. She hadn't thought of any of these details. It irritated the hell out of her that he had. "I'll pay for it, then."

"No." Brett grabbed her by the elbow and guided her to the edge of the sidewalk, out of the path of curious passersby. He dipped his head and whispered right into her ear. "I'm not so strapped for cash that I can't buy my girl a ring."

"I'm not your girl."

"Say it any louder and your cover will be completely blown."

She glared at him, clearly overpowered. Using a trick she'd learned at the academy, she twisted her arm free of his grip. "Teaming up with you was a bad idea."

"Should I remind you it was your idea?"

"Dammit, Taylor, will you be serious?"

He latched onto her arm again. "I am deadly serious." When she twisted this time, he was prepared. He snaked his arm around her waist and lifted her clear off the ground, trapping her in the vise of his hold. "I will do anything I can do to prove old man Bishop killed Mark. Even if it means putting up with an uptight, by-the-book workaholic like you."

"Like me?" They glared at each other, face-to-face. Dammit. She never lost her temper. But this Neanderthal had her wrestling for freedom on a public sidewalk in downtown Kansas City. "I'm the one who has to put up with a smooth-talking, immature show-off."

"Taylor." A crisp male voice called from behind the obstruction of Brett's wide shoulders.

The sudden paralysis in Brett's arms shocked her into curious silence. There was no mistaking the strength and hardness of the man as he slowly lowered her to the ground.

She watched the play of emotions across Brett's face. Recognition. Annoyance. Anger. Regret. Then, like a slate being wiped clean, he fixed a smile on his mouth. A smile that never reached his eyes.

"Chamberlain." Brett turned, opening up her view of the blond-haired man, but keeping the jut of his shoulder positioned between her and this Chamberlain.

Tall himself, though leaner in build than Brett's muscular bulk, he wore a tan trench coat over an impeccably cut spring wool suit. His gold watch and the black leather briefcase he carried added to the appearance of wealth and gentility.

But there was nothing gentle in the cold assessment of his dark eyes. "I just scheduled an appointment with your secretary. My investors aren't pleased with what they've seen in the news. One million dollars is a lot of money to be throwing away on a failing project like yours."

She expected Brett to bristle at the attack, but his expression never changed. "I didn't ask for your clients' money. It's just an opportunity for them to improve public relations.

They know no one around here wants that casino and the crime that comes with it.''

"Crime? Hasn't your family cleaned up the neighborhood yet? I thought that was the Taylor mission. To serve and protect us all, whether we want them to or not.''

The muscles bunched in Brett's shoulders. He shifted his feet to a defensive stance. Ginny latched onto his arm with both hands and tugged sharply against the explosive tension there. Her cop's instincts to defuse the antagonism between the two men melded with her curiosity at the cause of it. "Brett. Why don't you introduce us?''

The blond man's gaze swept over Ginny. "I'm Eric Chamberlain, an old high school acquaintance of Brett's. And you are…?''

She had no chance of holding on to Brett if he really wanted to take a swing at this guy. But as if he understood her silent request, he held himself still beneath her touch.

Acquaintance? Hell. Ginny might not know either man on a personal level, but she understood conflict. She recognized an old rivalry, a battle that had been fought before between these two men. She filed away her questions for later and extended her right hand.

"Ginny Rafferty. Better watch what you say about cops.'' She flashed her badge. "I'm one of them.''

Switching the grip on his briefcase, he took her hand. It was a doctor's hand, a lawyer's hand. Smooth-skinned, lacking the calluses and character of a hand like Brett's. "Waste of a pretty face.''

Ginny snatched her hand back. Apparently she hadn't received her due of chauvinistic quips yet today. But she never got to voice the retort on the tip of her tongue.

Brett jabbed Eric in the chest, *encouraging* him to take a step back. "Is there a reason you want to insult my fiancée?''

"Brett, I can defend…''

But both men had already excluded her from the conversation.

Eric's eyes widened. "Fiancée?" His surprise transformed into a smug smile. "No wonder Sophie couldn't reach you. While you were busy entertaining the police, they've been busy spreading the bad news."

"What are you talking about?" Brett challenged.

Eric's shoulders swaggered with some kind of victory. "Apparently that body you dug up was old man Bishop. Sophie got the news a couple of hours ago. Imagine her daddy being buried alive. She tried to reach you, but I see now you were..." He glanced over at Ginny, then back at Brett. "...otherwise occupied."

Brett lurched forward and Ginny darted between the two men. Ignoring the insult and Brett's defense against it, she flattened her hands on his chest and shoved. Hard. What she lacked in strength, she made up for in surprise, averting a possible assault charge against Brett. Judging by her first impression, Eric Chamberlain would be more than happy to file one.

Brett blinked twice and focused on her upturned face, as if just now remembering her presence.

But Eric Chamberlain forged ahead, taunting Brett. "She turned to me, Taylor. Me."

Brett shifted his gaze over the top of her head. "For what?"

"Comfort." The muscles across Brett's chest expanded beneath Ginny's fingers. "Seems you let her down. Again. Enjoy your day." With that insincere wish, Eric strode down the sidewalk.

Brett's chest deflated like a pricked balloon. "I'd better go to Sophie and tell her what's going on."

The sudden absence of danger turned their position into an embrace. Ginny quickly pulled her hands away. Fortunately, she could cover her self-conscious observation with professional concern. "You can't tell her about the case yet."

He shook his head, stirring the hair against his collar. "I meant us. Sophie and I have been friends for a lot of years. I don't want her to hear about our engagement from anyone but me. I didn't even think how this ruse might affect her."

Ginny's resentment of his overbearing tactics faded beneath intellectual curiosity. "What did Eric mean, you let her down? You just said you and Sophie are old friends."

"I let her down, all right. Real bad." He scraped his palm across his jaw and released an unexpected sigh of fatigue. "It's my fault her brother died."

Chapter Five

Ginny stared at the pink piece of paper in her hand and read the words one more time.

Amy will see you soon.

No name. No phone number.

Just a cryptic note lying in her in-box with a dozen other phone messages.

Setting aside the chill that crept across the back of her neck like the gaze of an unwanted admirer, she scanned her surroundings for a likely purveyor of the sick joke.

The Fourth Precinct office bustled about her in its usual end-of-the-day chaos. She tuned out the strident complaints of the handcuffed man crying for his lawyer. She dismissed the tapping of keyboards at various desks as day officers finished up reports before leaving. Her gaze darted to the raucous laughter over at the coffeepot as officers coming in for the evening shift filled their tanks with caffeine.

No strangers. No loiterers. No curious onlookers watching for her reaction.

So where had the note come from?

There had to be a million Amy's in the world. But only one had any significance in her life.

And Ginny Rafferty didn't believe in ghosts.

A bit of her Irish temper kicked in and dispelled the spooked feeling that had temporarily immobilized her. She showed the slip to the man sitting across from her at the adjoining desk.

"Merle, did you take this message?"

He looked up from his computer, scanned the pink slip and shook his head. "I picked up a stack for both of us from Sarge. Is it something important?"

"I'm not sure." She slipped out of her chair and crossed to the tall front desk near the elevators that greeted visitors to the Fourth Precinct. "Maggie?"

The blond, uniformed officer, built like a Viking princess, but with the sweet freckled face of a Kansas farm girl, looked up from her clipboard. "Yeah, Ginny. What's up?"

Although almost everyone, from rookie cop to top brass, called Maggie Wheeler by her rank, Sarge, she and Ginny made a point of calling each other by their first names in a show of feminine support in their male-dominated profession. Ginny laid the message on the countertop. "Did you take this phone call? Merle said he got it from your desk."

Maggie set her clipboard beside the paper and ran down the list of entries, flipping through several pages. Her perpetual smile straightened into a frown of confusion. "It's not in the log. Maybe Murphy took it when I was on break." She nudged up the dark blue sleeve at her wrist and checked her watch. "That was about half an hour ago."

"Could you ask if he remembers it?"

"He took off right at five to catch his son's soccer game. I can call him on his cell, if you want," she offered, already reaching for the phone.

"No, that's okay. I'll ask him in the morning."

Maggie pulled the pen from behind her ear and tapped her clipboard. "Every call that comes across this desk goes into the log. More than likely that came through someone else's line."

Ginny also considered the possibility that the message hadn't been phoned in at all, that someone in the building had written it and dropped it off, purposely losing it in the shuffle of papers on the sergeant's desk.

She picked up the note and read it again. Maybe the events of the past two days had her seeing a threat where none existed.

Still, the timing of the anonymous promise made her wonder if she had piqued someone's attention on Market Street. Someone who didn't appreciate her sudden interest in Alvin Bishop. Someone who knew of Alvin's connection to her sister.

"Is there a problem?" Maggie's question drew Ginny out of her speculation.

"No." There was no point in turning the message into a full-scale investigation. She had plenty of other work that needed her attention. She folded up the note and stuffed it into the pocket of her khakis. "It's just weird."

Maggie shrugged. "If it's important, they'll call back."

Ginny had an uneasy suspicion someone would.

"Rafferty!" Ginny snapped to attention, an automatic response to the sound of authority. A door opened at the far end of the room. "Get in here!" Mitch Taylor's voice boomed from the open doorway of the captain's office. Tall, broad-shouldered and barrel-chested, her boss wasn't a man to be kept waiting.

Maggie leaned across the counter and winked, offering support and dismissing herself at the same time. "I'll keep checking to see what I can find out."

"Thanks." The first thought that entered Ginny's head was that Mitch had found out about her unofficial investigation into Amy's murder. Refusing to panic, she straightened the placket of her blouse and walked calmly toward her desk, reminding herself that Mitch wasn't one to give stern lectures.

But he did control promotions and paychecks.

She hurried her pace.

She reached her chair and picked up the blazer hanging over the back of it. "Ginny!"

She dropped the jacket, deciding speed was more important than appearance at this point.

Merle met her as she walked around their desks. "That doesn't sound good. Want some backup?"

"No, thanks." Mitch would have called both their names if he wanted to talk about a case. She had a sneaking suspicion this was going to be something much more personal.

She hesitated for a moment, knowing she needed to tell Merle of her undercover ploy before he found out from anyone else—just as Brett had wanted to tell Sophie. "I think I've got us some help on the Bishop case."

"Yeah?"

"Detective!"

Mitch's demand forestalled the sharing of any confidences right then. Donning her most professional mask, she hurried past Mitch into his office. He gestured to one of the guest chairs. Ginny sat, hiding her trepidation behind a patient facade, waiting while Mitch sat in his own padded leather chair.

Despite the subtle flecks of gray in his coffee-dark hair, Mitch radiated an energy that commanded attention. He propped his elbows on the desktop and steepled his fingers beneath his chin, shaking his head. Though he was only ten years older than she, he looked downright fatherly.

"Ginny." Unlike his gruff summons, his voice now was remarkably gentle. If possible, she sat up even straighter, a note of alarm kicking in at his soft tone. "Here I am, all set to go out for a quiet, romantic dinner with my wife, and I get a call from my aunt, asking if I know anything about Brett marrying one of my detectives."

After the initial surprise passed, Ginny made a conscious effort to close her gaping jaw. "Your family knows?"

"Aunt Martha's received half a dozen phone calls already.

She wants to know why she found out about it through Pearl Jenkins, and not her own son.'' He flattened his palms on the top of his desk. ''I want to know why my smartest detective didn't tell me she was going to become part of the family.''

Brett had been right about one thing. In Pearl's able hands, news traveled fast.

Ginny searched her imagination for a plausible explanation.

She'd rather face down a perp with a gun than lie to Mitch. But she could hardly tell him she had embarked on an unsanctioned undercover investigation, and enlisted his cousin's aid to pull it off. ''Well, Brett and I, we—''

''I've got it under control, Mitch.'' The deep dark voice from behind her skittered along her skin, raising goose bumps. She turned to see Brett, and his equally dark, compelling blue gaze slipped over to her. ''Angel.'' With that single word, the rich timbre of his voice sank into her bones like a comforting caress.

She would never have labeled Brett Taylor as ''comforting.'' But the sight of his big, brawny body filling the doorway to Mitch's office did exactly that. If anyone could talk his way out of an awkward situation like this, he could.

She hoped her sigh of relief hadn't been audible to anyone's ears but her own.

Two easy strides carried him to the arm of her chair. ''I'll call Ma when I get home to explain things.''

Mitch sank back in his oversize chair and crossed his arms. But Ginny saw beyond the relief in his posture. She knew the look in his eyes that demanded answers. ''Maybe you'd better explain what's going on to me first.''

Oh God. She swiveled her gaze up to Brett. He wouldn't dare tell about her search for Amy's killer, would he?

Brett sat on the arm of her chair, butting his hip against her shoulder. She scooted away from that brief contact, her concerns briefly scattered by distracting thoughts about men with sexy legs. But Brett's hand settled on her shoulder, pulling her back to his side and back into the charade.

Ginny fixed a smile on her mouth and tried to sound as natural as Brett had. "We haven't made an official announcement. Work keeps getting in the way." She added the last bit of truth to soften the strain on her conscience.

Mitch shook his head, looking doubtful. "It just seems pretty sudden. I didn't even know you two were dating. And now this?"

Brett continued as if they'd been discussing any old case, and not the biggest, most necessary lie of her life. "I didn't want Ma to get her hopes up. You know, stir up the whole grandkid issue. But Pearl Jenkins got wind of the engagement, and, well, you know Pearl."

"I know." The suspicion eased from Mitch's eyes and he actually laughed. Brett stood to meet him when he came around the desk to shake his hand. "It's about time. Congratulations."

Ginny looked away as the two men shared a brotherly hug. She marveled at the friendly clash of titans. How could Brett embrace his cousin and lie through his teeth at the same time?

Just what kind of expertise made him such a smooth actor?

Mitch crossed to the coatrack beside the door. He rolled down his sleeves and pulled on his suit coat, smiling with a secret of his own. "And not to worry. Casey and I are working on the grandkid thing. We may have an announcement ourselves in a couple of weeks."

"That's great."

Ginny stood, setting aside her doubts and adding her own good wishes. Mitch's new wife had gone through an incredible ordeal with a vengeful stalker the past Thanksgiving, and the two had nearly lost their lives. They deserved the happiness that beamed from the captain's face.

"Gin. Who'd have thought." Mitch closed his hands around her shoulders, debating a moment whether to maintain professional distance or forget decorum. He ended up brushing a chaste kiss across her cheek. But he kept shaking his head in a way that made her wonder if they'd really pulled off the deception. "I don't know whether to congratulate you or send a sympathy card for taking on this big lug."

Flustered by the show of warmth and humor, Ginny made a gulping sound in her throat, unable to get the appropriate words past the lie stuck there.

She lost her breath completely when Brett's arms closed around her waist from behind, pulling her back into his chest. The differences in their heights forced him to curl his shoulders around hers, cocooning her in a web of strength and warmth.

His breath stirred a tendril of hair behind her left ear as he spoke to Mitch. "Once I saw how marriage agreed with you, I decided to take the plunge myself."

Mitch stepped back and looked at them both. The pleasure and approval in his eyes turned Ginny's stomach sour, but she kept the smile fixed on her face. "You've got a prize here, Brett."

"I know."

Brett's soft-spoken compliment blew a soft breeze against her neck, waking unknown wishes in a forgotten place deep in her soul.

She had to consciously remind herself that sincerity wasn't part of this game. She stiffened within the mock embrace. Brett's arms tightened around her, as if sensing her instinct to bolt.

Don't be afraid of me touching you, he'd said.

And yet she was.

Very afraid.

Afraid the ample shelter of his arms was something she wanted far too much. The wanting made her weak.

And he wanted her to show vulnerability? She pressed her lips together to keep from laughing out loud. Snugged inside this false embrace, she didn't think she could feel any more exposed.

After a round of goodbyes, Mitch left with a promise to lock the office when they were done. The instant the door clicked shut behind him, Ginny pushed away. This time, Brett didn't resist.

Her ragged breathing echoed in the room as Brett closed the blinds masking Mitch's office from the rest of the floor.

His chest expanded and fell with a deep breath as he turned to her. "You're a rotten liar, you know that?"

Ginny hugged her arms around her middle, feeling a sudden chill in the air that had nothing to do with the absence of his body heat surrounding her. "Me? What are you talking about? I didn't say anything wrong."

"It shows on your face. You think too much. A person who looks like they're telling the truth doesn't stop to analyze everything she says or does."

"I was worried you were going to tell him the truth. You two are like brothers, aren't you?" She reached up to tuck a curl behind her ear, keeping her hand there, sheltering more of her body from the glare in his narrowed eyes. "I don't want to make any mistakes. This is too important."

"I know what I have to do, Gin. We're in this together." He pointed in an angry gesture toward the door. "How would you have answered Mitch if I hadn't shown up when I did? He may be the toughest sell of all, if we plan to pull this off. And I intend to do just that."

Defensive hackles shot up along her spine, standing her up even straighter. "I would have come up with something."

His unexpected temper subsided as quickly as it had flared. He swiped a hand across his jaw. "How much trouble will you get into if Mitch finds out you're looking into Amy's murder?"

"A lot." Ginny's defiance deflated along with Brett's. "It's not exactly department policy to investigate a family member's death."

In her peripheral vision she saw Brett step closer. But when she looked up, he stopped. "Why can't you have a little faith in me? I know your job's important to you."

"This job is all I have. It's who I am."

"A job doesn't define who you are, Gin."

"Until I find out the truth about Amy, this one does." She'd never put that driving philosophy into words before. And now, hearing them out loud, she sounded as obsessive and empty as she felt inside. A man with Brett's attachments, his easy command of people and a wide range of emotions, couldn't understand a single-minded determination like hers. "As far as Mitch knows, I'm looking into Alvin Bishop's death. He doesn't know about the connection to my sister."

"Does anyone?"

His challenge hung in the air like an accusation.

Any number of people knew about her sister's death. They saw the tragedy as the inspiration for Ginny becoming a police officer in the first place. She embodied more than devotion to duty. She was the soul of justice. Cool-headed and detail-oriented, she'd fought her way through challenging physical training, endured sexual harassment from crooks and co-workers alike, and combatted every crime in the book from prostitution to homicide.

She'd earned the right to find out the truth about her sister's death.

Even if the entire legal system and her commanding officer wouldn't see it that way.

"No one *can* know," she finally said. "If I lose my badge, then I'll become a vigilante—because I won't give up. But I want to do this right. I want to take her killer into a court of law and find out *why*. I want to know why someone thought she had to die." She slipped her hand into her pocket and touched the mysterious note she'd received earlier. "Make no mistake. I will find out who killed my sister. No matter what it takes.

"And if you're worried about the consequences," she went on, "we'd better drop this now, while we can still explain away your involvement to your family as some sort of misunderstanding."

Brett eyed her steadily for several moments, no doubt rethinking his decision to help her after that soapbox tirade. She tipped her chin and matched his gaze, bracing herself for his resignation from their illicit partnership. It wouldn't be the first time she'd been abandoned and forced to forge ahead on her own.

"Here." He shook his head on a weary puff of air and slipped a small velvet ring box into her hand. "Maybe this will help you get into character so we can get the job done faster."

We.

He collapsed into the chair she'd used earlier. Though surprise kept her from moving, relief made her curl her fingers around the square box, grateful for the tangible symbol of his cooperation. He hadn't given up on the investigation yet. He was willing to take the risk right along with her.

Have a little faith in him?

She did. For now.

Unaccustomed to such a show of support, she silently debated how best to thank him. She wondered if she even should. Perhaps he didn't expect any thanks. Some men wanted a big fuss made over their gestures; others were uncomfortable with too much praise.

While her brain picked apart her next move, Brett's body rippled with a natural grace as he stretched the tension from his shoulders. The strain against the seams of his corduroy jacket distracted her from her thoughts. Not because of the healthy flex of muscle there, but because of the tired sag that followed it.

The subtle changes in his appearance suddenly registered. The loosened knot of his tie hanging below the unbuttoned collar. The dark stubble of beard growth shadowing his jaw. The red-rimmed weariness about his eyes.

Unbidden, a surge of compassion stirred inside her. She dropped into the chair beside him. "Are you all right?"

The question left her mouth before she could snatch it back. Judging by the rounding of Brett's eyes, her words startled him as much as her.

"I wondered what you were thinking back there. I could almost smell the smoke coming out your ears." He reached for her hand and gave it a squeeze, entwining his fingers with hers and pulling it across the gap between their chairs. Ginny held her breath, frightened, fascinated, as he pressed a kiss to her knuckles. The scruff of his beard abraded her skin, zinging a jolt of sensation up her arm.

"Open it." He nodded his chin toward the jewelry box in her lap.

His lack of an answer to her question seemed an answer in itself. If she could decipher it. Had his kiss meant she did have cause to worry? Or had he dismissed her concern?

Conscious of his unblinking gaze as he released her, she opened the box. The breath she held floated away on a soft breeze when she looked inside.

"I know it's not a traditional diamond," he said, "but I figure there's nothing traditional about us. I'd have to take out another loan to get a diamond of any size. I thought maybe the blue—with your eyes... But if you prefer a diamond, I'll go back..."

"No." She silenced his apology, slipping the ring onto her finger and losing herself in the simple perfection of the square-cut sapphire framed on either side by rectangular diamond baguettes. The white-gold setting added to the elegance of form and style.

She looked up and met eyes of the same sapphire blue. She'd never imagined a marriage proposal unfolding like this. Of course, she'd never imagined any proposal at all.

The expectant look in his eyes reminded her of a little boy seeking approval. "It's beautiful," she whispered.

But there was nothing childlike in the blunt planes and angles of his face moving toward her.

"Brett." Guessing his intention, she lifted her hand, blocking it against the solid wall of his chest and holding him at bay. "You don't have to. No one can see us now."

"I know."

"Then why...?" He pushed past her hand and silenced her lips with his own, communicating an elemental message that went far beyond a simple thanks or sharing of comfort. Unsure, unprepared, yet unexpectedly willing, she kissed him back.

She inhaled the clean, woodsy scent of him as she moved her lips beneath his, learning the different textures of mouth and man.

Gentle. Firm. Pliant. Persuasive.

His mouth was an evocative contrast to the evening shadow of beard that studded his skin. The roughness of it tormented her chin and cheeks, the tenderness of his lips soothed the path left behind.

Ginny tunneled her fingers into the long, silky hair at his temple and held on. Tasting and learning. Thanking and giving.

His tongue pressed between the seam of her lips and she opened for him. Her breath stuttered and caught as he stroked the softer skin inside. She angled her head in the opposite direction, investigating the rough, masculine taste and texture of his mouth, marveling at the sensual contrast to the lustrous mane of hair caught in the palm of her hand.

When they bumped noses, Ginny froze.

She should have laughed.

But she couldn't.

She remembered Jean-Pierre and a dozen laughing faces. Laughing at her and her rosy-eyed naiveté. She remembered Amy and her parents and all the reasons why she shouldn't drop her guard and surrender her heart to this man. To any man.

With her fingers still tangled in his hair, she pulled away. "What are you doing?" she accused on an uneven breath.

A lazy smile stretched across his face. "The same thing you're doing."

"You and I are business partners."

His smile flattened. He encircled her wrist in one big hand and extricated his hair from her grasping fingers. "You weren't conducting business just now, Detective."

"No. I was…you…" She couldn't blame Brett for forgetting their purpose for being together. Not entirely. She got up and turned away, licking her own lips in a useless effort to elude the stamp of Brett's possession there, idly noting that Jean-Pierre's kisses had never lingered this way. "I was thanking you for the ring. Comforting… You seemed so tired. That kiss didn't mean anything."

She heard the creak of a chair the instant before a rough hand at her elbow spun her back around. His fingers cut into the flesh beneath the short sleeve of her blouse. "Lie to me if you want, angel. Lie to everybody else—I'll even help you with that." He dipped his head, standing nose to nose with her. His hot breath washed in an angry gust across her face. "But don't lie to yourself."

In half a stride he was at the door, slinging it open. "If business is all you're interested in, then let's go."

"Go where?" she demanded, filing away her tumbled emotions to deal with later. She dodged through the doorway ahead of him as he charged through.

He paused only long enough to hit the lights and lock the door. He barely gave her time to snatch her purse and blazer, and say good-night to Merle. Then his hand was on her elbow, guiding her toward the elevators. "After I met with Sophie, I had an interesting talk with Frank Rascone while I was buying the ring. I think you should hear what he has to say for yourself."

IN THE APARTMENT over Frank Rascone's jewelry shop, Ginny put her hand over her cup, giving a polite refusal when he offered to pour more tea.

Judging by the rebellious rumble in her stomach, she needed more food and less caffeine. But she willingly endured the pangs of hunger so as not to break the hour-long spell of Mr. Rascone's stories about the "old days" on Market Street.

Brett's big hands dwarfed the cup he held as Mr. Rascone filled it with tea and milk again. "Tell Gin what you said about the year Mark Bishop worked for you."

Just like with Pearl and Ruby Jenkins, he deftly steered the conversation to the information she needed.

Frank doctored his own tea with milk and two cubes of sugar. Ginny waited patiently while he stirred and stirred. She understood his fascination with the spoon was merely a stall to gather his thoughts. Tonight he seemed older and more fragile than he had been at his shop that morning. His strong Italian nose and dark deep-set eyes gave the only hint of the robust young man he had once been.

"Mark was a good kid," he began finally. He set the spoon in his saucer and turned to Ginny, showing none of the avoidance he had earlier. Brett's presence at the far end of the table seemed to calm him. "He sported a black eye more than once. Had a broken nose one time. I hired him to clean the place, move boxes in the back room, that sort of thing.

"Alvin showed up one evening about closing time, spouting off about the electric bill not being paid, said the TV wouldn't work." Frank pressed his hand over his heart, trying to absolve himself of a pain that lingered in his eyes. "I told Alvin myself I didn't pay my employees until the end of the week. He started arguing with me, right in front of a customer. Mark took him out back to quiet him down. After the customer left, I went out to the alley to offer to pay him in advance, if that would help. Mark's nose was already bleeding."

Brett's hands tightened around his teacup. But he remained silent as Frank continued.

"I saw him pick Mark up by the shirt and throw him against the brick wall. Alvin was a big man. Tall, like Brett here. Not fit, though, the man drank too much. But Mark wasn't full-grown yet. I said something and Alvin left. He shoved me aside on his way out of the alley." Frank's volume rose and abated as he related the incident.

"Mark never said a word against his father. But there was something powerful angry brewing inside that boy."

Hurting for the jeweler's sorrowful memories, Ginny hesitated a moment before asking, "Did you ever see or hear Mark threaten his father?"

Frank glanced over at Brett, as if seeking his approval to answer the question. His good-ol'-boy demeanor long gone, Brett simply nodded. "I'd like to hear how you'd answer that, too."

Frank turned back to Ginny. He shrugged his bony shoulders before answering. "I'd never seen it myself. But I've heard that Alvin went after Sophie a few times. Mark would stand up to him then, get in the way, take the brunt of it."

Brett's cup clattered in his saucer. He pushed himself to

his feet and paced the tiny kitchen. Ginny watched him, an edgy combination of fatigue and pent-up energy. She hadn't considered how deeply his feelings for Mark ran, how difficult something like this would be to hear.

She gentled her inquiries for his sake as much as Mr. Rascone's. "Did you ever know Mark to 'take the brunt' of his father's rage to protect anyone else besides his sister?"

"How do you mean?"

"Would he interfere to protect a girlfriend?"

Frank thought for a moment. "I never knew him to date anyone except that Jenkins girl. I don't imagine Mark would ever let her get close enough for Alvin to hurt her. Of course, I didn't keep real good track of Mark after he quit my shop."

"When was that?"

"Summer. Before school started." The jeweler withdrew into himself, looking suddenly ancient beyond his years. "He died that fall…"

His voice trailed away as he shook his head and stared down into his teacup. His silence lasted so long that Ginny reached for his hand. She clasped the chilled, gnarled fingers, offering a human connection to the present, far away from those sad events of so long ago.

Brett stopped his pacing and watched them both, leaving Ginny with the impression that she was being tested somehow. But for what? She ignored the silent evaluation and pressed on. "Did you ever see Mark with a blond-haired girl? Almost towheaded, like my color?"

Frank's gaze followed her hand up as she touched her hair.

He shook his head. "I'd remember someone with a color like yours."

She wanted to ask Frank more about Alvin Bishop's behavior, but he seemed so weak, so frail, that she didn't have the heart to push. She gave his hand a gentle squeeze and started to pull away. "I know this was difficult for you, Mr. Rascone."

He gripped her fingers, refusing to let her go. "Last time I saw Mark was the day before he died. He came into my shop and bought a plain silver bracelet, asked me not to say a word to anyone about it. I expect he meant his father. Old Alvin wouldn't want him throwing away money on something like that." He looked over his shoulder at Brett. "Do you suppose that's what set Alvin off? Maybe I could have helped the boy by telling someone sooner."

Brett came over and squeezed the old man's shoulder. "Don't second-guess yourself, Mr. R. If Alvin had it in his mind to do someone harm, there'd be no stopping him."

Appearing grateful for the reassurance, Frank nodded his head.

"We'd better be going," said Brett, coming to the back of Ginny's chair and pulling it out. The polite gesture forced her to stand. "Mr. Rascone opens his shop early in the morning."

Taking into account Brett's mood and Frank's fatigue, Ginny reluctantly set aside her growing list of questions and allowed Brett to steer her to the door.

The abrupt departure didn't seem to faze Frank. He followed them onto the landing, asking about the fit of Ginny's new ring, congratulating them both, asking if any plans had been set.

"We'll put the word out as soon as we decide the details," promised Brett.

At the top of the stairwell leading down to the street, Mr. Rascone snagged Ginny's wrist, stopping her short. She started at the unexpected contact, but made no move to pull away when the glare from the naked lightbulb hanging above them revealed an almost desperate look on his face.

"Whoever killed Alvin Bishop did us all a favor." He held her a moment longer, anger and despair glowing in the watery depths of his eyes. "I know you're upholding the law, and Brett says you mean well, but..." He patted her hand before releasing her. "You won't make many friends around here trying to single out his killer."

Ginny stared after him until he closed himself inside his apartment and slipped the dead bolt into place.

"Ginny?" Brett's deep whisper reverberated off the peeling plaster walls and settled into her consciousness, bringing her back to the moment. He stood two steps below her, yet he was tall enough to face her at eye level. "He didn't mean that as a threat."

She slipped her hand into her pocket, felt the folded slip of paper that had hinted at her death. The anonymous phone message burned her fingertips. "Just a friendly warning, right?"

She dared a look deep into those handsome, weary, slightly distrusting blue eyes. The uncomfortable notion that he could see even deeper inside her, see her suspicion, see her fear, made Ginny blink and step to the side to circle around him. She headed down the steps to the street below.

Brett caught up to her and walked at her side, that ever-present hand of his lightly guiding her, guarding her, at the elbow. When they reached his white pickup, he unlocked the passenger door and she climbed inside. She put out a hand to hold the door open when he would have closed it.

Ginny waited the moment it took him to realize her intent and look at her. "Why do you second-guess *your*self?" she asked.

"Time to interrogate me, huh?" But the teasing in his voice didn't reflect in his face.

"I know it was hard for you to hear those details about Mark's injuries."

"I've seen Mark hurt plenty of times." He shrugged his shoulders, and the air of false nonchalance disappeared into the night. "I guess hearing Mr. R. describe that scene in the alley got me thinking about what I was trying to do to help Mark in the first place. And how, ultimately, I failed him. I guess a lot of us feel like we failed him.''

Ginny understood failure. She understood how debilitating the feeling could be.

"I failed Amy, too," she admitted. She wanted to reach out and touch Brett, offer him some bit of the comfort she herself had yet to find. But he was too big, too much, too hurt for her paltry skills to be of much help, so she simply shared her own story. "She tried to tell me something was going wrong in her life in that last month before she died. She wrote me letters while I was at school in Europe. But I was too caught up in my own stupid problems to listen."

"It eats you up inside, doesn't it."

He stood framed in the open door, one arm draped over the side of the truck bed, one hand hooked over the top of the door. From her perch on the seat, they formed a triangle, a connected unit.

The space between them sparked with electricity, an awareness of something more than physical. An embrace of like minds, of shared spirits, of battered souls. Ginny knew an overwhelming urge to touch, to close the distance between them. The tips of her breasts, her stomach, her fingertips tingled with the energy flowing between them. He needed... She wanted...

A single blink of his eyes broke the spell, reminded her of past mistakes, and finally, recalled the strength of her inexhaustible reason.

"I have to believe I'm helping her now. I will not let my sister be a statistic. She will not be some unsolved mystery." Her whispered vow caught in the trapped air between them. "Try to believe you're helping Mark now, too."

In the still silence of the night, Brett reached out. His broad hand hesitated in her peripheral vision. And when she didn't speak or flinch away, those rough-tipped fingers touched her hair ever so gently, catching a curl and tucking it behind her ear. She closed her eyes and savored the callused warmth of his hand along her jaw.

His low voice drizzled against her eardrum. "Thank you."

She opened her eyes, shaking her head. "For what?"

"For not being as tough as you want the rest of the world to believe."

Chapter Six

Ginny watched the numbers above the elevator doors light up one by one. She twisted her neck from right to left, trying to ease some of the tension there. She didn't know which spooked her more—the feeling that her investigation into Alvin Bishop's murder had stirred the interest of an anonymous fan, or the admission that Brett Taylor was getting under her skin despite her best efforts to remain unattached.

Four. Three more floors to go.

After their interview with Frank Rascone, she'd had the most illogical desire to throw her arms around Brett's neck and hold him close. She'd wanted to comfort him.

Five.

He'd do better wrapping up with his hard hat than to accept such a feminine gesture from her. She'd rejected his kisses, argued at every turn, misplayed his attempts to make their engagement look real. She'd even upset his chauvinistic sense of right and wrong by refusing to let him drive her home tonight.

Still, after talking about Mark, he'd been so…hurt.

It eats you up inside, doesn't it.

His words rang true, deep inside her soul. She understood the guilt he felt. For a few moments, she'd felt a connection to him that went beyond job stress or even physical attraction. Yet, while she buried her wishes and wants, and pains and sorrows, behind her badge and an attitude, he wore his for all to see—in those big smiles and on those broad shoulders.

She felt a coward, by comparison.

Imagine, thinking someone with her dysfunctional history could offer him some kind of comfort.

Six.

She laughed out loud. "Handsome playboy turns to neurotic lady cop. That'll be the day."

The bell dinged. Any humor, sarcastic or otherwise, was eclipsed by the ominous flash of the number seven.

As much as she hated the elevator ride up to the seventh floor of her apartment building, she dreaded stepping out into the hallway even more.

Fifty-fifty.

Those were her chances of having the hall light work. The window at the opposite end of the hall let in some light during the daytime. But at night, the place would be pitch black. And since her neighbors rarely opened their doors, she'd get no relief there either.

Ginny sucked in a deep breath and held it. She squeezed her eyes shut and waited for the elevator to open. Hardly a smart move for a lone female trained in the rules of self-defense. But it delayed the nightmare just a bit.

"Oh hell."

She focused her eyes on the long, black corridor that greeted her. Her breath whooshed out on a puff of air.

Little children and superstitious fools were afraid of the dark. Not mature adults, not cops.

But dark was dark, and she knew what kind of heartbreak and humiliation could lie hidden within the darkness.

With her key gripped in her hand, she hurried down the hall, trailing her fingertips past two, three, four doors. Flattening her palm against the door of 709, she used unerring rote memorization to find the dead bolt, insert her key and unlock it.

With her heart beating in her ears, she turned the knob. A sudden flood of light washed over her from behind.

"There you are."

She spun around, her key protruding between the knuckles of her fist. "Dammit, Dennis, you startled me."

She collapsed against her door and lowered her makeshift weapon as she identified the tenant from apartment 710 across the hall. Dressed in a bathrobe and slippers, Dennis Fitzgerald managed to look impeccable with his receding red hair and black plastic half-glasses perched below the bridge of his nose.

He tapped at the Timex on his wrist. "You're getting home awfully late. Is it that case from the Ludlow Arms?"

Ginny sighed deeply, emotionally drained and physically exhausted, but too well mannered to blow off his neighborly concern. "So you've been watching the news."

"You know I always watch the crime report. The description of Mr. Bishop's death reminded me of a story by Edgar Allan Poe that I read back in school." He pointed his thumb over his shoulder. "I pasted today's newspaper report in my scrapbook. Then I went to the library to get a copy of Poe's short stories so I could compare details. I can get the book for you, if you like."

Only one book? Dennis's lifelong hobby had been collecting police blotters from the newspapers, and accumulating photos and obits of assorted crime victims. Since his retirement, his amateur sleuthing had become a full-time profession. Ginny often wondered if he had chosen this particular apartment because he knew a detective lived across the hall.

"Maybe another time, Dennis. It's awfully late and I need to get some sleep."

He tipped his head to study her over the rim of his glasses.

"You do look tired. You'd best go straight to bed. I'll slip a copy under your door in the morning then, so I don't disturb you."

"I…" She rethought her protest. Dennis looked after her in an impersonal, good Samaritan kind of way. She trusted him to water her plants when she was gone on an extended assignment, after all. If helping her with a case gave him pleasure, or made him feel he could contribute something to the world, then she didn't have it in her to stop him. "You do that," she agreed, figuring that would earn her a quicker good-night.

"I will." He pointed to her door. "I'll wait until you lock up before I turn in."

"Thanks, Dennis."

"Good night."

She opened her door and stepped inside, immediately turning on the lamp she kept beside the door. She slipped the dead bolt and hooked the chain, then waited to hear the same sounds across the hall before moving on into her apartment.

Tossing her shoulder bag onto an overstuffed chair, she kicked off her shoes and walked down the hall, turning on lights as she went. Her hand grazed the doorknob to the room on her right and she paused.

For a moment she stopped breathing. This was always so hard.

Tightening her grip on the knob, she opened the door and flipped on the light. Unlike the rest of her apartment, this spare room was a study in chaos. Instead of carpeting, dropcloths covered the floor. A battered chest of drawers that had lost its handles long ago filled one corner. And on its paint-spattered top, she'd piled boxes of oils and pastels, and jars of pencils and paintbrushes. Ignoring the mess, she crossed the room to close the blinds that hung over the double windows.

Then she turned to the wooden easel and oversize canvas standing in the center of the room. Like the rows of canvases leaning against the north wall, this one, too, showed a hodgepodge of drab, muted colors. Olives and browns, grays and deep reds. Impressionistic in form, she'd created landscapes and cityscapes dotted with faceless people. Each painting reflected a mood, an observation about life, an attempt to escape the memories that refused to let go.

"God, you're depressing." She admonished her work and exited the room, closing the door behind her. When had her haven become such a dark, dour place?

Shaking off the downward spiral of her thoughts, she shed her blazer and carried it to the closet. After hanging it up, she removed her gun, holster and badge from her belt and locked them inside the metal box in the drawer of the bedside table.

Ginny hesitated for a moment before picking up the yellowed shoestring lying beside the box. Threaded onto the string was a tiny key.

Brett said a lot of people had failed Mark Bishop before his death. They'd failed Amy Rafferty, too.

Once, she and Amy had been more than sisters, they'd been best friends. They'd always talked. But when Ginny graduated from high school and went to Europe, she'd left her sister alone with two busy, distant parents. So they'd written letters.

Mostly, Amy had done the writing. Ginny had been too caught up in a new world, a new school, a new love.

Three letters had come the week after Jean-Pierre Dumage had hurt her so. A week she'd spent sulking in self-pity, questioning her talent, cursing her willingness to trust—a week to convince herself she had no more use for love.

Three letters came that week. Ginny didn't read them.

Until the phone call came from her father, telling her that Amy had been murdered.

She tossed up the key and caught it in her fist.

It was time to face those letters again.

When Ginny had on her ice-blue silk pajamas, she returned to the kitchen. A scan of her fridge and freezer revealed nothing more decadent than boxed microwave meals and bottles of salad dressing. Making a mental note to add ice cream to her shopping list, she poured herself a glass of milk and went into the living room. She set aside a bouquet of silk flowers and lifted the glass tabletop from the antique travel trunk that served as her coffee table.

She pulled the key from the shoestring looped around her neck and unlocked the trunk. The stale smell of mothballs and memories stung her nose as she pushed open the lid. She set aside a pilled and faded baby quilt and pulled out a stack of airmail o'grams tied up with a pink silk ribbon.

Curling her legs beneath her, Ginny sank onto the couch and untied the ribbon.

The first date and address actually made her smile. A safe place to start—before Paris and Jean-Pierre and shattered dreams.

London, England

Dear Ginny,

Too cool! Imagine writing to you in London! I am so jealous that Mom and Dad think you're old enough to study abroad. When I go to college, I'll probably end up at a state school. How dull is that?

I remember how you used to close yourself up in your room and paint all day. I always wanted to be creative like you. Mom used to send me up to get you for dinner. You'd be a mess, but you'd be so happy. Just think. Now you can be as messy as you want!

When I'm teaching kindergarten in five years, I plan to take my students to the Nelson Art Gallery to see your stuff.

Remember when Mom took us to the Egyptian exhibition there?

Ginny stopped reading and folded the letter. She closed her eyes and remembered. They were both in elementary school then, fourth and sixth grade. The sarcophagus had freaked them out. The idea of closing someone, even if he was dead, inside the ornate coffin had turned her into a quivering wreck.

Ginny's eyes shot open, thinking of Alvin Bishop's remains, chained to a wall and buried alive. How her flashlight had gone out and she'd been plunged into horrifying, haunting darkness.

She'd always hated the dark, she realized.

But Amy had recovered quickly. She might have marveled at her older sister's talent, but Ginny had always envied Amy's resiliency. Nothing kept her down for long.

Ginny's lips curved into a smile, remembering more about that trip to the Nelson Gallery. Minutes after leaving the Egyptian display, Amy was sliding down the wide marble banisters of the museum. She'd dared Ginny to try the ride, and throwing rules aside, she had.

She thought of Brett Taylor's assertion that she needed to break the rules. Once upon a time she would have. But now...

She set the letter aside and picked up the next one in the stack.

Paris, France
Dear Ginny,

Okay, 'fess up! Tell me more about this French professor of yours. He sounds really cute.

She refolded the letter and put it on top of the first.

"So much for a safe trip down memory lane."

Swallowing the last of her milk, Ginny got up and laid the letters back in the trunk and closed the lid. She'd try reading them in the morning, when she was rested and felt less at odds with herself.

On her way to rinse out her glass, the phone rang.

She glanced at the wall clock in the kitchen. No reason to panic. Anytime something broke on a case, she could get a call. Answering the phone at 12:00 a.m. was no big deal.

"Detective Rafferty."

"Gin?"

Professional detachment abandoned her and she hugged her arm around her waist in an automatic defense against the power of that hushed voice. "Brett."

After a breathless moment of silence, he asked, "Did you get home all right? It was so late, I wanted to double check."

His concern, couched in those seductive tones, made her knees and ankles tingle. She fought the feeling. "I'm a big girl. I've been getting home by myself for a long time now."

"Not when you're my responsibility, you haven't."

Her legs buckled. Preserving the shreds of her self-assurance, she climbed onto a stool and rested against the kitchen's center island. "I appreciate your concern, but—"

He cut her off. "I have a proposition for you."

Not again.

"Brett…"

"I feel guilty about making you miss two meals today." This was about food? She could almost see his shoulders relaxing, a mischievous smile tipping the corners of his mouth. She could almost feel a matching smile herself. "I don't want you to waste away into nothing."

Silly midnight talking. She hadn't done anything silly for so long. Maybe the late hour made it easier to give in to his boyish humor. Maybe the distance between them made it safe for her to play along.

"You missed two meals, too," she pointed out. "If you keep that up, you're gonna shrink down to my size."

The rich, musical laughter at the other end of the line made her smile. "No chance of that, angel."

The tension she'd felt from the phone message and the dark hallway and Amy's letters eased out of her like a gentle massage. It felt so good to just talk to someone, without trying to ferret out information or keep them at a professional distance.

"Did you really call just to check on me?" she asked, not quite trusting the shared moment.

"Not exactly." Her bottom lip slipped between her teeth as she braced for the reality check. "I just wanted to hear your voice."

She stopped her gentle gnawing. "My voice?"

"Yeah. Crazy, huh?" She heard a rustling sound over the line and imagined that he was up and moving around his...wherever he lived.

"Brett, where are you?"

"At home. I couldn't sleep."

In an unforeseen rush, her imagination conjured up a mental image of just how Brett might sleep. He didn't seem the pajama type. T-shirt? No, too confining for that much man and muscle. Shirtless? Yes, definitely. And shorts, maybe. They'd cling to those muscled thighs and show off the naked, masculine length of those powerful legs.

Ginny's nipples puckered as if a cool breeze had suddenly blown through her apartment.

"Oh, my..." she breathed, startled by her body's physical reaction to a mental image.

Shutting her eyes did nothing to dispel the image of broad shoulders and bare chest. Of a jutting jaw with a raspy need for a shave. Right on cue, her lips prickled with the memory of his gentle, commanding kiss.

"Brett." Was that croaky plea her own voice? She

slapped her palm over her mouth, embarrassed by all she might have revealed.

"Angel? What's wrong?" The snap of concern in his voice cut through the imaginative haze clouding her mind. She was dimly aware that he'd been apologizing for something. Moodiness, she thought she'd heard.

"I'm sorry. What were you wearing? Saying?" She shouted the correction, dismayed at how thoroughly her body had betrayed her rational mind. She stood up and circled the center island, struggling to dispel the lingering tension in her body.

"Ginny." The quiet word sounded like a sigh of pleasant surprise.

Great. That's all his ego needed, to know that her libido had temporarily overridden her logic and she'd been fantasizing about him.

"Business, Taylor," she warned him. And herself. "We have to keep it strictly business between us."

"I will if you will." She heard the laughter in his promise, wondered if it was at her expense. "As I said before, I have a proposition for you."

She carefully steered her brain away from the more lascivious definition of the word. "What kind of proposition?"

"Let me buy you breakfast. I'll get take-out. You can meet me at my office, and then I'll take you over to the Ludlow Arms."

The fact that he'd added the last didn't disappoint her. She was pleased that he'd remembered her earlier request. The offer took some of the sting out of her current embarrassment. But then this was Brett Taylor talking, and when he'd said *proposition*...

"What's the catch?" she asked.

"You tell me what *you're* wearing."

"Damn you, Taylor!" The heat in her cheeks was sudden

and intense. The indignation in her throat muffled any articulate response.

She slammed down the receiver, canceling out the sound of his seductive laughter.

When she crawled into bed that night, she clutched a pillow to her stomach and wrapped her body around it. She felt chilled and raw and completely out of her league after her midnight chat with Brett Taylor.

When she finally fell into an exhausted sleep, she'd left the light burning beside her bed.

"Mmm. I guess I was hungry."

Brett watched Ginny across the desk as she stuffed the last bite of a French-toast stick into her mouth. Then she proceeded to lick the gooey syrup from her thumb and first two fingers. One at a time, she pulled them between her lips and teeth with a delicate suction.

He put the disposable coffee cup to his mouth and swallowed a gulp of the warm liquid, thanking God for whomever had invented the desk, so that he could sit there and mask his body's response to the innocent, carnal movements of her mouth.

It didn't take much to feel the tightening in his jeans. He'd been off-kilter from the moment he realized why she'd sounded so breathy and distracted on the phone last night.

Making a joke out of it hadn't helped a bit. After hanging up, he'd spent an uncomfortable night trying to keep his mind from imagining what *she* slept in. Skimpy lingerie or practical cotton? It didn't matter. In his mind, he'd undressed her from a dozen different outfits with the same result—her sweet naked body, delicately proportioned and softly feminine, standing in shy perfection before him.

"Glad I could finally make good on my invitation," he managed to say. With casual efficiency, she cleaned up the paper wrappers and napkins, and carried the sack of trash to the wastebasket.

Man, he was a sorry celibate. Of all the women in the world who could be keeping him awake at night, it had to be this thorny rose of a woman.

With angelic hair and sensuous lips.

With fire cooking beneath that icy veneer.

And with the patience to listen and understand, without judging him for who he was and what he'd done or hadn't done.

That wounded spot, deep inside his heart, healed a bit under her care, just remembering how she'd been last night with Frank Rascone. Gentle and patient, with the right combination of push and give to get the job done without hurting the old man.

And the way she reached out to him afterward, with concern and compassion. He'd called her last night, hoping to recapture that soul-deep connection he'd felt. Hoping she'd admit to feeling something, too.

Today, though, he put on his game face, gearing himself up to hold his own against his fake fiancée, played this morning once again by the sensibly efficient Detective Rafferty.

He finished off his coffee, crushed the cup in his fist and followed her to the wastebasket. "Ready for the Ludlow Arms?"

"Let's do it." Today her professional uniform consisted of a peach-colored blazer over navy slacks. Despite the crisp lines of shoulder pads and lapels, the jacket's soft color highlighted the creamy complexion of her skin, making a mockery of his efforts to be as businesslike about working together as she was.

If he didn't quit noticing those little feminine details she tried so hard to hide, he'd never make it through this pretend relationship unscathed.

Grabbing his keys and cell phone, he led the way to the door. But he never made it outside.

"Brett?" The trailer door opened with the strident request. "Oh, Brett."

He backed up a step to brace himself as Sophie Bishop threw herself into his arms. She reached around his waist and tucked her nose into the collar of his shirt. He felt her sobs pushing in an erratic cadence against his chest before he felt the moist heat of her tears on his neck.

Automatically, he curled his arms around her and patted her shoulder. "Hey, it's all right," he offered, not sure what he was promising.

"It's all so horrible," she hiccuped. "I haven't done anything like this since Mark died."

Acutely aware of Ginny standing in mute courtesy behind him, he felt an unaccustomed discomfort at the pressure of Sophie's body pressed so tightly to his. He eased some space between them and nudged her chin up with the tip of his finger. "What are you talking about?" he asked. "What's wrong?"

With his focus split between the two women, he was only vaguely aware of the door opening a second time. Sophie pushed aside her tears with the palm of her hand and worked her mouth into a brave smile. "The arrangements for Daddy. My God, Brett, how could this happen?" She reached for him again, collapsing into tears.

Eric Chamberlain reached out and laid his hand on Sophie's shoulder, adding his solace to Brett's. Brett noticed an unexpected catch in the other man's voice. "She's talking about the funeral arrangements. The police released Alvin's body this morning. She wants to have a memorial service tomorrow."

Sophie tipped her head back. Through a sheen of tears, her brown eyes beseeched Brett. "You'll come, won't you?

I know Daddy wasn't a popular man, but I need you there for me."

"Of course I'll come. All the Taylors will, I'm sure. Even Cole, if we can find him. You're important to us."

She sniffed back tears and smiled. "Thank you." She threw her arms around his neck and hugged him tight. From the stiffening of her body, Brett knew the precise moment when Sophie recognized Ginny behind him. "Detective Rafferty."

At last she pulled away, smoothing the knit of her dark navy dress. Brett backed up a step to include Ginny in their circle. With her unique blend of authority and compassion, Ginny extended her hand. "My condolences, Ms. Bishop."

Sophie shook hands. "Thank you. I understand you've been assigned to my father's case. I trust you're doing everything you can to find his killer?"

Ginny nodded. "Right now we're going through the list of anyone who would have had a motive to kill your father."

Sophie pulled back, straightening her shoulders with a poignant pride. "I imagine that's quite a long list."

"Not so many as you might expect. It's a long way to go from disliking a person to actually killing him."

Eric slipped his arm around Sophie's waist, perhaps warning her before he shifted into his sharklike attorney's voice. "The way it was done, it had to have been premeditated. You're looking for opportunity as well as motive, aren't you?"

Brett clenched and unclenched his fists at his sides, damning the man's right to be here. But Ginny sounded unruffled by the subtle accusation of incompetence in his observation. "There was some planning involved, yes. I've been reading up on the method, in fact. I believe the inspiration for the plan comes from Edgar Allan Poe."

Sophie raised her eyebrows. "Really?"

Brett was curious to hear Ginny's explanation, too. "'The

Cask of Amontillado.' It's standard reading in any high-school American lit course. The story lays out an identical murder scenario to your father's death.''

"Tell me more.'' Sophie's curiosity seemed to briefly override her grief.

But Eric intruded on the intellectual meeting of female minds. "Sophie, you don't have to deal with this right now. Let's let Detective Rafferty do her job.'' He scaled his gaze from Ginny up to Brett. His lips curled into a charmless smile. "With your help, of course. Which comes first with you two? The job or the wedding plans?''

Brett's hands stayed fisted this time. It was one thing to play the game with him, but to involve Ginny... Suddenly he felt Ginny's hand on his arm, a tiny anchor of civility to latch onto. He looked down to see the subtle warning in her cobalt eyes. He covered her hand with his, promising to keep his temper, marveling how she could keep her own reactions in check.

"We were just on our way out.'' His glance included both Sophie and Eric. "Ginny wants to look around the Ludlow again. I'm her tour guide.''

Taking the hint better than Eric, Sophie backed toward the door. "You will keep me posted on anything you find out about my father's murder, won't you?''

"Of course.'' Ginny released Brett and reached into her pocket. "Here's my card. You can call me or my partner, Merle Banning, anytime, if you have a question, or if you think of something that might help us with the investigation.''

"I'll do that.'' Sophie dropped the card into her purse and tilted her lips to kiss Brett's cheek. "I won't keep you. I just needed to know you'd be there for me.''

Ignoring the glare in Eric's eyes, Brett nudged her chin with a playful fist. "Always, kiddo.''

She slipped her hand through the crook of Eric's arm. "Would you go on to the car? I'll be right there."

The obvious dismissal flushed Eric's cheeks. But apparently, he couldn't deny her request. With little more than a grunt of, "Later, Taylor," he shoved open the door and marched down the steps.

Sophie turned to Brett and straightened the collar of his chambray work shirt. Her long fingers brushed across his shoulders, smoothing out wrinkles and staking a familiar claim that, with Ginny standing by his side, made him want to squirm. "I apologize for Eric's rudeness. He's just trying to protect me. He always has."

"No problem," Brett lied, taking her hands and pulling them away from his shoulders before releasing her.

"I almost forgot. Congratulations on your engagement." She looked down at Ginny, her smile for him thinning into a taut line. *A test.* He read Sophie's expression as clearly as a billboard. He prayed Ginny could read it, too. "You're stealing one of the finest men I've known away from our little neighborhood."

Ginny locked up at the suddenly personal turn in the conversation. Like always. Several appropriate responses danced on the tip of Brett's tongue. If she didn't lose that wide-eyed, deer-in-the-headlights look every time the subject of their engagement came up, they'd never be able to pull this off.

As the seconds ticked into aeons, Brett opened his mouth to speak. But Ginny found her voice. "Stealing's such a strong word."

She hooked one hand around his bicep, entwined her fingers through his and curled her body along the length of his arm. With her snuggled so close, he felt the imprint of a small, firm breast at his elbow. And when she laid her head against his shoulder, that delicate scent of freesia stirred from her hair.

Articulated with throaty precision, even her words suckered him into believing the authenticity of the impromptu embrace. "I'd like to think he volunteered to become my husband."

With her face tipped up, her lips mere inches away, he bought into the wordplay. "Willingly."

Then, because the tentative confidence sparkling in those clear blue eyes was impossible to resist, he angled his mouth and kissed her. He felt her strain against his arm, stretching her body up to meet him. Her lips moved beneath his, equal partners for the first time.

His body hummed with excitement, her bold move fanning to life the embers she had forged in his feverish dreams. He caught the nape of her neck with his right hand, twisting to catch the fall of silky curls between his fingertips.

A polite cough filtered through the potent desire clouding his brain. It took Sophie clearing her throat a second time for him to remember himself and forcibly pull his lips from the sweet heaven he'd just discovered in Ginny's willing kiss.

It was easy to smile when he turned to apologize to Sophie. "Sometimes we get carried away."

"Yes, I see."

A breeze of cool air chilled his arm as Ginny started to back away. A quick glance at her rosy cheeks warned him that she, too, had temporarily forgotten their audience. He tightened his grip on her hand so she couldn't release him entirely.

Perhaps it was the strain of her father's funeral, and the investigation surrounding his death that seemed to make it impossible for Sophie to smile along with him. "I'll see you tomorrow then. At ten o'clock."

"We'll be there."

After Sophie left, he felt the inevitable tugging on his hand. "She's gone now. You can let go."

But he wasn't ready to let Ginny escape. It had been real. To his body and heart, that kiss had been for real.

He spun around and grasped her by the shoulders, delicate points of muscle and bone that fit easily into his hands. He dared her to admit the same. "You had me believing you."

She writhed within his grip, the flat of her hands pushed against his chest. "I've been working on my acting skills."

The flippant remark left a sour taste in his mouth. But like the keeper of a frightened bird caught in a trap, he let her go.

Her haste to open the door insulted his sense of honesty, inflamed a craving inside him for her to feel something, anything, of the misplaced need he felt for her.

Coming up behind her, he pushed the door shut and trapped her there. The curve of her rump butted against his thighs, her shoulders heaved against his chest. But he was bigger and stronger and refused to budge. He held her there, feeling her heat, inhaling her scent, sensing her anger and distrust like an undeserved slap in the face.

Hating himself, he whispered into her ear. "Is it really so impossible for you to admit there's something between us?"

Her struggles stilled instantly. "It doesn't make any difference, Brett. When this investigation is over, you'll go your way and I'll go mine."

"You don't know that," he argued. "You won't even give us a chance."

"You said I shouldn't lie to myself." She threw his own words back at him with clear, logical cunning. "Okay, so maybe I feel some attraction to you, some kinship because of Mark and Amy. But that's it."

"Kinship?" He spun her around, pinned her with his hands at her shoulders, his hips pressing into hers. "I don't feel…"

"I'm no good at relationships, Brett." She curled her hands into fists between them, clutching up handfuls of chambray, softly beating her message into him. "I can barely act my way through one, much less deal with one in real life. So I am not going to care. I am not going to give in to passionate kisses or any other damn thing that's going to hurt me ever again. You included."

He shook his head, denying the sheen of tears held in check in her eyes. Not believing what she'd just admitted.

"You're a coward."

"Yes."

She boldly held his gaze. He searched her flushed cheeks, her shining eyes, her trembling mouth, for any sign that he'd misheard her. He searched inside himself, in his memory, in his heart, for any clue she might have dropped that would explain this deep, irrational fear. But he discovered he knew as little about Ginny now as he had that first day down in the subbasement of the Ludlow Arms.

He released her and stepped back, holding his hands out to either side of his body in apologetic surrender. "I'm sorry. I don't know what you want me to do."

"It's not up to you to do anything." The way she hugged herself, rubbing her hands up and down her arms, made him regret giving rein to his frustration, made him wish she'd allow him to give her that comfort she sought for herself. "I came to you to help me find my sister's killer. Not to fix my love life."

Chapter Seven

Brett granted Ginny her silence as they walked to the Ludlow Arms. Other than a perfunctory request to put on a hard-hat once they crossed beneath the yellow crime-scene tape blocking off the entrance, he, too, had little to say.

He wasn't sure what he felt for her beyond respect, lust, fascination, admiration. Hell, he'd been thinking with his hormones instead of his head. Tough as Detective Rafferty might be on the outside, she was more fragile than he'd ever have guessed on the inside.

Someone had hurt her. Badly. Scared her enough that she wouldn't trust her own feelings anymore. Maybe it had been the epitome of arrogance for him to assume she had any of those feelings for him. She'd need someone solid, reliable, as good as his word, to help her through whatever she needed to get through.

Brett was smart enough to know the job description didn't fit him.

"What are those for?" Ginny had asked to go up to the fourth-floor apartment where the Bishops had lived. After climbing the relative stability of the first two flights of stairs, she pointed out the red X's spray-painted on some of the risers going up to the third floor.

Construction sounded like a safe enough topic for them to discuss. "They mark where the support structure is weak.

You can crash through to the bottom of the stairwell if you put too much weight on those particular timbers.''

''Why label them if you're going to tear down the building?''

''Originally, I wanted to save the Ludlow. There's some real architectural history here.'' He remembered the day he made the decision to pour his money into the other two buildings because the Ludlow needed so much work. He'd felt as if he'd let her down.

He skimmed his hand along the painted walnut paneling, still wishing he could repair the ravages of time and bad taste. The stale dust that tickled his nose gave way to Ginny's clean, flowery scent. She wasn't interested in his emotional attachment to the building, she'd simply asked a polite question. He gave a polite answer. ''The cost to restructure her was too prohibitive. Let's keep moving.''

He negotiated a path around the first of the marked stairs. Leading the way, he easily stretched over two rotted steps. But with her shorter legs, it proved a more challenging climb. He kept a close eye on her as she matched his footing.

As she shifted her balance, she rocked back on her heels, automatically reaching out for the railing that was no longer there. He lunged quickly, grabbed her hand and pulled her up onto the step beside him. ''Easy.''

Ever the practical detective, she hesitated only a moment before turning her clasp into his, allowing him to help her over the dangerous stretch of stairs and onto the fourth-floor landing.

Once on a level surface she let go. She breathed in through her nose and out through her mouth, revealing a need to calm herself. ''Do I want to know how far down this stairwell goes?''

''You're four stories up now. Plus the basement. That's a good sixty feet before you hit bottom. Unless you get skewered by an exposed timber or support pylon along the way.''

Her gaze darted up to his, satisfying herself that the danger he described was real. "At least my phobias don't include a fear of heights."

Whether that was an attempt at humor or just a statement of fact, Brett didn't try to decipher. He shied away from trying to understand Ginny, and stuck to what he knew best. "You want to walk as close to the walls as you can. There's more support there than over an open expanse of floor."

He practiced what he preached and led her down the hallway, past a gaping hole in the middle of the floor where the linoleum and woodwork had given way to water leaks and age and gravity. To her credit, she respected his expertise and followed along in his footsteps.

"Here." He turned into one of the many doorways without a door. "This was the Bishops' humble abode. Sophie moved out after Alvin disappeared. Stayed in a foster home until she graduated high school and left for college. It's been abandoned ever since. I don't know what you expect to find here."

"Neither do I." Trailing her hand along the outer wall as she had done in the hallway, she scouted the perimeter of the tiny one-bedroom apartment. "How did three people fit in here?"

Brett idly opened the one remaining cupboard door in the kitchenette area and peered inside. "Sophie used the bedroom. Mark slept on a sofa bed out here. Alvin spent most of his time passed out in a recliner in front of the TV, with his coffee cup full of whiskey and java."

"Coffee cup?" A light of possibilities sparked in her eyes.

He imagined a set of precision gears twirling inside her head as her curiosity kicked in. Despite his mood, he'd always been drawn to fine-tuned machines, and found her intensity hard to resist. "I never saw him drink the booze straight. He liked to pretend he was *handling* his addiction.

Whether it was here or at a bar, I don't think I ever saw him without his Irish coffee.''

"When did he start drinking?'' she asked, jotting his responses in her notebook.

"When his wife left him. Mark said old Alvin never was the same after that.''

Ginny's breath rushed out on a compassionate sigh. "Did he abuse her, too? Did drinking worsen an already existing problem?''

He'd been little more than a kid himself the last time he saw Mrs. Bishop. He vaguely remembered dark hair pulled back into a bun, and a stern but pretty face. "You'd have to ask Sophie that. Mark never said much about his mom.''

Ginny tucked her notebook back into her pocket. "It's a wonder Sophie survived as well as she has.''

He reported his findings instead of commenting on the obvious. Mark *hadn't* survived that home life. "Nothing here, unless a mouse hole's important.''

She poked her head into the bedroom, but didn't go in. Instead, she worked her way back to the kitchen. "Mr. Rascone said Alvin Bishop was as big as you, right?''

"Yeah. Fatter, but probably just as tall.'' He wondered what tangent of the case she was calculating now.

"Could you carry a man that size down four flights of stairs and on into the basement or subbasement?''

"It wouldn't be easy. If he's passed out or unconscious I'd have to drag him.''

She shook her head. "That would draw too much attention.''

"Then I'd need help to carry him that far.'' He caught on to her train of thought. "You think more than one person killed Alvin?''

That light blazed in her eyes. "I think something happened up here that made him go downstairs on his own.''

"Like what?''

"Like finding out his meal ticket was running away with my sister. How many loved ones can one man stand to lose? I think he went downstairs to stop them."

Brett stared at her. Hard. "You're saying he tracked them down? Followed them so he could stop them by whatever means he deemed necessary?"

She sucked in a deep breath and studied him. He had a feeling she wasn't evaluating his ability to follow her line of thinking. But there was no way he could prepare himself for her question. "You found Mark's body, right?"

"Hell." He hooked his thumbs into his front pockets and turned away, unable to keep the horrible scene from popping into his mind. So much blood. So much waste.

He jumped as a soft spot of heat singed his shoulder blade. He stiffened, unprepared for the touch of Ginny's hand. But he needed that touch to stay in the moment, to stay sane enough to help her. He leaned back, allowing himself to feel the imprint of each finger against his back, cherishing the bit of comfort she offered.

He wanted to turn and swallow her up in his arms, bury his face in her hair, lose himself inside her. Then maybe he could find enough warmth to chase away the utter chill of holding a lifeless friend in his arms.

But Ginny wouldn't do that for him. He had no right to ask for anything more than what she was willing to offer him, a *strictly business* partnership. The hell of the matter was, her business was taking a toll on his big ol' heart.

He opened his eyes and faced her, setting aside all emotion just as she so often did. It was the only way he could get through this. "I found him. He was already dead. When the paramedics rushed in, I got pushed aside. Then Sophie came home. She got hysterical. I took her outside and we just walked. For hours. Then the police caught up to us and, you know the rest."

He pounded his fist on the warped countertop. "He'd

asked me to meet him in the basement. He wanted to borrow some money for bus tickets. I was going to try to talk him out of eloping. He was too young. He had his whole life…'' His words failed him as he fought back the angry tears burning his eyes.

"Was Amy there?''

"No, dammit!'' His hoarse shout echoed in the empty room. "It was just him. His skull broken, his ribs crushed, his life seeping away into the cracks of this hellhole.'' It took Ginny cowering back a step for him to realize he'd been advancing on her.

Twelve years of anger and hate and guilt dashed out on a single breath. "I'm sorry.'' She nervously tucked a perfect curl behind her ear. The best way to atone for his outburst was to answer her question. "I was late meeting him. If Amy was there she'd already gone.''

"She wouldn't have left him if she knew he was hurt. My sister could never leave anyone who was in pain. She wouldn't have left Mark to die alone. Not voluntarily.''

She spoke quietly, keeping her eyes locked on his, offering that same empathy from the night before. But no, she'd made herself clear. This was the good cop prodding him along. Not a fiancée, not even a friend. She meant nothing personal with that reassurance. He had no right taking the compassion from her she didn't consciously want to give.

He moved past her to the living-room window, needing the benefit of space between them to keep from reaching for her. He could tell by the pinpoint articulation in her voice that whatever trepidation he might have caused her was being crushed beneath the gears of that analytical mind of hers. "No Amy. No Sophie. No Alvin. How late were you that night?''

He looked outside into the bright, normal sunlight that couldn't seem to pierce the grimy, cracked windowpanes. "An hour, hour and a half.''

"*You* didn't call the paramedics?"

"No."

He didn't get the significance of the questions until she added, "So who called 911?"

The discovery in her voice beckoned him to turn. Forget the sunshine. Ginny's blue eyes blazed with intensity, and made him feel one step closer to the truth. "The only people who knew Mark was down there were Alvin and me."

"And Alvin's killer."

She pulled out her cell phone and punched in an autodial number. "I'll call Merle and have him check the 911 records. Keep your fingers crossed there's a name or number we can trace."

"We can leave now, right?" He wasn't sure how visiting the old apartment had helped Ginny with the case, though apparently it had. But if she'd seen enough, he'd rather they returned to solid ground to figure out the rest of it. Straying from the outside wall, he hurried across the room.

With his third step, the floor dipped beneath his boot. His sense of the building's flaws made his reaction quick. He jumped to the bedroom doorjamb as the flooring cracked and began to sink.

"Brett!"

He put out his hand to stop her in her tracks and keep her from running toward him. "Don't move."

She froze.

The cracking sound gave way to the erratic trickle of bits of wood and plaster hitting the framework between this and the apartment below them. Ginny held her breath the way he held his.

Like a sudden spring storm, the patter of falling debris gradually increased its tempo to a steady staccato beat as chunks grew bigger and set off a chain reaction of floor hitting ceiling, and breaking through and hitting the floor below.

Without a word he motioned her away from the extra weight of the kitchen counters to the relative safety of the front doorway. Below his feet he felt the groaning stretch of a century-old structure trying to support itself.

"C'mon, old lady," he breathed, willing Victorian craftsmanship to hold together for a few minutes longer.

"Brett, let's go. I've seen enough. This isn't safe."

"You don't have to tell me twice."

As if the floor itself was crying out in pain, a bellowing moan followed the path of his quick, nimble steps to the doorway. He caught her up around the waist and leaped with her to the open archway across the hall.

"My phone!" It flew from her hand and disappeared through the broadening rift as the Bishops' living room fell away. He pushed Ginny against the jamb and turned his body to shield her from flying plaster and a snowfall of dust. The crash of the heavier timbers jarred Brett as they smashed into the floor below.

Seconds later, minutes perhaps, once the chorus of falling debris had reduced itself to the normal creaks and crumbles of a settling building, Brett eased his hold on Ginny. Her fingers relaxed their death grip on his forearm, but he didn't allow her to move away. Fear of more floor giving way, he rationalized, ignoring the way their bodies still trembled in unison.

Even from this distance, he could see the yawning hole in the center of the apartment. It split the length of the room and gave them a view of the pile of wood and rubble on the floor below.

"You don't need your phone back, right?"

He didn't really want her answer. They were leaving. Now.

"I guess not." She let him take her hand and lead her back down the stairs. Even though the broken steps had been marked, he tested each riser himself before allowing Ginny to follow.

Not until they hit the main floor did he dare to release her. Then, with his hand pushing slightly at the small of her back, he hurried toward the front door. "You see why I have to raze her, don't you? There's no way to bring this death-trap up to code."

"You mean 'raze' as in tear down, right?" He nodded at the definition. "How do you raze a building of this size?"

"Usually we use explosives. You create an implosion so it collapses on itself without damaging neighboring build-ings." He paused at the entrance to touch the sculpted arch-way that would have to be destroyed. "I'll take a wrecking ball to this old lady, though. She's too unstable to count on her falling the right way."

Ginny had stopped listening to his explanation. She an-gled her head back toward the stairwell. "Do you hear voices?"

He stopped her by the elbow when she took a step in that direction. "The place is falling down around us, remember? It makes lots of noises."

She shook him off but respected his concern. "I need to check the subbasement, anyway, before you raze the build-ing."

"Didn't Mac and his crew take enough pictures for you?"

"I want to see it for myself one more time. Get all the puzzle pieces in my head before I start pinning down an-swers."

Then he heard a sharp cry, a squeal of sorrow, followed by some incoherent mutterings, and knew he wasn't done with the Ludlow Arms just yet. "Damn. It's got to be the homeless guys. We have to get them out of here."

He ran down to the basement with Ginny right behind him. When they reached the trapdoor and the top of the ladder that led to the subbasement, he hesitated. "I didn't bring a flashlight with me. Are you okay to go down there?"

She very nearly smiled, surprising him yet again. "As long as the roof doesn't cave in on me, I can handle the dark for a few minutes."

Once Brett's boots hit the dirt floor, he reached up to Ginny's waist to lift her from the ladder. With her gun in the way, he had to move his hands higher, cursing his own gallantry when his fingertips caught beneath the firm curve of her breasts. When he set her down, she stepped away quickly, pulling her jacket and blouse and personal armor back into place.

He wished he could do the same.

"We won't talk. You can't make us talk."

The defiant taunts came from the same direction as the pungent odor of sweat and dirt. He waited for his eyes to adjust to the darkness before taking stock of his surroundings.

Little had changed since his last visit down here. The hole in the wall where Alvin was found had been opened up to facilitate removing the body. Sitting on the pile of bricks nearby was a gray-haired man with a greasy beard. From the whimpering sound he made, Brett assumed he was crying. Next to him stood a wiry, stooped man dressed in World War II–issue fatigues. He had his hands raised in the air and was backing away from Ginny.

"He's gone. What did you do with him?" he accused, clearly agitated by Ginny's arrival.

She had her hands in front of her, patting the air, trying to calm his fear. "I don't know what you're talking about, Mr. Jones. Right now, I need you to come with me."

She turned her head to the silent man, who clutched his gnarled hands together as if saying a prayer. "Charlie, is it?"

Brett crossed under the ladder and stood beside her. "You know these guys?"

"They discovered Alvin's body. I tried to interview them, but they think I'm the enemy. For whatever reason, they're lost in the middle of a war. Zeke Jones and Charlie something."

"Zeke? Charlie?" Brett tried common-sense persuasion. "This building isn't safe. I can take you to a shelter instead."

"We never leave a comrade," insisted Zeke.

"Guys, you have to go." Ginny stepped forward. Zeke grabbed Charlie and backed against the wall.

"I don't have to tell you nothing but name, rank and serial number."

Ginny turned to Brett. Even in the dim light, he could see the thoughts gleaming in her eyes. "Use a commanding voice. Order them to listen."

She wanted him to play along with the two intruders. Pulling up to his full height, he barked an order. "Men. Stand to."

They shut up, glared at him wide-eyed, then snapped to attention.

"At ease, men." In a softer voice, he whispered to Ginny, "You realize I've never been in the military."

"It doesn't matter. They're listening to you."

Taking a risk, Zeke spoke. "Why did the guard stop coming?"

"What guard?"

Zeke and Charlie exchanged curious looks before Zeke continued. "Kept the POW locked up here. Tortured him. Tried to break him."

Brett turned to Ginny. "Any idea what he's talking about?"

"Alvin Bishop." Safety took a temporary back seat to her

investigation. "Did you know the POW? Was it Alvin Bishop?"

"Answer her," ordered Brett.

"Sir, yes, sir." Zeke curled back into his eighty-something stoop. "Private Bishop. The guard checked him every day, until he stopped making that noise."

"The bell around his neck." She latched onto Brett's sleeve, the discovery filling her with an energy he could almost touch. "My God, that's how he knew Bishop was dead. The bell didn't ring anymore."

He smiled into her upturned face, knowing, as she did, that they'd found an eyewitness to Alvin's murder.

She kept hold of him as she asked, "Who was the guard? Did you know the guard?"

"Came every day."

Like an evil reminder, the building shifted above them. "We need to get out of here," Brett reminded her.

Ginny tried one more time. "Would you recognize the guard if you saw him again? Can you describe him?"

Zeke stared at her wildly. Then blinked, as if surrendering to the inevitable. "Not like you. Tall." He pointed a twisted, grubby finger at Brett. "Like him."

"THEY'LL EXPECT to see us together."

Ginny glared daggers up at Brett. "When you said to meet you here, I thought the service was over and we were going to pick up Zeke and Charlie from the shelter."

She rolled her eyes in frustration and turned away, hugging her arms around her middle, trying to rid herself of the goose bumps that pricked her skin. Pacing to the secluded corner of the elegantly appointed lobby wasn't nearly far enough to escape the suffocating air of the Stegmeier Mortuary.

It wasn't far enough to escape Brett's persistent arguments, either. She felt him at her right shoulder before he spoke. "It's just a memorial service. Sophie had Alvin cremated, so there's no coffin. It'll last twenty minutes, tops."

The piped-in organ music whispered at the fringes of her subconscious mind like tiny voices telling her to run away as fast as she could. She tried to ignore the impulse, find a more dignified way to make her escape. "But I don't *do* funerals."

"What does that mean?"

She spun around, thinking that facing him would help drive her point home. "I don't like them. I never have. I've been to too many of them." With a gesture of her hands, she swept the air clear between them. "I am not staying for this one."

His hands closed around her arms, right above each elbow, preventing her from leaving. He dipped his head closer to her level and looked her in the eye. "I'm concerned about maintaining your cover."

"You're kidding, right?" How the hell would sitting through twenty minutes of torturous flashbacks to her family's deaths help maintain her cover?

"I don't know how you handle tragedies in your family. But the Taylors stick together. Anyone who knows us would expect the people we care about to show up and support us, too."

"But..."

"Now I know you don't really care about me. But others believe that you do. Sophie. Mitch. Frank Rascone. Pearl Jenkins." The ruthless set of his features seemed out of place on his laugh-lined face. "If they don't see us together, they'll question how serious our relationship is. If they question it, they'll question you. You'll become enemy number one on Market Street again, and your investigation will be over."

A joking, flirtatious Brett she could argue with. When she'd first brainstormed this outrageous charade, she thought she could order his actions to fit her predictable, regimented life. But what she had mistaken for a lack of committment to any serious cause was merely a front for a man who did what he thought was right in a kinder, friendlier way than most.

Brett Taylor was a man with a long memory and a huge heart, instinctively smart, fiercely loyal to anyone or any cause he cared about. Just because he concentrated on the joys in life didn't mean he didn't feel its sorrows, too.

It was this harder, hurting man beneath the surface that she couldn't argue with.

She twisted within his grasp, pleading for her freedom, ignoring the gathering stream of mourners waiting to sign the guest registry before going into the chapel. He might have understood her silent request, but he didn't budge.

That left reasoning with him. She used that clipped tone he'd once said commanded authority. "We can give a plausible excuse. I have to work."

He didn't buy it. "Mitch is taking time off to be here."

She snatched the lapels of his navy worsted suit, grasping at the opportunity. "Then I need to go back to the office and hold down the fort while he's gone."

"Kansas City will survive for twenty minutes without two of its finest."

His sarcasm hurt when he turned it on her. Maybe she deserved it, for sidestepping the truth. But it hurt all the same. Feeling trapped now, feeling helpless, she started to squirm, kneading her fingers into his jacket and shirtfront, meeting the resistance of immovable muscle underneath it all.

"Brett, please." His chest expanded beneath her hands in a weary sigh. She might have worn him down. He might let her go.

She was wrong.

"I've done everything you've asked of me." His low

voice was barely a vibration. "It's your turn to do something for me."

"Not this." His viselike grip slackened, but she saw it as a gesture of trust that she would stay, not a gateway to freedom.

She'd tracked down rapists and murderers, drawn her gun giving chase and in self-defense. In the past week she'd proved she could lie in any number of ways.

But she had no strength, no weapon against what he was asking of her. She gentled her grip on his clothes, smoothed out the wrinkles in the cotton and wool. But ultimately, to be truly honest, she had to tilt her chin and look all those miles up into his deep blue eyes.

"Didn't you ever wonder why my father has never called you to check out what kind of man his little girl is marrying? Why my mother has never taken me to lunch to talk flowers and bridesmaids' dresses?"

"I assumed your folks live out of town." She saw the first chink in that unfamiliar cold armor he wore. "Ah, hell."

"I'm an expert at funerals, Brett. You already know about Amy. It's just me in the Rafferty family. The rest are all gone."

His hands rubbed soothing circles where he'd gripped her. One slipped up to squeeze her shoulder, cup her jaw. But the dam had already opened. And no amount of gentleness or regret or compassion could stop it now.

"To be more precise, my sister was murdered, my mother killed herself, and my father died of a broken heart." A pain welled up in her gut, sharp and piercing, making it hard for her to breathe.

Without asking permission, Brett gathered her in to his chest, wrapping her snugly in the cocoon of his arms. "Angel, I'm sorry. I'm so sorry."

His lips stirred the crown of her hair as he spoke. She

turned her cheek into the front of his jacket, seeking the steady beating of his heart beneath her ear. There were no tears to shed, that well had gone dry. There was only the pain, the choking, squeezing pain in her chest.

She couldn't control it. She couldn't keep it in. "Brett?" She forced his name out on a strangled whisper of air, a cry for help before the panic consumed her.

"Shh, angel, shh." Locking her hands at his waist, he pulled his shoulders back to create a space between them. He feathered his fingers into her hair and tipped her face up, forcing her to meet the concern etched in his eyes. His face swam before her. She couldn't focus.

The softest of kisses touched her lips, startling the breath into her lungs. He kissed her again. She could feel her own heart beating once more. His lips touched hers a third time, and Ginny kissed him back. Curious. Hopeful.

At that slightest of responses, he claimed her mouth with a force that stunned her. The essence of Brett Taylor poured into her, seeking that empty part of her that once knew how to love and be loved. She raised up on tiptoe and met his challenge, absorbing his scent, his strength, his healing touch.

When she knew herself again, knew Brett, she broke the kiss and buried her face in the front of his jacket. The rasp of wool at her cheek, the soft silk tie at her nose, the scent of soap and man, the enveloping warmth all comforted her.

And with comfort came rational thinking. "I think I just had a panic attack."

His hands rubbed life and warmth into her shoulders and back. "You should have said something. I wouldn't have asked you to come." His hands stilled, allowing reality to creep into their hidden corner of the room. "But then, you don't share things like that, do you. If it's personal, it's a state secret with you."

Ginny stepped back, hearing regret, not spite in his voice. "That's not fair. This isn't a real relationship."

"So you keep reminding me."

She broke contact entirely, struggling to close the wounds inside her that a stiff chin and cool words could never really heal. "I'm just trying to protect myself."

"Ah, hell." To her surprise, he slipped an arm around her shoulders and steered her toward the exit. "I'll get you out of here."

Unlike Sophie's pessimistic complaint yesterday, a good number of people had shown up to pay their respects to Alvin. Or more likely, as Brett had intimated, to show their support for Sophie. With a few brief nods and acknowledgments, Brett moved them closer to the door. When he stopped abruptly, Ginny had to double-step to keep from stumbling.

"Too late."

She glanced up at the ominous import of his words. She saw nothing but the bottom of his jaw as he stared straight ahead.

"Brett!"

Ginny turned toward the unfamiliar female voice. A tall woman, with striking silver hair and deep blue eyes opened her arms and stepped away from the crowd.

Brett removed the security of his arm from Ginny's shoulders and bent to exchange hugs and plant a kiss on the older woman's lips. "Ma."

Ginny stiffened.

A large, stocky man, only a couple inches shorter than Brett, with streaks of gray peppering his dark hair, joined them. The two men shook hands and hugged. He pulled away, slightly breathless. "Son."

Oh no.

The walls closed in on her chance of escape when she saw Brett's cousin Mitch guiding his beautiful, flame-haired wife toward them. Though she walked with a perpetual limp, she had a natural style and grace about her that made Ginny feel small and gangly by comparison.

She thought about a back door. But that meant going through the chapel.

A dark-haired woman, about her own age, got scooped up off the floor into a Brett-size bear hug. "Jessie."

"Ginny, it's good to see you again." Casey Taylor, the captain's wife, ever gracious, had made several efforts to cultivate Ginny's friendship in the past. Now that she'd noticed her, the trap was complete.

"Hi, Casey." The two women shook hands, and a flurry of introductions began.

Brett caught hold of Ginny's hand and pulled her to his side, anchoring her in the oncoming storm. "Ma. Dad. This is Ginny Rafferty. My folks, Martha and Sid Taylor."

"Oh my. You're the one who finally caught our Brett." Martha clasped her hands together, then held them out. A gentle nudge from Brett pushed Ginny forward, and his mother wrapped her arms around her.

Shocked by the unexpected hug, Ginny said nothing, did nothing. But Martha's delight wasn't daunted by her lack of a response. "I'm so pleased to meet you. I'm just sorry it isn't under better circumstances." She stepped back and pressed her hands together again. "Poor Sophie. This is so sad."

Sid settled for a handshake. Mac and Mitch, she knew through work. Then there was Jessie. Gideon. All tall. All Taylors.

A police officer in his starched blue uniform jogged up behind them. "Sorry I'm late, Ma."

This one was as big as Brett, but a decade younger. They punched playfully at each other, then traded a hug. "This is Josh," explained Brett. "He's the baby of the family."

Ginny shrank back, overwhelmed by the lively give-and-take of so many people talking at once. When she felt Brett's saving hand at her back, she leaned into him and whispered, "How many of you are there?"

"Six kids. Seven, counting Mitch. And we always count him."

"How many did I meet?"

"All but Cole."

Martha had a true mother's hearing. "I saw Cole's name in the registry. He must not have been able to stay." The wistful concern in her voice captured Ginny's curiosity. "I hope that boy's taking good care of himself."

And then Sophie Bishop walked through the chapel doors and all conversation stopped. Despite the grief of the occasion, she looked stunning in a black figure-hugging pantsuit trimmed with a long silver necklace that dipped into the jacket's neckline, and a silver bangle bracelet. With her long hair pulled back into an elegant twist by an antique silver comb, it struck Ginny that Sophie wanted this service to be more about her than her father.

"Martha. Sid." She greeted them with a familiar kiss, hugged each Taylor son or nephew like an old friend. She held on to Brett longer than the others, eyeing him expectantly until he dropped a kiss onto her cheek.

Then she turned to Ginny. "Detective Rafferty."

Not Ginny. Not Ms. Rafferty. Not thank you for coming. *Detective.*

Ginny knew about exclusion. A big family, close friends. She hadn't been a part of anything like this for years. The conscious choice to avoid such painful connections had become second nature to her after being alone for so long.

That aloneness never hit home the way it did now.

But the isolation she felt never had a chance to take root. Brett untangled himself from Sophie's embrace and slipped his arm around Ginny, silently identifying them as a couple, silently saying that she belonged.

She didn't care if it was for show. She didn't care if he was playing the part of her fiancé to perfection. She was grateful to have him as an ally, grateful to think of him as a friend.

She could only imagine what the protection and compassion of Brett Taylor would be like if he really loved a woman.

An unexpected fissure opened inside her armored heart as her mind jumped to the next logical question. What would it be like if Brett really loved her?

"Are you making any progress in my father's case, Detective?"

She'd been thinking the impossible. What could Brett see in her beyond a challenge resistant to his charms? Or the link to answers in Mark Bishop's death. What difference did it make to wonder about the way Brett loved?

"Y-yes," she stuttered, not quite able to recapture control of the calm rationality that had served her so well over the years. "I believe we've located a witness who may have seen your father's killer at the Ludlow Arms. A homeless man."

"Really?" Astonishment lit her dark eyes, disrupting the cool mask of grief. "That's wonderful news. I'll want to hear more, but…"

With an artful swish of her long, elegant hands, Sophie linked arms with the Taylor patriarch, Sid. "We'd better get this started." Ginny set aside her foolish speculation and braced herself for the task at hand. Standing at the center of the Taylor clan, Sophie added, "I'm so glad you all could come."

Seated in the second row behind Sophie and her escort, Eric Chamberlain, Ginny blanked her mind to the minister's eulogy. She'd heard similar words before and knew them by heart. But when a faceless soprano sang a hymn from behind a curtain, Ginny had the urge to crawl right out of her skin.

In an instant, Brett's hand was there. One big hand swallowed up both white-knuckled fists in her lap. She distracted herself by studying the nicks and calluses along his blunt-tipped fingers. She recognized it as the hand of a man who had experienced his share of hard work and hard times. The strength of his hand bespoke endurance, a steel will, courage; the gentleness of it bespoke kindness, patience and a big heart.

What could a hand like that gain from holding a hand like hers?

She still had no answer.

When the music ended, Eric Chamberlain crossed to the podium. He looked impeccable in his black pin-striped suit, a perfect match for Sophie's fashion-model sophistication. His remembrances focused on Sophie, how she'd caught his eye when she was still in high school, even though he was eight years her senior. He talked of her educational and professional accomplishments and how her perseverance had helped her rise from poverty to enormous success. Alvin Bishop would have been proud of his daughter.

Eric ended by saying, "I'm just glad I've been able to help her when she needed it along the way."

With those words, three things popped into Ginny's mind. Sophie's claim that Eric had always taken care of her. An unknown party who called 911 the night of Mark's death. Zeke Jones's mysterious guard, described only as 'tall.'

Her fears receded and the sharp-eyed detective took over. She tipped her chin and stretched toward Brett's shoulder to whisper, "How tall do you think Eric Chamberlain is?"

His blue eyes widened. He understood where her thoughts had taken her. He glanced at Eric, then lowered his mouth to her ear. "I'm six-four and I can look him in the eye."

"Tall?"

He nodded. ''Tall.''

Her mind leaped ahead to the pictures she wanted Zeke to look at, and she wondered if one crazy old man's identification of a suspect would stand up in court.

Chapter Eight

Ginny fought the usual urge to close her eyes as the elevator neared the seventh floor. Her tall, dark and silent companion would question her about that, too, no doubt. But she'd already revealed too many of her well-guarded secrets to Brett Taylor.

No amount of bargaining or begging had convinced him to let her drive herself, or drop her off at the curb in front of her building. He was going to see her safely to her door before she'd ever get rid of him. Something about feeling responsible for screwing up her day, he'd said. So he'd volunteered to be her second shadow until he knew she was all right.

But she needed to be alone right now. She needed to sort through all the unwanted emotions he'd forced out of her today, to tuck them neatly back into place so she could get on with the painless precision of her life.

As long as Brett was around, there'd be no peace, there'd be no dull comfort. As long as Brett was around, she couldn't just think, she had to *feel*.

She dared a glance across the elevator where he stood with hands in pockets, fixedly watching the numbers for each floor light up, poised on the balls of his feet as if ready to defend her against the elevator itself if it didn't open its doors on the right floor.

He looked so different today from the easygoing flirt she'd first met. Though the tie had disappeared the moment they'd stepped outside the mortuary, the unbuttoned navy suit he wore emphasized the breadth of his shoulders and length of his legs. The white shirt set off his working man's tan to healthy perfection. His long, dark hair curled over the collar and tangled in the nubby weave of the spring-weight wool.

He reminded her of an untamed animal on the prowl, poorly disguised in civilized dress. She felt ill equipped to be his keeper. Or even stand in the same cage with him.

"Is something wrong?" He'd caught her staring. The memorial service must have rattled her more than she realized for her to be so careless.

"No." She quickly looked away, unable to come up with any excuse, and unwilling to admit how much she'd been thinking about him. "We're here." She'd never again complain about clichés as the ding of the elevator bell saved her from further explanation.

She'd excused herself from an offer to share lunch with the Taylor clan under the pretext of not feeling well. By doing so she'd taken Brett from his meal, and now, as they stepped into the hallway and apartment 709 came into view, she wondered if he expected to be invited in for lunch.

She lowered her face to look in her purse for her keys and hide her wry smile. Poor Brett. If he only knew what kind of hostess she was, that her cooking skills were limited to the microwave and the toaster.

The man would have to be starving before she'd invite him into her sanctuary. Before she'd allow the emotional roller-coaster ride that was Brett Taylor disturb her sublime refuge from the real world.

His hand grazed her back, blanking her smile. "It's 709, right?"

She nodded and inserted her key into the dead bolt. But

she didn't unlock it. Brett deserved more than a goodbye and a door shut in his face. Without him at her side, she couldn't have gotten through the morning.

Still debating her words, she turned and tipped her chin up. "Thank you. Thank you for..." For what? Forcing me to face my fears? Helping me cope with them? Making me wish I still had some faith in myself?

"You're welcome."

"But..." He shushed her open mouth by pressing a finger to her lips. Didn't he realize she hadn't finished explaining her gratitude? That she wasn't sure how to finish?

Maybe he did. He drew that same finger along her cheek, caught a tendril of hair and tucked it behind her ear. She watched his eyes as they followed the movement of his hand, until his palm came to rest against her jaw.

She should have moved away. She could have simply turned her head to deny him the contact. But she couldn't. He was warmth and strength. And she seemed to be in short supply of both right then.

The corner of his mouth curved into a half smile. "I should have listened to you this morning, and not put you through that. I can be pretty bullheaded sometimes."

"I noticed."

A full smile blossomed on his mouth. The familiar laugh lines crinkled beside his eyes. "Feeling better, I see."

"It's a big job to cut you down to size, Taylor. I have to stay in practice."

"Ooh, strike two."

Without thinking, she reached out and spread the flat of her hand across the center of his chest, drawn to the movement of laughter. Crisp cotton teased her palm. Warm man radiated through the thin material. "I think you like it when I call you on your ego." Ginny barely recognized the sound of teasing in her voice.

He leaned one arm on the door frame beside her head,

angling his body so close that she had to lean back against the door to maintain eye contact with him. The fingers at her jaw tunneled into her hair and cupped the nape of her neck. "Careful, angel. I'm going to think you're flirting with me."

"Me, flirt?" She was genuinely puzzled. "I don't think I know how."

"Probably not. You don't play games. That's one of the things I admire about you."

"Admire?" A twinge of warning made her curl her hand into a fist, though she still didn't pull away.

"Yeah. I want you to feel you can be honest with me. Like you were this morning. That meant a lot to me."

He began to gently knead her scalp, releasing the tension gathering within her. "You have to know that sharing something like that isn't easy for me," she admitted.

"I'll be patient."

She frowned, trying to keep the upper hand in this conversation, but feeling herself falling behind. "I know you better than that, Taylor."

A boyish smile lit his face. He rephrased himself. "I'll keep trying?"

Her fingers relaxed as she fell under his earnest spell. She leaned into him for balance and rose on tiptoe, rewarding him for putting up with her foibles and phobias, rewarding herself. "So will I."

She waited in anticipation for his mouth to close the gap between them, forgetting that she might be making a promise she couldn't keep.

The slide of a dead bolt jolted her eardrums. She dropped to her heels, just beyond the reach of Brett's kiss.

"Oh. I'm sorry." A hushed, erudite voice intruded. "Is this a bad time?"

Brett's lips flattened out in a frustrated sigh. When she

nudged at his chest, the sigh seemed to expand throughout his entire body.

She didn't wait for him to step away. She scooted around him and confronted her neighbor. "Dennis. Do you spy on me all the time?"

He pulled those little half-glasses off his nose and pointed them at her in self-defense. "How was I to know you were coming home for lunch? I heard a noise in the hall and thought I'd check it out."

Brett stepped in front of her. He splayed his hands on his hips and puffed up to an intimidating size. "She's fine."

She tugged at Brett's elbow. "I don't need you to protect me."

Dennis was no slouch in the proprietary-male department, either. "She doesn't usually bring men home, you know."

"Dennis!"

Brett grabbed her left hand and held it up for Dennis to see. "I happen to be her fiancé. Who the hell are you?"

Suppressing a few choice words of her own, Ginny freed herself. She fisted her hands in royal frustration and shook them at the two men. Flustered, angry and embarrassed, she unlocked her apartment and stormed inside, leaving Brett and Dennis to verbally duke it out. She didn't have time or patience or interest in seeing which male earned the right to be king of the hallway.

She tossed her purse onto the chair and made a beeline for the kitchen. By habit, she punched the answering machine to play her messages. She opened the fridge, pulled out a bottle of water and bolted two large swallows. She relished the icy chill running down her throat, cooling her blast of temper as it settled into her stomach.

The first message was from Merle. "I've tried your cell phone twice, but there's no answer. Call me when you get in. I have some info on that 911 search."

The ending beep diverted her attention to the voices in

the hall. Less intense, more wordy. At too low a volume to make out anything specific.

She listened to another message from Merle. His sweetly persistent voice reminded her that she needed to contact Maggie Wheeler and requisition another cellular phone.

After the third beep, she noticed that she didn't hear anything from the hallway at all. Good. Providence had spared her a firsthand view of the overbearing behavior of the Neanderthal-male species. And she'd made her escape from Brett.

She took another, slower drink, and gave thanks that she'd been given time to recover from her emotional battering that morning. She'd almost made a dangerous mistake by kissing him. She'd already revealed too much of her personal life to him. She'd gone so far as to depend on him, to enjoy the ongoing battle of words and wills between them.

As she replaced the water bottle, she saw the rich blue sapphire on her left hand. Suddenly, that white-gold band felt like a lead weight.

She felt a similar weight in the pit of her stomach. This whole relationship with Brett was just a game. She had a job to do. "My feelings for Brett aren't real," she muttered to herself.

So why did he make her so angry? Why had she wanted him to kiss her?

The machine beeped with yet another message as Ginny stood in front of the open refrigerator and breathed in the cool air.

"Stay away from things that don't concern you, Detective." Her blood ran cold all on its own. The mechanically altered voice played through her apartment in shrill, robotic tones. She shut the refrigerator and stared at the answering machine as if it were creating the message itself. "I warned you. Let the past stay buried."

"Son of a bitch."

Ginny whirled around at Brett's emphatic curse. "What are you doing here?" She tromped across the room to the man whose brawn filled the open doorway. She'd left the apartment unlocked, and he had the gall to invite himself in. "Get out."

Her hand hit his chest. She shoved.

He didn't budge.

Dennis peeked his head around Brett's shoulder. "Is there a problem?" he asked, so full of innocent concern that Ginny wanted to scream.

"Go home, Dennis."

They'd violated her haven. Brought the outside world to her sanctuary.

"Call the police and report that." Brett crossed to the phone even as he gave her the order.

"I *am* the police." Ginny hustled after him. She snatched the receiver from his hand and slammed it back down onto the phone. She leaned her shoulder into his rib cage and pushed again.

His hands closed around her arms and he set her back a step, stopping her momentum as easily as if she were a child. "What do you do in a case like this?" he asked, refusing to let go. "Does the precinct assign some sort of protection?"

She twisted inside his grip and raised her foot with every intention of grinding it down on his instep. "They trained me to protect myself."

"I'm not the bad guy here." With amazingly quick speed for such a big man, he sidestepped her attack and picked her up off the floor as he had done twice before, pinning her to his chest, dangling her in space.

"Stop doing that!" Eye to eye, heartbeat to heartbeat, she stared him down. "I am a grown woman. A professional police officer." She enunciated each syllable. "Let me do my job."

He dropped her. Her feet hit the floor with a hard jolt and he backed away, his head shaking, his hands raised in surrender.

"Dammit, Ginny. That was a threat on your life. He said *warned you,* past tense. Have there been other threats? Aren't you going to take it seriously?"

"I'm always serious. Remember?"

She stormed to the door and held it open, impatiently waiting for him to walk through so she could slam it on his backside. An eternity passed between each step as he followed her across the room. He paused in front of her. His fingers perched at his hips and he leaned his shoulders slightly forward in that overtly masculine stance of his.

"You've been threatened before, haven't you?" She turned her face to the side to avoid eye contact with him. With his finger and thumb, he forced her chin back to face him. "Haven't you?"

"Once."

Her breathing skipped its natural rhythm. The same panic that had attacked her at the mortuary tried to seize her again. She jerked her chin from his gentle grip, fighting off the traitorous desire to share her fears and hurt with him. She had to be strong. She had to get through this. Alone. She couldn't afford to get used to his comfort, his compassion. She couldn't expect him to be there for her when her job or her life got to be too much. She shouldn't want him to be.

"I received a note at work," she admitted. She intended to end this personal conversation. "I handled it."

The gentle concern shading his eyes absorbed the brunt of her dismissive glare. "I'll just bet you did. You'll take on anything life throws at you, won't you?"

"You can leave anytime. The door's open."

"You're not mad at me." He called her bluff. "You're scared."

She clasped one hand at her throat, hiding the proof of her leaping pulse at the pinpoint accuracy of his statement.

His deep gentle voice almost made her believe in trust again. "Angel, it's okay to be scared."

She stepped back and pointed to the hallway, refusing to succumb to his seductive lies. "Get out."

Dennis Fitzgerald suddenly appeared in the open doorway across the hall. His agitated shifting from foot to foot distracted her from her mission to get Brett out of her apartment. "Ginny. Turn on your television. There's a story on the noon news about the Ludlow Arms."

"I don't want to watch television."

"You'll want to watch this. They found another dead body."

FEELING TOO RAW to argue with Brett, to even speak to him, Ginny mutely agreed to let him drive her down to the Ludlow Arms.

Strangely enough, the familiar flurry of police cars and yellow tape, the technicians and medical examiner's van, even the crush of reporters and curious onlookers, returned a sense of normalcy to Ginny's mind. This kind of stress she could handle. She could even distance herself from the tragedy of death so long as she could focus on her job and didn't have to cope with big bossy Neanderthals turning her personal life upside down.

She climbed out of his truck and clipped her badge onto her belt. Brett fell into step beside her as she crossed the street and pushed her way through the crowd toward the front steps of the Ludlow.

When he lifted the yellow tape for her to pass under, she stopped. "Where do you think you're going?"

"It's my building."

"It's my case."

"It's *our* case." He took her by the hand and pulled her

through beside him. He caught her fingers again and flashed the ring before her eyes. "Equal partners, remember?"

"You're never going to let me forget."

She snatched her hand free and climbed the steps into the lobby. Brett lingered behind, scanning the crowd, then tipping his face up toward the Ludlow's roofline. After his dogged insistence on staying with her, the unexpected pause made her come back outside. She, too, looked up, wondering what it was about the towering bricks that had caught his attention.

"Is something wrong?"

"We have to move these people back, and cut down to the bare minimum of personnel and equipment inside." He looked down at her and shrugged. "It's just a feeling. This old girl doesn't have much life left in her. You touch it and she falls apart."

To demonstrate his point he reached out and swiped his fingers across the outside wall. The open hand he held in front of her face had picked up red brick-dust and pea-size chunks of mortar. "I don't think she's too happy to give up all her secrets." He clutched his hand into a fist and dropped it to his side before brushing it clean on the pant leg of his good suit. "I wonder how many people have to die before she surrenders."

"It's just a building, not an entity. She's not a suspect."

She heard herself use the feminine appellation, saw the grim acceptance in Brett's tight expression, and realized she half believed him.

The Ludlow Arms was an elegantly engineered mix of steel and brick and wood and stone. But she remembered the collapse of the Bishops' fourth-floor apartment, the way the split in the floor had seemed to chase after Brett.

Ginny shivered in the warm April sunshine. "I'll find out who the scene commander is and you can fill the officer in."

When Brett's hand settled at the small of her back to guide her inside, she didn't mind.

Soon enough she fell into the routine where she functioned so naturally. Turning on her calm, rational mind and shutting off her emotions, she pointed out the officer in charge of the scene and waited for Brett to take him off to the side before seeking out Merle.

Mac Taylor and his crew were scattered about, taking photographs and marking blood samples. She found Merle kneeling beside the covered body itself at the bottom of the basement stairwell. She touched his shoulder, indicating her presence before stooping down beside him.

"What do we have?" She lifted the corner of the tarp and gasped. She identified the man on a whispered prayer. "Zeke Jones."

She covered the old man's face and pulled out her pen and notepad to mark down Merle's observations. "That's why I didn't label it accidental death. He was your witness, wasn't he?"

Ginny nodded. "He said he could describe Bishop's killer."

Merle's surprise was obvious. "How'd you get that out of him?"

"Brett Taylor. He acted like a commanding officer, and Zeke reported in to the real world long enough to respond to him."

Merle pushed himself to his feet. "What's the deal with you and Taylor, anyway?"

Ginny took a deep breath before standing. She found it hard to choke the words past the lie in her throat. "We're engaged."

"So I heard. How come I never heard of you two being an item before now?"

She poked around in the corner, ostensibly looking for clues. "You know I like to keep my private life private."

"Still, as your partner, I figured you'd clue me in on a major life change like that."

She faced him, feeling defensive. "How much do you tell me about your personal life?"

"As much as you let me." He met her challenge with a dose of reality. "I like you, Ginny. I like the way your mind works. I think I'm lucky to have you for my partner. You've got enough experience so I don't feel like such a rookie, but not so much that I can't relate to you. But you're a tough nut to crack in the friendship department."

He surprised her by giving her arm a supportive squeeze. "I'm glad Taylor managed to get through to you. I hope he makes you happy. I'd like to see you happy."

Did she really seem so negative? So dissatisfied with life? Maybe what she'd seen as self-protection others had interpreted as disinterest or disdain. And why the hell was she worrying about this right now? Had she allowed Brett to tear down so many of her walls that she couldn't control her own reactions anymore?

Judging by the worried look on Merle's face, she needed to give some kind of response. "I like you, too," she admitted, avoiding mentioning Brett altogether. "You keep me sharp. On my toes. You're not afraid of hard work. And nobody handles that computer like you do." Why had she never told him that before? They'd been teamed up nearly a year ago. They'd shared a few working lunches, discussed the merits and myths of *Star Trek*. But she'd never really gotten to know him. Or more accurately, she conceded, she'd never given him a chance to get to know her.

How many other connections in her life had she limited to such a shallow, safe relationship?

Damn Brett, anyway, for forcing her to deal with the personal side of her life right now. She already had three homicides to solve, and her best lead had just become victim number four of the Ludlow Arms.

Fortunately though, Merle seemed to have agreed to an unspoken truce, and let the issue of their friendship take a back seat to the investigation at hand. He pulled out his flashlight and shined it up through the jagged stumps and shards of wood that used to be the interior stairwell support structure. "Zeke crashed through from the fourth floor. Mac says his neck's broken. He places the time of death late last night or early this morning."

"What was he doing up there?" Ginny found it easy to slip into the role of partner once more. "He and Charlie camped out in the subbasement. Brett and I took the two of them to a shelter yesterday. We were going to clean them up and have them make a formal statement."

"Charlie Adkins has disappeared, too. There's no sign of him in the building. We checked the place as best we could. We had to jerry-rig a suspension system to get up to the top floors. Nobody's going up those stairs anymore."

"Nobody should." She heard herself echoing Brett's warning. "This place isn't safe."

"No kidding." When the forensics team lowered a gurney to lift Zeke's body from the basement, Ginny and Merle climbed up the surviving stairs to the first floor. "I already put out an APB for Charlie Adkins. Anything else you want me to check?"

"Did you get an ID on the 911 caller for Mark Bishop?"

Merle flipped through his notepad and found the information. "Nothing specific. Records say it was an anonymous woman. And get this, the call originated from the pay phone that used to hang here in the lobby. That's less than thirty feet from where Mark's body was found."

"A woman?" She immediately thought of Amy. Maybe her sister *had* been here that night. But if she left Mark's side to make the call, what happened to her? Why didn't she return?

Merle had a suggestion. "Maybe you were hoping Alvin had second thoughts after hurting his son?"

"That's not likely." She sensed Brett's presence an instant before his voice rumbled behind her. "Instead of destroying his liver, drinking killed his conscience. He'd do his worst to someone, then forget it ever happened."

"Where have you been?" she asked. A mantle of dirt and sawdust clung to his shoulders, standing out in stark relief to the dark material of his jacket. She brushed off what she could, dispersing nervous energy and concern under the pretense of saving the poor suit.

"Nosing around." He caught Ginny's hand and clasped it down at his side. When it came to his building, the man was all business. "Detective Banning, did your people stick to the main stairwell when they conducted their search?"

Merle frowned in confusion. "Is there another way upstairs?"

Brett nodded. "What used to be the servant stairs off the kitchen. They were sealed off years ago when they converted the hotel into apartments. With the building's decay, it's easy to knock out a wall. I found a loose section of paneling in the back hallway." His gaze swept up to the arches and high ceilings, as if the Ludlow would share her secrets with him if he only listened closely enough.

Ginny squeezed Brett's hand, asking him to look her in the eye. "Do I want to hear why this is important?"

He dropped his chin to meet her upturned gaze. "Somebody's been using those stairs. Recently, too. There's a clean set of footprints in the dust."

NOT FOR THE FIRST TIME, Brett wondered at the stamina of the law enforcement officers he knew. Before his arrival with Ginny, Mac and his team had spent hours documenting possible clues. Now, for over an hour, Ginny and her partner had taken notes, asked questions and played out various scenarios that could explain Zeke Jones's death.

Brett's discovery of the back stairwell added another forty-five minutes of tracing paths and measuring distances, stretching their visit well into the long part of the afternoon. He hovered at the fringes of the mini think tank, keeping a watchful eye on the building while Ginny, Mac and Merle focused on the footprints leading to the fourth floor.

Mac adjusted the glasses on his nose and stood from where the three had been kneeling. "Offhand, I'd guess the prints belong to a small man or to a woman."

Ginny stood next. She crossed her arms in front of her and tapped at her lower lip with her index finger. Brett's gaze zeroed in on the gesture, drawn to the thoughtful pout on her lips. "To be honest with you, I was leaning toward Eric Chamberlain as our tall man. If he's Sophie's champion, as he claims, then he might murder Alvin to protect her from any more abuse."

Mac shook his head. "If it's the same Eric Chamberlain I knew in school, there's no way those footprints could be his."

"Maybe Zeke's?" offered Merle.

"Without Charlie?" said Ginny. "Those two were bound at the hip. There'd be another set of prints. This is one clear set going up to the fourth floor and coming down."

Brett watched as the wheels of speculation danced in her eyes. She might use that intellect as a defensive weapon at times, controlling her emotions and denying herself the opportunity to trust or laugh or love, but he marveled at it now. Watching her work like this, she radiated a power, a confidence. His pulse throbbed inside his veins like an answering beacon.

He didn't like the danger she faced as a cop. Didn't like the things she had to see and discuss as a homicide investigator.

But he worried a little less, knowing that she was good at this job. Her co-workers believed in her abilities, and she delivered.

"Let me think on it," Ginny said. The movement of her lips disrupted his own train of thought. "I have a feeling the clues are all here. But if they won't add up to Chamberlain, I need to put them together in a different way." She ducked through the hole in the wall with Merle at her heels. "Let's walk through it one more time."

Brett slung his jacket over his shoulder and started to follow. He'd momentarily forgotten the presence of the second eldest Taylor brother. "Is she always like that?" Mac asked.

The imprint of Ginny's bottom, cupped in those sensible slacks she always wore, as she bent over to pass through to the lobby was the last impression that stayed with him. Hardly a noble sentiment. But he'd shared worse with his brother. "Beautiful, you mean?"

Mac came up beside him and grinned. "Well, I was going for analytical or driven. But yeah. I can see it with the eyes and the hair. The whole package is pretty hot."

Brett turned his head and looked him straight in the eye. "If you weren't wearing glasses, I'd knock you down where you stand." If they weren't brothers, the glasses wouldn't have made a difference. For him to see Ginny as *pretty hot* was one thing. For another man to notice her the same way fired his blood in an embarrassingly primitive way.

"If you hit me, I'll tell Ma," Mac teased.

Reverting to their childhood, Brett flattened his hand on Mac's forehead and pushed him aside. He crouched to climb through the exit himself.

"When the big ones fall, they fall hard."

Wary of the hundred-eighty-degree turnabout in his brother's tone, Brett straightened and asked, "What are you talking about?"

Mac's gray eyes leveled with the cool excitement of a

scientist testing a new theory. "Do you have any idea how crazy you are about her?"

Brett shifted his jacket to the opposite shoulder, uncomfortable with this line of questioning. He bluffed his way past the inquiry by donning his toughest big-brother voice. "We're getting married, aren't we? What do you know about relationships anyway, Professor? You claim you never have any time for the stuff."

"I'm smart enough to know that a week ago Ginny didn't want to have a thing to do with you. I know you love a challenge like that. But just a few days later you're engaged to be married? C'mon." Mac covered his heart in mock-melodramatic fashion. "You're breaking my heart, big brother. I thought you were the perennial bachelor of the family."

"That's Josh's job." He was floundering in avoidance of Mac's original question, and he had a feeling his brother knew it. "Besides, it's not unheard of to fall in love quickly."

"No, it's not." When Mac squeezed his shoulder in apologetic reassurance, Brett knew he was in trouble. "But I surprised you when I mentioned your feelings for Ginny just now, judging by how nervous this whole conversation makes you. Whatever game you're playing, Brett, be careful. Ginny's a friend and you're my brother. I'd hate to see either one of you get hurt."

Chapter Nine

"I heard about the Ludlow Arms murder on the news this afternoon." John McBride leaned on his rake, pulled off his faded red Kansas City Chiefs ball cap and wiped the sweat from his forehead with the back of his hand. "The homeless folks have a tough enough life without getting in the way of someone who doesn't want them around."

"Yeah. I'd love to nail that someone." Ginny looked up from her seat on the grass where she'd been culling dead leaves and blown trash from the rosebush planted beside the Rafferty monument. "He was a confused old man who his killer ignored for twelve years, either because he didn't know there'd been a witness, or he didn't think anyone would believe his story. Then Zeke Jones talks to me, and the next day he's dead."

"You're making someone nervous."

She thought about the pink phone message at work, and the threat on her answering machine at home. She shivered despite the warmth of the evening sun. "I guess I am."

Ginny picked up her trash and carried it over to the plastic bag next to John. "You know what I can't figure out?" She posed the question out loud.

"What's that?" John resumed raking the dead grass from the new green shoots.

"How the killer got Zeke up the stairs in the first place."

"The news said Zeke discovered the body buried below the Ludlow Arms, right?"

At this point Ginny was willing to listen to any new ideas. She'd worried with this puzzle so much that it seemed more confusing and unsolvable than ever. "He thought of the place like a POW camp. He told us that he was rescuing a fallen comrade."

"How did he know the body was there? Unless he killed him."

Ginny had already ruled out that possibility. She opened the bag and held it for John to stuff a pile of lawn clippings into. "Zeke had no motive. He told us he heard a noise that prompted him to check it out. I believe it was a bell that the victim was wearing around his neck."

"That was twelve years ago." John stopped with an armful of debris. "Why did he tell the police about the body now? Why didn't he report it sooner?"

The kernel of an idea took root in her mind, sending out tiny little inklings. The idea searched for sunlight. "He didn't hear the sound until a few days ago."

"A corpse doesn't ring a bell on its own."

"The killer came back and moved the body." The discovery grew like a wild vine. "The building's about to be torn down. You want to make sure your secrets and old ghosts are buried with it. So you check to see the body for yourself one more time."

She dropped the bag at John's feet and crossed her arms, tapping her index finger against her lip. "The killer got away with murder twelve years ago. But last week, when he revisited the scene, there was a witness. An incoherent old man who thinks he's serving his country by reporting what he saw."

John picked up on the possibilities unfolding before her. "So doddering or not, the old man's a liability. Someone just might make sense of his story."

"I did." She tipped her face up to the waning sunlight. For some inexplicable reason, she felt her time to solve Alvin Bishop's murder and the chain of events surrounding it was slipping through her fingers just as quickly as that setting sun. "Somebody else thought he made sense, too. And that somebody lured him upstairs and pushed him to his death."

"So back to your original question. Why'd he go up all those stairs?"

"He went to save a comrade."

The wrinkles in John's forehead deepened with confusion.

She explained. "He answered a bell."

"You lost me with that one. But I guess that's why I'm the groundskeeper and you're the homicide detective."

"I have to get back to work." She took a couple of steps before she recognized the rudeness of her abrupt departure. Breathless with excitement, on the verge of breaking the case wide open, she came back. On impulse, she squeezed John's forearm. Then, holding on to balance herself, she inched up on tiptoe and kissed his cheek. "Thank you."

The ruddy blush in his dark cheeks made her smile. "What was that for?" he asked.

"Maybe my family isn't the only reason I come here."

He put his rake to the ground and resumed his work, pretending not to be flustered by the unplanned overture of friendship. "I've always enjoyed our talks, too."

Feeling his soft-spoken admission like a great big hug, Ginny sped down the hill to her car. This tired old case had been given new life. She'd been given new energy.

She knew what to look for now.

A set of twelve-year-old wind-chime bells.

"YOU'RE POSITIVE it was Alvin Bishop who stole those wind chimes off your fire-escape balcony?"

Ginny refused to back out of the open door of Pearl's

Diner until she got the answers she needed. Pearl pulled a light blue coat on over her white uniform and tucked a zippered leather bag under her arm. "Ms. Rafferty, it's after nine o'clock. I need to get my deposit to the bank."

"I know it's late. I'll drive you there myself." She patted the bulge of her gun beneath her jacket. "Police escort."

Pearl's gaze followed the movement of Ginny's hand. She shifted back and forth on her feet, as if testing whether she had the energy left to make the walk without taking her up on the invitation. Then she shook her head, unable or unwilling to accept the offer.

"Look, all I know is that old Alvin is the only one who ever complained about my chimes. I woke up one morning and they were gone. My Freddie made those for me with his own hands."

When Pearl raised a fist to her heart, Ginny knew she'd taken a trip down memory lane, and her usefulness in answering questions had ended. Ginny hit the light switch herself before preceding Pearl out onto the sidewalk.

Ginny tried another option. "Would Ruby remember the incident?"

Pearl locked the door and pocketed the key before answering. She puffed up her ample chest. "My Ruby is on a date this evening, and I do not want you to disturb her. It's hard enough finding a man to marry around this neighborhood without you outsiders coming in and snatching up all the good ones."

"Excuse me?"

"My Ruby isn't slim and gorgeous. I know her limitations." Ginny wasn't sure where this outpouring of skewed motherly pride was coming from. "But she can cook up a storm, and make a man laugh. She has a good heart. It's been broken a few times along the way, but she keeps smiling."

A distant eclipse of a memory tried to work its way into Ginny's conscious mind. "Who broke her heart?"

"Mark Bishop was the first one. They were back in high school then, probably too young to really think about marriage. I couldn't stand the thought of being related to Alvin, but Mark was good to my girl." She clicked her tongue behind her teeth, tutting with disgust at her next thought. "Alvin found out Mark was buying trinkets for Ruby. Little things, you know. A necklace. A pair of barrettes. Alvin put a stop to that."

"How?"

"Threatened her." Her fist moved to her mouth as the memory became more difficult. "Came up to our apartment. Told her no girl was going to take what belonged to him."

So Alvin hadn't been afraid to bully teenage girls, either. He'd lost his wife already. He couldn't stand to lose his son, too. Ginny's stomach flip-flopped. Had he made the same threat to Amy? Steeling herself for the answer, she asked, "Did he hurt her? Ruby, I mean?"

"Mark broke up with her. Isn't that hurt enough?"

Oh Lord, she wished she had Brett around to make these questions easier. "Did he hit Ruby?"

Pearl drew back, horrified. She didn't answer. "I have to get to the bank."

"Pearl, please."

The older woman ignored Ginny's plea and bustled off down the sidewalk. Damning her foolishness for trying this on her own, Ginny released a weary sigh, punched the unlock button on her remote and headed for her car.

"Ms. Rafferty?" Ginny turned. Pearl had stopped at the corner. In the light from the overhead street lamp, her face reflected more life experience than her sixty-something years should. "He never hit my girl. That's why Mark broke up with her. To protect her. To keep Ruby from being the target of his father's wrath. He didn't start seeing that Amy girl until sometime later. Ruby likes to say she lost Mark to another girl. But the truth is, she lost him to old Alvin.''

Chalk up two more suspects with a motive for killing Alvin. And Amy, too, for that matter. They could have lied about him stealing those wind chimes. Living in the same building would have given either mother or daughter the opportunity to kill him.

But neither Pearl nor Ruby fit Zeke's description of a ''tall'' guard.

Had Alvin made good on the same kind of threat to her sister? Or had Mark tried to save Amy's life by keeping her away from his father?

''Thank you.'' She felt she owed Pearl for dredging up such an unpleasant memory. ''I'd still be happy to give you that ride.''

''No thanks, hon. Tonight I feel the need to walk.''

Ginny headed the opposite direction. She climbed into her car and buckled up. Every time she took a step closer to Alvin's killer, someone pushed her two steps back. She clasped her hands at the top of the steering wheel and rested her forehead there.

''Oh, Amy,'' she breathed on a frustrated sigh. ''Why couldn't I have just been there for you that night?''

She had one more call to make. She knew she wouldn't be popular when she phoned Sophie Bishop about Alvin's personal belongings. But then, she was getting used to that.

Sitting up, she started the car and shifted it into gear. As she sat there waiting for another vehicle to pass, a whisper of cool air made the hairs at the back of her neck stand on end. Taking care not to panic, she looked out at the sidewalk, thinking Pearl had changed her mind about accepting a ride. But the City Market had been abandoned for the night.

In her rearview mirror, she spotted the empty eyes of the Ludlow Arms looming behind her. Maybe it was the building itself that gave her the feeling of being watched.

She shook off the shiver running down her spine, dismissing the sensation as the fanciful imagining of a tired mind. She checked the mirror again, assuring herself that an old brick building couldn't walk or talk or see.

Her gaze dropped to the back seat and her pulse stopped in her veins. "What the hell?"

She slammed the car into Park and scrambled out the door. In one swift sure move, she planted her feet on the pavement, unsnapped her holster and pulled out her sleek 9 mm handgun. She cradled the cold steel in both hands, willing the trembling in her fingers to subside as she crouched behind the relative safety of the door and scanned her surroundings.

Every ninety degrees she altered her stance so that she was always balanced, always prepared to strike. Pearl Jenkins had disappeared into the shadowy distance of the night. The neon archway that lit the entrance to the market during the day was a dark canopy above her. The businesses across the street had locked their caged facades and bolted their doors. The car that had passed her was a flash of red as it turned the corner, too far away to read the license plate.

Alone.

She was completely, utterly alone.

So who put the four-foot-long cardboard tube in her back seat?

You wouldn't listen. The ominous warning had been scrawled with a faded black marker across the cardboard.

Ginny straightened her legs and forced herself to breathe normally, in and out through her nose. She turned and faced the silent menace of the Ludlow Arms and spoke to the two broken windows near the top. "I'm listening now."

With habitual ease, she let curiosity outweigh her fears. Ignoring the scribbled threat, she holstered her weapon and opened the back door. With a handkerchief in hand to avoid

damaging any fingerprints, she picked up the tube and
peered inside the open end of the dusty cardboard cylinder.

"Blueprints."

An odd warning. The first two messages had been anonymous, advising her to steer clear of the neighborhood. This
one seemed to be inviting her right into the heart of downtown Kansas City.

The corner of the top sheet crumbled between her fingers
as she unrolled the stack of drawings on the hood of her car.
Though yellowed and faded, the label at the bottom of each
page was clear: Ludlow Arms Hotel.

The obvious antique value of the blueprints registered
along with the black X drawn by hand in the center of a
sharp-cut rectangle. As she thumbed through the remaining
prints, she found four more X's.

That feeling of being watched crept along her skin once
more. This time she didn't hesitate to look up at the Ludlow
Arms.

"So what are you trying to tell me?"

"I'M SORRY, ma'am." The courteous voice clipped an impersonal apology. "But until the City Market fund-raiser ball
is over tomorrow night, Ms. Bishop is not accepting any
new appointments."

Ginny changed the receiver to the other ear. "I'm asking
for five minutes of Sophie's time over the telephone, not a
sit-down meeting."

"I'm sorry," the woman repeated. "I'll give Ms. Bishop
your number and the message that you called."

"Fine, then. Goodbye."

Ginny hung up the phone and took a bite of the apple
she'd washed off in the sink. The tart crunch woke up her
mouth and recharged her drained energy cells in a way her
restless sleep and early-morning shower hadn't.

"I'd bet you'd drop everything to talk to Brett, wouldn't

you, Soph?'' She asked the question out loud, needing to hear a voice in the deafening quiet of her apartment.

The only person willing to talk to her this morning was Merle. She punched in the office number and carried the receiver over to the couch.

''Detective Banning.''

''Hey, Merle, it's me again.''

His good-natured laughter eased the stiff tension in her. ''What, fifteen minutes and you miss me already? There's still no news about Charlie Adkins. I just talked to the director of the shelter to see if anyone visited or phoned Zeke and Charlie before they checked out yesterday.''

Ginny quickly swallowed. ''And?''

''Phone call.'' He was already a step ahead of her. ''Don't worry. The phone company's running the number for me right now.''

''Good man.'' Maybe there really was something in getting to know Merle better. They seemed more in tune with each other's thoughts since she'd opened up to him about her relationship with Brett.

She chomped another bite of apple. Okay, so maybe lying to him about her engagement wasn't exactly ''opening up.'' But at least they were negotiating the twists and turns of this investigation more efficiently than their previous cases.

Her extended silence prompted him to ask, ''Did you need something else?''

''Yeah.'' She swallowed and focused. Her mind seemed to stray whenever the topic of Brett or their engagement came up. ''I wondered if the lab has finished running the tests on those blueprints?''

''They're sending them over later this morning. No fingerprints, though. They're analyzing the type of marker ink used. It's not much, but it might give us something to go on.''

Ginny inhaled and caught her breath. "You didn't tell Captain Taylor, did you?"

She knew she'd been asking a big favor when she instructed him to send in the blueprints without reporting the obvious threat attached to them. "The old man doesn't know. He hasn't been in yet this morning."

Ginny relaxed enough to breathe again. "Thanks, Merle. I owe you one."

"No sweat, partner." She could envision the smile spreading across his sweet, trusting face. She almost smiled back. "Need anything else?" he asked.

"No. Thanks." She hung up, wondering if she had ever been that young and innocent. Maybe. Once. When she still had a family. When her sister had been her confidante. When she still believed in love.

The echo of her own thoughts depressed her. "Get a grip, Rafferty," she scolded herself. "You have a job to do."

She cinched the belt around the waist of her robe and finger-combed her damp hair. Work was the answer. Work had always been the antidote to the emptiness in her life.

Tossing her apple core into the trash, she padded down the hall to her art room. Deprived of the blueprints, she'd sketched a rough drawing of her own.

Impressionistic shadings gentled the imposing lines of the Ludlow Arms. Concrete steps, brick facade, ribbons of lemon-yellow crime-scene tape.

She stood back and studied the unfinished painting. Had it been a clue or coincidence that those drawings had been included with the threat? Ginny suspected the former. The idea that someone had watched her closely enough to know when her back was turned so he could get into her unlocked car didn't bother her half so much as knowing the answer to her investigation had been placed in her hands—if only she could decipher what they meant.

She squeezed a dollop of black oil onto a palette, selected

a brush and began dotting windows. Up a row. One, two, three, four. She stopped. The paintbrush hovered in the air above the fourth dot. The creative side of her brain shut down as the analytical side rifled through messages and observations, snatches of conversations and faces of dead bodies. Alvin Bishop. Zeke Jones. Amy.

Ginny squeezed her eyes shut and averted her face, trying to turn away from the crystal-clear memory of Amy's perfect young face, framed in a coffin, devoid of color, devoid of life. A moan rose within her, an almost physical pain that squeezed up from her gut and choked her throat.

Suddenly, deep within her mind, the lights went out. The horrible darkness descended upon her. Closed caskets. Dirt above her.

The darkness she feared assailed her in varied, insidious ways. Whispered breaths lay in the shadows. A lover laughed. A trust was shattered. And then the lights.

Bright, blinding lights.

Ginny fought through the terrible darkness and pushed her eyelids up. She forced her way back into her tiny room. She breathed in deeply, welcoming the sting of paint fumes in her nostrils, waking her, bringing her back to the moment, back to the work at hand.

Back to the X she'd painted where the fourth-floor window should be.

"What the...?" Her shaking hand pointed straight to the X. She needed to see those blueprints again. She needed to know what the five X's meant.

She needed to talk to Brett.

He could interpret the blueprints for her.

Brett could keep the darkness at bay.

"Damn." Her heart skipped a beat as her overactive senses created a vivid image of the tall, dark man who pretended to love her. A picture complete with the sound of a deep, teasing voice, and the remembrance of a tough, tender hand gently caressing her cheek.

"Double damn."

Ginny felt hot. She hated the instant leap her mind made to form Brett's image so perfectly. She hated her body's traitorous response to that image.

She quickly busied her hands by cleaning her brush. She tried to talk herself out of the mental and physical longing that consumed her. "It's just an illusion," she warned aloud. "Nothing with Brett is real."

With ruthless focus, she turned her mind to the one task that could still distract her from this annoying obsession with Brett Taylor. Returning to the living room, she curled up on the couch and picked up Amy's last three letters.

Sliding her thumb under the first flap, she opened it. Inside she saw Amy's familiar flowery script. The i's were dotted with hearts.

Dear Gin,
    We're going to do it. We're eloping. We're meeting the seventeenth and taking the bus to Las Vegas. We'll have to lie low for a couple of months until I turn eighteen, but...

The passions of young love followed, along with the frustrations of parents who didn't understand, the pleas of one sister to another to call or come home.

Make Mom and Dad understand. Mark says his dad will be no help at all. But he has a friend...

Brett.

Ginny nearly laughed out loud. Maybe it was impossible to escape thoughts of Brett. She rubbed her thumb against the sapphire adorning her left hand. After all, she'd share a connection with him all these years. What if she had met him back then? Before she'd been disillusioned by love and trust. Before they'd both missed the chance to help two young people who hadn't been able to help themselves.

She shut down the pointless speculation and picked up the next letter.

> Gin,
>   Please call. I need to talk to someone.
>   Mark had a black eye last night. He says he wrecked his motorcycle, but I think his father did it. Mark won't let me meet him, says it's for my own good. I'm scared. He needs my help, but I don't know how.
>   We're serious about getting married. Mark gave me a beautiful silver bracelet as a symbol of our love. I thought a ring would raise too many questions, and Mom and Dad have already grounded me until my birthday. If they saw a ring, they'd lock me in my room and I'd have no chance of sneaking out to help Mark.
>   How did you get around all their rules when you fell in love?

Ginny choked down a surge of guilt and let the letter slide to her lap. Love? "I ran away to Europe."

The only passion she'd ever felt had been for her art. Until she met Jean-Pierre in Paris. The dynamic, hands-on portrait instructor tapped in to more than her creative inspiration. He charmed his way into her innocent heart and untested soul. He taught her more than brushstrokes and shading. He taught her to overlook her shy inhibitions and give free rein to her emotions. He taught her about love and lust.

And humiliating betrayal.

The temperature in Ginny's apartment dropped a good ten degrees. She rubbed at her upper arms, trying to find the warmth that eluded her.

She thought of Brett's hands on her arms. A lifeline to warmth and strength. His gentle touch at the small of her back, his fingers at her elbow, his hand swallowing up both of hers. He gave so much reassurance, so much caring with a look or a touch.

She moaned aloud at the awful loneliness that consumed her.

A survey around her apartment revealed the pristine perfection in which she lived, the cold predictability of the life she had sentenced herself to. Amy had rushed headlong into love, willing to take chances. Able to risk facing tragic consequences.

Ginny might have taken off for Europe, but she lacked her sister's brave heart. A sobering truth hit her square in the chest, weighing her down, trapping her in a cold, lonely lie.

She wasn't afraid of Brett being a playboy or a flirt.

She was afraid of his laughter, his hugs, his kisses. She was afraid of needing him, wanting him.

She was afraid of falling in love.

Tucking the last unread letter into her purse, Ginny marched back to her bedroom. "Damn you, Brett Taylor."

Love was a weakness, a setup, a guarantee of getting hurt. She'd already been hurt so much. Too much. She couldn't allow herself to fall in love. She couldn't afford to be that kind of fool again.

Repeating a mantra on the benefits of independence, she pulled on a pair of jeans and tucked in a blouse. She was threading her belt through her holster and cinching it at her waist when the telephone rang.

The phone beside her bed suffered the fury of all the emotions she'd tried to bury inside her. "Detective Rafferty."

Her sharp tone reverberated in her own ears.

"Ginny?" Brett. His bass-deep whisper popped her defenses like a balloon. "Is this a bad time?"

She summoned the scattered remnants of her composure and threw up a makeshift wall of bravado against the lure of that mesmerizing voice. "I'm glad you called. I need you to earn your keep," she demanded. "I have a set of blueprints I want you to look at. And I need you to talk to Sophie Bishop for me. She won't return my calls…"

"Gin…"

"I need to ask her about a set of wind chimes. I think the bells…"

"Virginia." The use of her full name stunned her into silence. Who was she kidding? She had no real defense against her feelings for Brett. "I'm sorry." His voice sank to a low, guttural murmur. "I don't even know if that's your given name."

"It is. I only heard it when I was in trouble, though." Her cheeks heated with self-conscious awareness as she paused long enough to listen. She allowed herself a moment of curiosity. "Am I in trouble?"

A long-drawn breath that might have passed for a weary laugh answered her.

Curiosity gave way to concern. "Brett?"

"You're not in trouble. Wind chimes, huh? I'll phone Sophie."

"No, wait." She recognized the fading sound of his breathing as the intention of hanging up. The volume increased as he returned the receiver to his ear. "Why did you call?"

His long pause made her wonder if he had hung up.

"To hear your voice." Something hard and hurtful melted inside her at his throaty admission, taking with it the walls of loneliness she'd hid behind for so long. "I gotta go. I'll call Sophie for you."

"No." But an ominous click disconnected her protest.

She'd missed something very important here. By attacking first, she'd denied him any opportunity to explain why he'd called. Maybe he'd found another clue about the Ludlow. Maybe he really had just wanted to talk. To her.

Maybe she really had no emotional self-preservation instincts after all.

She dug into her purse and pulled out Brett's business card. She punched in his office number. After the first ring, his secretary answered.

"Brett Taylor, please."

"He's not in the office today, may I take a message?"

What was it with personal assistants this morning? Ginny bit her tongue. The woman was only doing her job. "I just spoke to him. Is he at a job site?" She added some leverage to her polite request. "This is his fiancée."

"Ms. Rafferty? I'm sorry, I thought you knew."

"Knew what?"

"Brett's at the hospital. St. Luke's."

Ginny's heart plummeted to her toes. Another collapse at the Ludlow? A stray wrecking ball knocking some sense into his handsome hard head? She struggled to put professional detachment into her next question. Her ragged whisper hardly qualified. "Was there an accident?"

"Oh no, he's fine. But his father, Mr. Taylor, had a heart attack early this morning. If you need to get a hold of Brett, I could page him at the hospital. Ms. Rafferty?"

The receiver hit the cradle before Brett's secretary finished her offer. Answering a very different call from a place deep inside that wasn't as immune to big hearts and broad smiles as she'd like to think, Ginny grabbed her jacket and purse, and ran out the door.

Chapter Ten

"What would I do without him?" Martha Taylor sniffed back the tears that had already turned her eyes red.

Brett tightened his grip around his mother's shoulders, worried at the downward spiral of her thoughts. "We're not going to lose him, Ma."

"Then why won't they tell us anything?"

When she turned her face into his chest, Brett snuggled her inside the dubious comfort of his hug. He was way out of his league with this one. Though the doctors in the E.R. and cardiac unit of St. Luke's Hospital had all spoken positively about his father's chances for recovery, his mother was taking this threat to her family with uncharacteristic pessimism.

Sid Taylor had never suffered anything worse than a cold or the flu, she'd insisted. Strong as a bull, he rarely missed a day of work in his butcher shop.

"Why didn't I see this happening to him? I've been baking too many desserts. I let him sleep in front of the TV when he should be out walking."

Brett understood that kind of guilt born out of love. He tightened his hug and spoke words that Sid had once told him, shortly after Mark Bishop's death. "You can't predict the future. You can't always know what's going on in someone else's life. We just have to do the best we can with what we know.''

The words made logical sense, but still couldn't blot out the shadow of failure that had plagued him all these years. Mark's tragedy could have been prevented. *He* should have prevented it.

''I know.'' Martha stepped back. She breathed in through her nose and out through her mouth, calming herself. He wondered if she had found comfort in those words, or if she, like him, was simply going through the motions of moving on so her family wouldn't worry about her. ''I suppose it's Alvin Bishop's funeral that's making me think this way. They were the same age.''

''Dad is nothing like old Alvin was.'' Brett refused to even compare the two men. One knew nothing about fatherhood, while Sid could write a book about how to do it right. ''I know I'm prejudiced,'' he conceded. ''But Dad takes a lot better care of himself than Alvin ever did.''

Martha nodded. ''He takes good care of all of us.''

Gideon pushed to his feet from the waiting room's velour couch. He massaged his hand across their mother's back. ''Bypass operations are a routine procedure. They've done hundreds of them here at St. Luke's. Dad'll pull through and get back to keeping us all in line in no time.''

Mac added his support. ''You handled everything the way you're supposed to, Ma. The doc said there won't be any permanent damage to his heart muscle. When Dad felt the pressure in his chest, he called 911. And the aspirin you gave him may have helped prevent more serious side effects.''

''But they're cutting him open.'' She touched her hand to her sternum where Sid's incision would be. ''He's old enough to retire. He shouldn't have to work in that shop every day.''

Josh shrugged his fingers through his sandy-brown hair

and grinned. "But Ma, how would he meet all his friends? He's a mainstay at the City Market. Going to work is a social event for him." His remark earned him his mother's indulgent smile.

Jessie stood and linked her arm through Martha's. "Come and sit for a while. You've been up since two this morning. You don't want Dad worrying about you not taking care of yourself."

"I know you're right. But waiting is so hard." Martha still clung tenaciously to Brett's hand. "Will you find out what's going on?"

Seeing her surrounded by his younger siblings—all strong, competent, caring adults now—Brett felt safe enough to leave her side. "I'll go ask the nurse for an update."

"I just wish Cole was here." Martha's gaze swung up to his. The responsibility she entrusted him with settled like a mantle about his shoulders. With Sid temporarily incapacitated, she looked to him to serve as head of the family. "I know he and your father haven't always seen eye to eye. But he should be here."

That mantle grew a little heavier. He looked beyond the family circle to his cousin and best friend, Mitch. "Last I knew, he was working at that Italian restaurant over on Harrison."

"I'll get on the horn and track him down." Mitch turned to his wife before stepping away. "You okay?"

Casey Taylor nodded and slipped her arms around his neck, hugging him tight. "I'll stay and keep Martha company."

An unexpected ache clenched inside Brett at the unabashed kiss they shared. He immediately thought of Ginny. She was so strong, so driven and mentally focused. A pint-size fireball of temper and passion who hid her vulnerabilities beneath an icy control. He'd called her earlier, hoping to draw on some of that strength.

Or maybe it was the vulnerability he sought. She might be the one person who could understand this fear of letting down his family. Of not being the person his mother and father and brothers and sister needed him to be right now.

He'd failed before.

He might fail again.

But it wouldn't be for lack of trying. Determined to see his family through this crisis, he left the plush waiting room and strode down the hallway to the surgical ICU desk.

"Excuse me." He leaned over the counter to prompt the attention of the two attendants sharing a conversation over their monitors. "Can you tell me if my father's out of surgery yet?"

The younger of the two desk clerks answered. "One of the surgical aides buzzed a couple of minutes ago, Mr. Taylor. They're closing up now."

"That's good, right?" he asked, knowing he'd never shake this sense of unease until he saw his father's mischievous grin for himself. "The surgery hasn't taken too long, has it?"

"I don't know those kind of details." She smiled in sympathy. "But the doctor will come out in a few minutes to give you a status report."

She spun her chair around to resume her conversation with her friend. Her hair twirled with the movement, stirring up the clean scent of her shampoo. But as he inhaled, the fragrance changed. A subtle perfume of flowers teased his nose, the rich texture of freesia. The familiar scent of...

...an angel.

Brett looked to the elevator doors and watched a miraculous ray of sunshine step toward him. His breath caught in his throat, and something hot stung the corners of his eyes as Ginny closed the distance between them. A shy frown puckered the smooth skin of her forehead.

"How's your father?" she asked, as if she was breathless from rushing to the hospital, yet unsure of her welcome.

So strong, he thought. *So vulnerable.*

He stared at her for a moment in disbelief that she had come, absorbing the beauty of her bright blue eyes. He hadn't asked, yet she was here. He gaped long enough to see her fingers reach up to nervously tuck that stray silver-blond curl behind her ear.

"Brett?"

Like a statue suddenly brought to life by some divine magic, he leaned down and closed himself around her, wrapping her in his embrace, burying his nose in the flowery scent of her hair. He dared to speak only when her arms snuck around his waist and held on to him with that unique feminine strength that made him feel whole and supremely masculine. The tips of her small fingers pressed into his back, aligning them together in a way that had him believing the past could really stay in the past, and he could look forward to the future once more.

"You're here."

She turned her cheek into his chest and snuggled closer. "The Taylors, and anyone who cares about them, come together in times of crisis, right?"

A cold splash of reality doused his soaring spirit. He raised his head and inched back, resting his hands on her shoulders, reluctant to break contact with her completely. The confused expression on her face when she tipped her chin did her credit. Her acting skills were improving.

"Your cover." He'd come too far through the emotional wringer to mask his disappointment. "Smart move to show up here. I'll get that call in to Sophie for you as soon as I find out about Dad."

Her hands latched onto his belt and jerked him back as he turned away. Her cheeks flushed a brilliant rose.

"Dammit, Brett. I *want* to be here. I…" Her gaze dropped

to the buttons of his shirt as she seemed to search for a particularly difficult word to express herself. Then her hands tightened into fists and she lifted her face to zap him with a bolt of clear cobalt blue. "I was trying to say that I care about you. I wanted you to know that if there's something I can do to help, I will. You've helped me with Amy and Alvin. I owe you. I just wanted you to know that."

He trailed his fingers along her jaw, testing the combination of softness and strength there, of silky skin and resolute determination. He traced the curl behind her ear and let her hair tangle in his fingers as he framed her face in his hands.

Perhaps she *had* come simply to repay a debt. Maybe it was beyond the capacity of her guarded heart to feel love. Maybe her sense of fair play was the best she could give him at the moment. Maybe it was the most she would ever be willing to give.

Brett was too smart and too tired and too full of need for this woman to let that little window of opportunity pass him by. He wanted only one thing from her. He had only one request.

He dared her to meet his challenge.

"Stay."

"DAMMIT, Cole, you plant your butt in the chair and wait until Ma gets back out here." Brett fisted his hands at his sides, fighting the urge to grab his younger brother by his long brown ponytail and drag him back to the waiting room.

At Mitch's request, the prodigal son had shown up at the hospital. But after twenty minutes, Cole Taylor had slipped into his black leather jacket and headed for the elevators.

"Look." Strong, unsmiling features, so like his own at the moment, defied him. "I made my peace with Dad. I can't stay."

"It sounds like you read him the last rites. You want Ma

to hear you talk that way?'' Brett's temperature rose right along with his concern over the look on their mother's face when she walked out of Sid's room and found she had missed Cole again.

''I can't stay.'' He articulated each word with a finality that hinted at some underlying message.

But with only a couple hours of sleep to get him through this family crisis, Brett didn't have the patience to figure it out. ''You run out on us so often, I forget what you look like. Which side of the law is taking up your time today?''

A flash of fire in Cole's dark eyes flared and went out. Brother number three could mask his feelings as quickly and completely as…as Ginny.

''Don't you think I want to come back and be a part of this family?''

Still rattled by the comparison he'd just made, Brett reached out to his brother the way he wanted to reach out to Ginny. He clasped his hands around Cole's thick shoulders. ''Then do it.''

''I can't, big brother.''

''Are you in that much trouble?''

An edgy control that kept people at a distance softened a fraction. Cole gripped Brett's wrist and squeezed, the closest thing to a hug that he would allow. ''I watch my back.''

''You better.'' Brett released him, but cuffed a friendly fist at his shoulder. ''Or I will.''

''I'll get back when I can. Take care of Ma, okay? Jessie, too.''

The request went without saying. Cole was the Taylor who seemed to need help right now. ''Is there something I can do?''

''Nah.'' He pressed the down button on the elevator, telling Brett the conversation was over.

The words to keep his family together failed Brett. He searched for the right thing to say or do. In the end, he could only stand shoulder to shoulder with his brother, and doff a goodbye salute as the elevator doors shut behind him.

"Brett?" Ginny's crisp voice snuck through his over-worked mind, pinpointing that raw inner core that carried the burden of his family's troubles. He failed to muster a smile before turning to face her. "Your father's asking for you."

A full day at the hospital hadn't dulled the beauty in the symmetry of her heart-shaped face. Dealing with insurance forms and wayward brothers and the threat to his father's life hadn't dulled his desire for her, either. Soft yet strong, sure of herself yet shy, Ginny Rafferty had gotten into his blood somehow.

But murders and this damn charade between them got in the way of telling her how he felt, of proving to himself he had the right to feel this way.

Brett reached for her hand and pulled her into step beside him as he marched down the hallway to his father's room. True to an unpredictable nature he might never understand, she tugged against his grip.

"I'm just the messenger, Brett. Your mother said Sid wanted to talk to you."

"He'll talk to us." He emphasized the group pronoun and lengthened his stride.

Ginny doubled her speed to keep up. "But I don't be-long—"

"You belong to me."

Brett stopped and looked down into her stunned face. "That ring says as much. My father believes you love me, that we're getting married. I don't intend to let him think any differently until he's better."

"I just thought—"

"Don't think." He placed his hand on her shoulder and let the heel of his palm slide down to the upper curve of her right breast. "Feel. Open up that cold, frightened heart of yours and just feel something for a change."

A sheen of moisture brightened her eyes. "That's not fair. I don't want to hurt your family. But I'm an outsider. This is hardly the time or place to promote our engagement."

"Then why did you come this morning?" He asked the question knowing that he pushed those emotional buttons she tried so hard to avoid. "Why did you stay?"

She dropped her focus to the front of his shirt, a sure sign that she didn't know the answer herself. "Because you asked?"

Brett shook his head and pressed his hand closer to her heart. "Doesn't some small part of you care about me? For real?"

Ginny bowed her head and pulled away from his touch. "You shouldn't keep your father waiting."

He felt the space opening between them like a yawning chasm. He ached to bring her closer, physically, mentally and emotionally. He wanted to teach Ginny about love. He wanted to teach her about trust.

But how? When? Would she even give him a chance?

Brett had a sinking suspicion that his time to reach Ginny's battered heart was growing short. Soon she'd find Alvin's killer, and his usefulness to her would end.

With Ginny's help, he could put Mark Bishop's memory to rest. She could help him come to terms with his past. But it seemed she had little faith that there could be any future with him.

With a weary sigh, he took her hand, more gently this time, and raised it to his lips. He pressed a kiss to the silky skin at her knuckles, glad that she had stayed the day with him, regretful that she hadn't stayed for the reason he wanted.

"Let's go see Dad."

Brett pushed the door open and paused as his eyes adjusted to the dimmer light of the SICU room. Chilled air danced along his skin and a sharp whiff of alcohol and iodine tingled in his nose.

But a familiar face, a shade more pale than usual, yet creased with laughter and love, smiled at him from the white pillow. "Brett?"

A steady, healthy beep repeated itself from the monitor beside Sid Taylor's bed. Behind Brett, Ginny freed her hand and urged him to his father's side. Brett stepped forward at her gentle insistence. He knew an ironic sense of calm at having the detective behind him to back him up—though the support he took from Ginny's quiet presence had nothing to do with her badge.

Sid lifted his hand from the sheet atop the bed. Brett linked their thumbs and caught his father's hand between both of his. Brett couldn't help but note that Sid's big grip wasn't as firm as before. "It's good to see you."

"It's good to be seen." Sid smiled, though the effort to laugh made him catch at his side with pain. "Damn tubes. Scared your mother. I tried to tell her I don't feel as bad as I look. Have one of the nurses explain to her what everything's for."

"Relax, Dad." Brett squeezed his father's hand. "I've got everything under control. All you need to concentrate on is getting your strength back. Despite the trouble you had with the anesthesia, the doctors say you'll be fine."

Sid nodded and sank back into the pillows, clearly exhausted by the eighteen-hour ordeal. "Your ma's depending on you."

"I know."

As his eyes drifted shut, Sid summoned the strength to tighten his hold on Brett's hand. "Don't carry the weight of all this yourself, son. Let that young woman of yours share the burden."

Sid turned his cheek into the pillow and looked past Brett.

Despite pain, exhaustion and a sewed-up hole in his chest, the original Taylor charmer flashed a smile. "I'll be up and out of here in no time. I expect to be dancing at your wedding reception soon. I get the first dance after Brett, right?"

Feeling the waning strength in his father's grip, Brett turned and sent a silent message to Ginny, willing her to play her part so Sid wouldn't question their relationship. He didn't need any kind of stress right now.

She huddled in the doorway, arms crossed protectively in front of her. Her cheeks blushed a rosy pink at Sid's flirtations, but she had that stricken look of surprise in her eyes that broadcast her mind's search for the right lie to tell.

Disappointed, Brett hurried to cover her silence with a plausible excuse. "Ginny and I haven't set—"

"Absolutely." That crisp detective voice cut him off. Ginny brushed up against Brett's side and linked her arm through his. She laid her left hand—the one with the glint of his ring on her finger—over his hand and Sid's, aligning them as a team. Proclaiming they belonged together. Making it all look—and feel—real. "Maybe even the next two or three dances," she teased.

Sid winked. "If we can ditch Brett."

Her breathtaking laughter worked its magic on Sid. It had a bewitching effect on Brett, too. A pang of jealousy for his own father twitched deep in his gut. Ginny had rarely dropped her guard long enough to reveal the sunny beauty of a real smile to him. But here she was, joking and smiling with his father. And Sid believed every last word. Brett almost believed the magic himself. For an instant, his own heart flip-flopped at the notion of a real future with her.

"I'll hold you to that promise." Sid grinned weakly. He rolled his face back up toward the ceiling and closed his eyes. "She's a keeper, son." His hand went slack inside Brett's as fatigue and the effects of pain medication won out. "A real keeper."

"I love you, Dad."

But sleep had already claimed the Taylor patriarch. A wealth of suppressed emotion tightened like a vise deep inside Brett. He squeezed his eyes shut and dropped his head, sending up a silent prayer to heal his stricken hero.

"Brett."

A gentle tug on his arm matched the soft voice. He opened his eyes at the unspoken request and looked down into Ginny's upturned face. A halo of silver-gold hair fell in shimmering wisps against the lines of concern and compassion etched beside her eyes.

He toyed with the urge to bend down and kiss her, to take the compassion she offered. But her rationality was rubbing off on him, and he couldn't quite trust that the offer was real.

Still, she had come through for Sid when he needed her. And for that, Brett would always be grateful. "Thank you."

"For what?" Her lips compressed into a tiny frown.

He covered her hand where it rested on his arm, and studied the contrasts of callused and smooth, large and small, male and female between them. The vise inside him tightened a notch. "For making Dad believe in us."

Ginny pulled away and left the room. Unwilling to break the tenuous connection of comfort between them, Brett followed. He fell into step beside her. Their unhurried pace took them past another patient's room and on toward the empty staff lounge at the end of the hall.

"Your dad's easy to like," Ginny explained. "I wouldn't want to cause him any more pain."

Yeah, Brett conceded, his family was easy to like. Safe, loving and supportive. Plus, they had nothing to do with the case against Alvin Bishop's killer.

But maybe it wasn't so easy to like him. For Ginny, at any rate.

He was her last chance to solve a murder and find the

truth about her sister's death. He was the risk she'd had to take, the ally she didn't want, but couldn't help needing.

And he'd taken advantage of that. Lord, how he'd needed her today. Her feminine scent, her soft hair, her shy presence and succinct voice. The vise inside him broke beneath the twist of emotion and he reached out.

He snatched her wrist and pulled her into the lounge and shut the door behind him.

"What are you doing?"

In answer, he gathered Ginny into his arms and buried his nose in her hair, inhaling her sweet softness. Miraculously, her arms curled around his waist and he felt her fingertips pressing into his spine, holding him close, drawing him near.

The delicate weight of her breasts branded him through his shirt. He ran his hands along the length of her back, skimming her from shoulders to hips, finding the hard bulk of her gun and the soft indentation of her waist. He pulled his hands back up, underneath her blazer. His palms tickled at the friction of denim, soothed at the touch of soft cotton, zinged to life at the discovery of silk and lace and feminine curves beneath it all.

"Ginny," he whispered a ragged plea against her ear, and turned to press his lips to the silky hair at her temple. "I need you."

He longed to feel the heat of her, skin to skin. He longed to taste her. She was life and strength and escape for a man whose foundations were broken, whose well of faith had run dry.

"I can't." She squirmed in his arms, blindly seeking to free herself, though her hands had balled into fists at his waist, grabbing on to his shirt and refusing to let go. "I don't know what you want."

"Just let me," he promised, finding a strength all his own in her tentative surrender. He framed her face in his hands and stilled her halfhearted struggles. He locked on to her gaze, calming the turbulence there with a smile of pleasures yet to come. "Just let me."

Brett closed the distance between them and kissed her. A light sweep of his tongue coaxed her lips to part and he claimed her for his own. Leaving the splendor of her moonlit curls, he lifted her hands to his neck. She rewarded him by stretching up on tiptoe and holding on, pulling herself into his kiss.

As their tongues and lips played a heady game of search and surrender, he moved his hands to her waist. With desperate speed he untucked her blouse and slipped his hands inside. A groan of sheer delight rumbled in his throat at the tactile heat of creamy skin and supple muscle there. His suddenly unsteady feet shifted beneath him.

Ginny tumbled into his chest. He carried her with him as he backed up, seeking to brace himself against the unexpected mix of passion and compassion in her soft, seeking lips.

When his hips butted against a desktop, he sat and pulled her snug into the V of his legs. She slid down the length of him until her feet touched the floor, tormenting his body and bringing hope to his aching heart.

He left her mouth to run his lips along the delicate line of her jaw. He tipped her back over his arm and explored lower, supping at the sensitive curve of her neck, drinking his fill at the fragile bone beneath her collar.

He dragged his fingers to the front hem of her blouse and pushed it higher, exposing the flat of her stomach. With one broad hand, he soothed the ragged catch of breath there. He inched the material even higher, and pressed his mouth to the boundary of silk and breast, right above her pounding heart.

His own pulse hammered in his ears at this reckless abandonment of rationality. He'd broken through to Ginny's precious emotions. That volatile heat she locked inside her forged them into one, lifting him high above the concerns for his family, the fears for himself and the impending destruction of the future he wanted to build with her.

Ginny teetered on the edge of an abyss. She'd lowered her guard and Brett had quickly rushed in.

She gasped for air as his tongue teased the tip of her breast. Soft flannel gave way to the hard heat of Brett's massive shoulders and chest as he crushed her in his arms. Surrounded by his strength, she felt so weak, so vulnerable. The darkness surrounded them and could destroy her at any moment. But right now Brett needed her.

He needed *her*.

And so she let him in.

The scruff of his day-old beard nearly burned her hands as she caught him to her breast. His mouth closed over the distended nipple, claiming her through the sheer lace of her bra.

Ginny tumbled over the edge at the raw jolt of electricity that shot through her. Crying out his name, she struggled to save herself. She tangled her fingers in the silky mane of his hair, holding on as he murmured lusty little praises against her skin.

But it was too much.

Too much, too fast, too dangerous. She flattened her palms against the sensuous curve of his skull and guided his mouth back to hers.

She wanted the reassurance that Brett knew this was her. Ginny. She wanted him to know that he sought comfort from a woman who had loved unwisely, a woman who had shamed herself before a group of her peers, a woman who had steeled her heart in self-defense. A woman who knew more about guns and criminals than she knew about trust and love.

"Brett?" He allowed her a breath between a smattering of kisses.

"Hmm?"

Her own lips scudded across the square jut of his chin as she tried to pull back. "We need to talk."

"Right this minute?" A heavy puff of air lifted the curl beside her ear as he sighed. Fascinated by the movement, he turned his attentions to the soft skin of her earlobe. "Put the badge aside for now, angel."

His dark voice skittered along her neck and made her catch her breath. He adjusted her in his arms to give his lips better access to that tender spot. Her hip brushed against his jeans, leaving her no doubt that she had some effect on him, too.

Her teeth stuttered together as she tried to form words. "It's not about the investigation."

At last he lifted his head and looked at her. If the drowsy shadows in his sapphire eyes counted as a look.

Ginny moved her hands to his chest and pushed a little space between them. The subtle shove didn't go unnoticed. His breathing slowed into a steady pattern, and the tiny crow's-feet beside his eyes deepened as his expression grew serious.

"What's bothering you?"

"This."

"There's not a damn thing wrong with *this*."

She shook her head, caught the loose curl at her jaw and tucked it behind her ear. "It's me."

"There's not a damn thing wrong with you, either."

His dark blue eyes drilled into hers, daring her to contradict him.

Ginny stepped back, fighting to gather her scattered thoughts and turn them into reason. But Brett's hands held firm on her hips, as if he knew she'd slip away entirely if he let go. She pulled down the hem of her blouse, feeling exposed enough without the air-conditioning chilling her heated skin.

"You're worried about your father," she began.

"Yeah."

"We've been through some heavy stuff lately. We've had to deal with the worst memories of our lives."

He didn't argue with her. "What's your point, Sherlock?"

"My point is, you're not thinking clearly right now." She held up her left hand between them, waving her fingers until the twin diamonds caught the light. "These might be real gems, but it's not the real thing between us."

"It can be."

"Can it?" She curled her hand into a fist and dropped it to her side. His words stirred a longing within her. But she could tell his desire was cooling, and she was starting to make sense.

Holding her now by one hand, he used the other to flip the lapel of her blazer back into place. "You're fire and I'm water, is that it? The two can never exist together?"

Finally, he let her move away. When she had the length of the room between them, she turned. "The last real relationship I had was twelve years ago. And I screwed it up." He stood, swallowing up the space of the room. His overwhelming size made her point easier to make. "I need my distance, Brett. It's how I keep myself from screwing up again. If you get too close to me, I know…" She crossed her arms over her stomach, afraid of baring her soul to this man. "I know you'll be disappointed."

Ginny withered in the dreadful silence that followed. Brett's low-pitched whisper shivered through her veins. "That bastard must have hurt you pretty badly."

Her heart hadn't been broken so much as her faith in her own judgment had been shattered.

"He kept me from being here for my sister. He kept me from possibly saving her life."

Brett raked all ten fingers through his hair, and caught it

behind his neck. "Maybe we have more in common than you think."

He lowered his arms, splayed his hands on his hips and took in a deep breath to add something more. But the lounge door opened, and a flick of a switch flooded the room with fluorescent light.

"There you are."

Half hidden behind the open door, Ginny watched Sophie Bishop sashay across the room and throw her arms around Brett's neck. Without rising on tiptoe, she kissed him full on the mouth. Ginny's own lips compressed into a resigned frown.

Both tall, both dark, Brett and Sophie fit together. They shared history. "I've been looking all over this hospital for you. How are you holding up?"

"Your timing stinks, Sophie." Even Ginny started at the dismissive growl in his voice. He grabbed Sophie's wrists and unwound her from his neck.

"I know you're upset, but I came as soon as I could." Ginny wondered if Brett could hear the hurt in her voice. "I've been up to my eyeballs getting the last-minute details taken care of for your fund-raiser."

"What?"

"The ball at Union Station. Five hundred dollars a head to raise money for your renovation project?" Sophie reached for Brett again. "Oh God, Sid must be worse off than I thought."

This time, he dropped his arm around her waist and accepted the hug she wanted to give. "Sid's going to be fine."

With an old friend to supply him the comfort he needed, Ginny snuck around the door, intending to leave while she still had any pride left.

But Brett had no intention of letting her take the cowardly way out. "This conversation isn't over." His promise stopped Ginny in her tracks.

A possessive gleam in Sophie's smile warned her it had to be over. "Are you two lovebirds having a tiff?"

A bit of the Irish toughness that had seen her through grisly crimes and wasted heartache stiffened Ginny's spine. "It's none of your business. We were talking about you earlier, though."

"Really?" Sophie looked less stunned by the switch in topic than Brett.

Slipping into the one role she knew how to play well, Ginny asked, "I wondered if you know about a set of wind-chime bells your father stole from Pearl Jenkins's apartment."

"This is hardly the time to bring up something like that."

"Tell us about the chimes, Sophie." To her surprise, Brett joined the questioning.

At Brett's urging, Sophie finally answered. "Yes. He took them from the Jenkinses upstairs and kept them." Turning her back squarely on Ginny, Sophie sidled up to Brett. "Is that the best your detective fiancée can do? Can't she find a real clue to who lured my father downstairs and left him to die?"

"The chimes," he insisted. "We need to see them."

"I don't have them. Eric packed up Dad's things for me and put them into storage."

He pushed on while Ginny listened. "Where?"

"I don't know."

"Soph, honey. We're trying to help you here. We're trying to help Mark."

Ginny watched the play of Sophie's shoulders tensing, then forcibly relaxing, as Brett's words stirred an unpleasant memory. But her voice revealed nothing but detached co-operation. "I'll ask Eric. He's meeting with some associates at the casino this evening. But I'll see him in the morning."

Brett looked beyond Sophie's shoulder to Ginny. "Is that what you needed to know?"

"I need to see those chimes. See if there's a bell missing."

Brett looked intently at Sophie. She threw her hands up and shrugged. "Fine. If you think it will help, Eric and I will go to the storage unit and bring you the chimes tomorrow."

"Thanks." He squeezed Sophie's hand. "I'll see you tomorrow night at the ball."

"With a tie," she reminded him.

"With a tie." The strain of the day, maybe even of their last few minutes together, told in the weary tilt of Brett's smile. "Now, if you'll excuse me, I'm going to drive my fiancée home."

Chapter Eleven

"You don't have to do this." Ginny watched the elevator buttons light up, steadfastly ignoring the way Brett's big body consumed the tiny space around her.

"Yes, I do. I'm not letting you run away this time."

He stood close enough for her to smell the odors on his clothes, the faint detergent, his mother's delicate perfume. Even the scent of her own skin lingered on him, reminding her of how close they'd been, how close she'd come to forgetting everything but kissing him, loving him.

She didn't bother to argue. She *was* running. But apparently not fast enough nor far enough to escape and give herself some time to get her head on straight.

A real relationship with Brett could never work. He was big and brash and seized the world with both hands. She was woefully ill equipped to be his equal. She doubted he would settle for anything less. She didn't want him to.

As the elevator neared her floor, she tried one last time to keep him out of her sanctuary. She had a terrible feeling that if he broke through her self-protective walls there, she wouldn't have the strength to push him away a second time.

"We can talk later. You must be exhausted." She ventured a glance up at the dark stubble of beard shading his jaw and neck. Telltale shadows ringed the stern expression in his eyes. A tender compassion swallowed up her heart and squeezed it tight.

"I'm fine." He punctuated the lie with a Brett-size yawn. She wanted to smile at the boyish contradiction, but his next words sobered her. "You were about to tell me something important, and I intend to hear it. Tonight."

Before she could think about the wisdom of her action, she reached out and touched her fingers gently to his forearm. "Please, Brett." But was she asking him to take care of himself? Or to leave her alone?

His larger hand covered her own, thanking her for the gesture, but not allowing her to dissuade him. "I can be as single-minded about things as you are, Gin. And right now, *you* are the only thing on my mind."

As he bent closer, Ginny pulled away. If she could just get to her apartment and close her door—with Brett in the hallway—she could get some precious time to herself, regroup, think of a way to make him see that he wouldn't want to be with her once the investigation was over.

She could spare herself the humiliation of giving her heart to a man, then finding out he didn't want it, after all.

When the doors opened on the seventh floor, she quickly stepped out, not even worrying about whether the lights were on or off. She had to get away from Brett, put distance between them. She set off at a brisk pace, restraining the urge to run from him to the haven of her apartment.

But Ginny's life had never been about easy escapes from conflict.

Halfway down, the door across from hers opened and Dennis Fitzgerald appeared. "Ginny." He hurried down the center of the hall, blocking her path. "Thank God you're here." The flush of excitement staining his face all the way up to his receding hairline turned her sense of urgency in a new direction. "I didn't know how to contact you, so I called the police."

"The police?" Ginny halted, automatically checking him from head to toe for some kind of injury. "Are you all right?"

She linked her hand through the crook of his elbow and turned him back toward his apartment. She scanned his open door for signs of forced entry.

"Ginny." Brett's deep voice from behind her left shoulder turned her focus to the real problem.

Her apartment.

The same creepy foreboding that had assaulted her senses at the City Market last night returned with a renewed suspicion that pumped ice into her veins.

She heard the sounds of conversation and laughter before the band of light outlining her door registered. Reaching inside her jacket, she unsnapped her holster. With gun in hand, she pushed the unresisting door open.

Instantly, Brett was there, his hand on her arm pushing her back. Heroic intentions aside, she was the one with the weapon. She should enter first.

"Move." She commanded him to step aside.

He didn't budge. But at his ripe, damning curse, she pushed her way past him to see the apartment for herself. She froze.

"Oh my God."

Her sanctuary had been violated. The tiny haven of all she held dear in the world had been slashed, broken and tossed about with a violent disregard for the few belongings she had in the world that held any real meaning for her.

Feeling violated herself at the sight, she sank back into Brett's hands at her shoulders, leaning into his strength.

"Angel, I'm sorry. I'm so sorry."

She very nearly turned her face into his chest to hide the chaos from her sight, but Merle Banning and another man walked out of her bedroom. Summoning dwindling reserves of energy, she stepped out of Brett's embrace and holstered her weapon. She drew on the cold, calculating side of herself, and ordered the kick-butt cop inside her to take charge of the situation.

"Merle, what happened?"

Her partner gave her arm a reassuring squeeze before answering. "Sorry, Gin. We were going to be out of here before you got back. Your cell phone is still out of order, so I had no way to reach you when the call came in."

"From Dennis Fitzgerald?" She picked up a remnant of Japanese silk that had been sliced from the shards of bamboo screen that had once masked her kitchen. She crushed the material in her hand and assessed the damage.

"Right. About five-thirty this evening. Your neighbor said he was out buying newspapers. When he came back, he saw the lock had been broken."

She hadn't realized Dennis had joined the party until he spoke. "I opened the door to see if you were here, if you were hurt. Then I went back to my apartment and called it in." His black half-glasses hung from a chain he fiddled with around his neck. "I didn't touch anything but the doors."

Jeff Ringlein, an assistant on Mac Taylor's forensics team, peeled off his plastic gloves and dropped them into his black leather briefcase. "His story checks out. I've dusted for prints, bagged a few samples and taken pictures, so you can clean up whenever you're ready. Whoever came in was wearing gloves. The only other prints I got match Mr. Fitzgerald's."

Merle finished the report. "Nothing of value appears to have been taken. Your stereo system is intact. TV's untouched. It doesn't look like a robbery to me."

"You know damn well what this is, Gin." Brett rose from the center of the living room and pieced together two broken plates of glass that had once been her coffee table. "Another threat. More intimidation."

She felt her sense of fear and injustice transforming itself into anger. Brett provided an easy target. "Every other contact has had a message," she argued. She righted one of the stools at her kitchen counter. "What does this mess prove?"

"That he can get to you."

His tone of deadly certainty rattled her more than she let on. She turned and snapped an order at Merle. "Find Eric Chamberlain. If he's not at the river casino, track him down and bring him in for questioning. I want him to account for every minute of his day today."

She kicked aside the stuffing that had been ripped from her oversize chair and headed down the hall to check for any further damage. The room where she painted had provided a grand playground for slashing canvas and squirting paint on the walls. The easel lay in a muddy mix of oils that had pooled on the floor.

The knife she used to cut paint protruded from the X she'd drawn on the canvas that morning. She pointed out the short blade with its stainless handle. "Did you check that for prints?"

Jeff Ringlein answered. "It's been wiped clean."

"Bag it as the probable tool used to cut everything up in here."

"Sure thing." He scuttled out of the room to get his bag.

It was easier to play the cop than the victim, she discovered. If she busied herself figuring out the cause of the break-in and vandalism, then she wouldn't have time to feel the anger and violation.

Merle fell in behind her as she examined the sticky web of toilet paper, lotions and shampoo globbed on the floor in the bathroom, then moved on to the last room, her bedroom.

Amazingly enough, little had been touched here. Her bed was still as neatly made as it had been that morning. The clothes in her closet hung with wrinkle-free familiarity. The personal items in front of her dresser mirror had been rearranged, but nothing was broken.

"Was he interrupted before he finished ransacking the place?" she speculated out loud.

Merle crossed to the table beside her bed and pulled the drawer open with the tip of his pen. "I think he finally found what he was looking for."

She knelt beside him and pulled out the open metal box. The lock had been broken off. Ginny shook her head, not yet comprehending the significance of what she held in her hands. "I keep my gun and badge in here. I had those with me today."

And then it hit her. She set the box aside and dived into the drawer itself, running her fingers along every empty corner.

"Where's the key?" she asked.

"What key?"

Her feverish search clearly perplexed him. But she didn't take time to explain. She was already running to the living room and tossing things aside to make a path. "My trunk." She pushed the remaining chunk of glass to the floor and unhooked the clasps on either side of the locking hinge. "I keep sentimental things in my trunk."

Brett knelt beside her and studied the antique. "It's locked."

Merle took his place when Brett got up. "Why would anyone bother to lock it after they've looked inside?"

"Let's find out." Brett returned with a large screwdriver from a kitchen drawer. He slipped it under the edge of the locking hasp and forced it open. Ginny pushed up the lid to see what was inside.

She lifted the baby quilt and stared at the wrinkled pink ribbon lying beneath it. A quick dig through music boxes and old sweaters revealed what she feared the most. "My letters. He took Amy's letters."

"Gin." Brett's hand on her shoulder stilled her. She followed his gaze to the message scrawled inside the lid of the trunk.

Your sister never learned her lesson. But you will.

Ginny felt light-headed. Dizzy enough that she swayed when she tried to stand.

Brett caught her around the waist and steadied her. But when he tried to wrap her in his arms, she resisted. She flattened her palms against his chest and pushed. "No. This is a police matter. We'll handle it."

She curled her fingers around the badge on her belt, finding little comfort in the cold brass and leather. She sucked in deep lungfuls of air and walked away from Brett. If she gave in to his easy strength now, she'd lose it. She'd break down in one of those useless fits of panic. She might never find her own strength.

With those letters stolen, she felt as if she'd lost Amy all over again.

"If he wants to play games, I'll play." She made her voice sound tougher than she felt. She found a perverse sense of power by turning this personal invasion into an objective police investigation. "Have the lab compare the trunk to the ink in the message I got last night."

Brett's eyes narrowed in a proprietary scowl. "What message?"

She couldn't look at him and maintain that all-business voice he'd once taken exception to. So she walked to the kitchen and pulled a box of trash bags from under the sink. "The Ludlow Arms blueprints I wanted you to look at."

Ginny stuffed the ruined cloth from her Japanese screen into the bag, then moved on to the foam stuffing from the chair.

Unfortunately, Merle wasn't put off by her silence. He even added a tinge of impatience to his voice. "The tube the blueprints came in said *'You wouldn't listen.'* She found them in the back of her car.''

Brett grabbed her by the upper arm and pulled her to her feet, knocking the trash bag to the floor. ''You knew that when you came to the hospital this morning? Why didn't you tell me?''

His accusation ticked her off. She'd been scared last night, but she'd gotten through it. She'd had no knight in shining armor to save her then. She didn't need one now.

Twisting free of his grasp, she marched to the door and opened it wide. ''Thanks for bringing me home, but I want you to leave now.''

He didn't budge an inch. He propped his hands on his hips, pushing his shoulders out to stubborn proportions. But he spoke with calm reason, not his usual challenge. ''I think it's time we told Mitch what was going on. This has gotten too personal for you *and* the killer. I don't want you to get hurt.''

''It's not your decision to make.''

Brett erased the distance between them in two long strides. She pressed her back into the door and tipped her chin, determined to defy the protection of this gentle giant. He made a mockery of her false bravado by tucking that independent curl behind her ear. She jerked her jaw away from that tender touch.

''Dammit, Ginny. Think. You're scared right now. You don't know what you're saying.''

''I have a job to do. I can't deal with you right now.'' She turned her head, refusing to look at him. ''Please leave.''

Brett stood there for endless seconds, never blinking, waiting for her to relent and ask him to stay. Her eyes burned with the effort to hold back tears. Her gaze landed on the ruined trunk, and she almost gave in. But Brett had had enough.

With nothing more than a disgusted grunt, he strode down the hallway and disappeared through the stairwell door. Ginny stepped out to see that he was gone. Truly gone.

When the door slammed shut behind him, she gave in to the tears.

TWO HOURS LATER, Ginny was on her own again. Merle and Jeff Ringlein had stayed long enough to clean up the black powder used to take fingerprints. They loaded the trunk into Jeff's van, and came back to pick up the mess in the living room while she cleaned the kitchen.

She'd even endured a visit from her captain, Mitch Taylor. His initial concern had quickly eroded into one of those paternal frowns that made her feel young and foolish. He praised the legwork she had done on the case thus far, but his approval of her tactics vanished once Merle recited his version of the investigation, including the threats that she'd left out of her own reports.

He didn't have to remind her of the rules. She knew she had broken them. But Mitch never asked for her badge. He never mentioned the reprimand that should go into her file.

Instead, he placed a call to the precinct and ordered a round-the-clock watch on her building. He told Maggie to reassign Ginny's caseload except for the Bishop and Jones murders. And then he dismissed Merle and sat her down on the couch.

"Can you prove Alvin Bishop killed your sister?"

Not the question she was expecting. Ginny shook her head.

"Can you prove Eric Chamberlain killed Alvin?"

"I'm getting close." All the evidence pointed to him. He had a motive. He had the opportunity to go to Alvin's apartment and lure him downstairs. "I need Charlie Adkins's testimony to make it stick."

"I'll make locating Charlie the precinct's top priority."

He loosened his tie and stood, relaxing the hard edge that made him such an intimidating officer. That he could be so commanding, yet treat his officers like human beings, had earned Ginny's respect from the day she transferred to the Fourth Precinct.

His big barrel chest puffed out with a meaningful sigh. She stood, preparing herself for what he was about to say. "If you can make this case hold up in a courtroom, I'll sign my name off as arresting officer on your sister's killer. We'll keep the conflict-of-interest charge and Internal Affairs out of your file."

Ginny stood. "Why?"

"I'm tired of finding dead bodies in my precinct." He crossed to the door, apparently ready to leave.

She hurried after him, confused by the generous gesture. "But why would you bend the rules for me?"

He frowned at the broken dead bolt on her door, then tested the lock on the knob to be sure it worked. When he turned to face her, the old man actually smiled. "Because you're family. Brett was there for Casey when she needed protection. It seems fair that I look out for you, too."

Now she sat in the middle of her bathroom floor, using a wet sponge to mop up the shampoo and shower gel that had been dumped there. She squeezed the gummy liquid into the sink, twisting the sponge tighter and tighter between her fists. She imagined that the sponge was her worn-out spirit, and she could squeeze a few more drops of sanity out of it if she just worked hard enough and kept her mind focused on the investigation.

She still cringed at the lie she had perpetuated by not telling Mitch the truth about her engagement to Brett. Merle didn't know their match was a fake, so he hadn't revealed her secret, either.

Only Brett knew the truth. Brett seemed to know all her truths.

She rinsed the sponge and attacked the tile floor again. Brett knew she was a fraud. A by-the-book detective valued for her intelligence and perseverance who was afraid of the dark. A cool-thinking woman who lost her ability to carry on a rational conversation whenever he took her in his arms and kissed her. An emotional coward who couldn't even do a good job pretending to be in love with him.

And she was so very terrified that she *was* in love with him.

She had nothing in common with Brett. He joked, she frowned. He took action, she thought things through. He was comfortable with his emotions, and she was afraid of hers.

Ginny dropped the sponge in the sink and sought a different job that would keep Brett Taylor out of her thoughts. But there was really only one job that had ever consumed her. And though she'd been ordered to stay put for the night, she remembered one avenue that a curious detective could still pursue.

A firm knock brought Dennis Fitzgerald to his door. He identified her through the peephole and let her in. When she saw that he had changed into his pajamas and robe, she apologized. "I didn't check my watch. I'll talk to you in the morning."

"No, no, come in." When he gestured to the chairs in the dining room, she accepted his offer. "I was up, working on my scrapbooks. Would you like some tea? I have a special herbal blend that might help you sleep after what happened."

"No, thanks." She doubted anything could get her to sleep tonight. "I did want to ask you about the break-in, though."

He pulled out a chair and she sat. Dennis hurried to the opposite side of the table, his flushed face betraying his excitement. "I thought you might. I know I bug you about cases you're working on, but this time I might be able to help you.''

She shared his interest, but not his enthusiasm for the subject at hand. ''When exactly were you gone this evening?''

''I always leave at four-thirty to visit the kiosk on the corner. I buy the *Star,* the *Denver Post,* and *USA Today.* Then I go to the coffee shop across the street and have a café mocha. I head home right at five-fifteen. Depending on how the elevator is working, I'm back in my apartment by five-thirty.''

''Were you here at five-thirty this evening?''

''Right on the dot. I saw your door standing open and went inside. I was here the rest of the day, so I must have just missed the break-in. Otherwise, I would have heard something.''

One of his stack of scrapbooks lay open at the end of the table. A few clipped articles sat on top of the folded newspapers he had mentioned. A name in one of the articles jumped out at her. Zeke Jones.

Dennis said nothing when she picked up the articles and thumbed through them. Alvin Bishop. Mark Bishop. She stopped at the picture of a hauntingly familiar brick building. She looked at Dennis expectantly.

He rubbed his hands together. ''I follow all the murder cases, waiting for a moment like this when I can be of some real help to the police.''

Ginny got up and walked to the end of the table, flipping through the pages of the open scrapbook. Ten, eleven, twelve pages all dedicated to one place. At the beginning of the book, the articles were yellowed with age. She found a physical description of Alvin Bishop, listed as a missing person.

The secrets of the Ludlow Arms crept under her skin and

chilled her. She looked at Dennis and asked, "What's your interest in the Ludlow Arms?"

His ruddy face paled beneath her scrutiny.

"Dennis?" she prompted.

"I used to live there."

Her uprooted world spun in a maddening new direction. "You knew I was working on this case, and you didn't tell me you used to be a resident?"

He stood, halfheartedly defending himself. "I showed you 'The Cask of Amontillado' story. It helped you figure out how the murder was accomplished, didn't it?"

"Did you know Alvin Bishop?"

He didn't have to answer. His shoulders sagged and he dropped his gaze to the table. "Yes. Everything you've heard about him is true. No one was sorry when he died."

"His daughter, maybe."

Dennis looked up and shook his head. "I doubt it. My daughter, Lydia, used to go to school with her. Some days she said Sophie wore sunglasses to class. She'd get in trouble, but she'd rather go to the principal's office than take them off."

"It's no secret that Alvin was an abusive man." She picked up the articles and dropped them in front of Dennis. "If you really wanted to help me, you should have told me you had a connection."

"I didn't want you to think I had a motive for killing him."

"Did you?"

Dennis straightened the papers into a tidy pile before answering. "I moved my family out of the Ludlow after my daughter was attacked."

"Attacked?" A sinking suspicion settled in the pit of her stomach. "Did she by any chance date one of the tenants in the building?"

"My Lydia was knocked down. She hit her head on the

concrete stoop. We had her in the hospital for two days before she regained consciousness.''

A horrible pattern seemed to be repeating itself. "Did your daughter date Mark Bishop?"

Dennis made no pretense of being a nosy neighbor with an annoying hobby anymore. The dull resignation in his eyes told her he'd been an unwilling participant in the hell of the Ludlow Arms. "To earn extra money toward college, she tutored students who needed help in English. She worked with Mark for three weeks. Then she had her accident and we moved.''

"But you don't think it was an accident."

"Lydia has never remembered what happened. But I know.'' He put his glasses back on and stuck the articles in the spine of the scrapbook and closed it. "Old Alvin couldn't tolerate the thought of Mark getting married or going off to college.''

"You believe Alvin pushed Lydia down the steps?" Zeke Jones's death popped to mind, but the matching M.O. didn't make sense. Alvin Bishop had been dead twelve years before Zeke was murdered.

"Who else could it be?"

Ginny clutched at her stomach, unable to absorb anyone else's grief and anger right now. She needed to get back to her place, among her own things, and regroup. Thanking Dennis for his help, she showed herself out the door.

She stepped across the hall and reached for her own doorknob. But then the old lightbulb in the hallway shorted and went out, plunging her into darkness.

She couldn't stop the cry of pain that escaped her. She closed her eyes and buried her face in her hands. She'd forgotten about the break-in. There was no sanctuary for her anymore. There was no safe place where she could nurse her wounds and conquer her fears and go out and face the world again.

And then the elevator dinged. She peered through the darkness at the dot of light that indicated the doors were about to open. She caught her breath, hugged herself and waited for whatever fate was about to throw her way.

The doors opened. Lighted from behind, a tall, bulky silhouette emerged. She heard the jingle of metal and a thunking sound, like that of a low drumbeat.

She shivered and her skin prickled with goose bumps as the figure came closer. Then the dimensions took shape. The long length of denim-clad legs, the broad shoulders, the silky waterfall of hair framing a bold face and catching in the collar of a soft flannel shirt.

"Brett?"

She breathed his name in prayer and relief.

"The light went out." A silly, meaningless thing to say to the man who now stood in front of her. "I'm not really claustrophobic. It's the dark I can't stand."

His eyes deepened to pools of midnight in the shadowed hallway. But they didn't frighten her. He swung a leather tool belt off his shoulder and hooked it over the tool box he carried in his hand. "I came to fix your lock."

That dark rasp of his voice filled her ears and seeped into her bones, making her weak, making her strong.

And then, because she was too overcome to be anything less than honest, she simply said, "I'd like that."

GINNY FINISHED cleaning the bathroom while Brett installed a new dead bolt on her door. He worked in diligent silence, probably afraid that she'd order him out again if he stated an opinion. Without asking, he checked her windows. He replaced a missing screw and mounted a spring-lock rod to her bedroom window.

She was in the art room, picking up emptied tubes of oil paint when he finally called to her. Dropping the mess into the wastebasket, she pulled the door closed and found him in her bedroom.

He was kneeling in front of her bedside table. She saw the end of a black metal box as he shut the drawer. When he stood, he held out a small key ring. ''I bought you a new security box. I already locked your gun and badge inside. Here's the key.''

He dropped it into her outstretched hand without touching her. This completely businesslike demeanor surprised her. He didn't act like the Brett she knew. Had she done so good a job at making him feel unwelcome that he couldn't see how grateful she was that he should come back and take care of her like this?

She brainstormed ways she could thank him, ways to show that his very presence helped her feel secure. She needed something straight to the point, something tangible so he would believe her sincerity.

She took the key out to the kitchen and dropped it into her purse. She looked at the clock: 10:00 p.m.

He'd been with his father the night before, at the hospital all day long, with her this evening. When had the man taken time to eat and sleep?

''How's your father doing?'' she asked when he came down the hallway and put his tools away by the front door.

''Resting comfortably.'' He closed the toolbox and faced her. His two-day beard stubble gave him a dangerous look, and the haggard circles beneath his eyes turned his jovial countenance into the face of a man with little left to lose. ''He has to change his diet. Take some pills for his blood pressure. But you can't keep Sid Taylor off his feet for long.''

He almost smiled then. But his stomach grumbled instead.

That's when the inspiration hit her. ''I don't think I saw you eat a thing all day. Can I feed you a late dinner?''

He hesitated, not like Brett Taylor at all. But then he accepted the truce she offered. "Sure. Why not? We'll call it an even trade. I'll get washed up."

After Brett disappeared into the bathroom, Ginny opened her freezer and discovered two boxes to choose from. She opted for the chicken and potatoes. She vented the plastic cover, put the tray in the microwave and set the timer for six minutes.

She checked the fridge for anything to make a salad with, and ended up slicing an apple and arranging it on a plate. She set a place at the counter and poured him a glass of milk. When Brett pulled out one of the wooden stools and sat, she pulled out the microwave tray and set it on his plate with a flourish.

What might have been an ample portion for her shrank in front of Brett. The black plastic cook-tray was no bigger than Brett's hand, the four fingers of chicken shorter than his own fingers.

Ginny felt the telltale heat creeping into her cheeks. "I'm sorry. When I offered to cook, I didn't mean I actually knew how to cook."

Brett stared at the tiny servings until she felt compelled to apologize again. He busted out laughing, putting up a hand to wave off her offer to heat the last frozen dinner she had. In that moment, the Brett she knew best returned. The rich laughter that shook his chest absolved her of embarrassment and triggered an unfamiliar sound from deep behind her own diaphragm.

Ginny laughed.

A noiseless giggle that lifted her shoulders at first. Then it crept into her throat and became a broken hum. Then she opened her mouth and truly laughed.

Brett's eyes danced and focused on her mouth. She tried to contain herself by covering her mouth, but he reached across the counter and pulled her hand away.

Her laughter became a shortness of breath when he

brought her hand to his lips and pressed a lingering kiss to her palm. "Thank you."

His softening beard teased her with hundreds of little kisses, inflaming the sensitive nerve endings in her hand. She pulled away, surprised by how quickly the atmosphere between them had changed from light, easy laughter to something much more sultry.

Feeling a need to cool down, Ginny pulled the ice cream out of the freezer and started talking. "My building has a super who could have fixed the door, you know."

Brett picked up his fork and made quick work of the snack she had served him. "He wouldn't get to it until the morning."

She set out two bowls and two spoons. "He probably wouldn't have done such a neat, thorough job, either. Thank you."

"You're welcome."

While Brett polished off the apple, Ginny dipped up heaping dishes of ice cream. She licked the milky sweetness from her fingers, oblivious to the way his eyes narrowed and followed the movement. "Wait. Better idea," she announced.

He carried his plate to the sink and was standing beside her when she pulled the plastic bottle of chocolate syrup out of the fridge. She turned the bottle upside down over the ice cream and squeezed. Nothing came out.

"Need some help?"

"No. This happens all the time." She banged the bottle against the side of the counter and tried it again. Still no chocolate. "It gets too cold in the fridge and won't come out."

"Try zapping it in the microwave."

She put the bottle in for ten seconds. She turned it upside down again but had no success. "Maybe the syrup's stuck in the bottom."

Ginny pounded the bottle against the counter again, then

placed it between her hands and squeezed as hard as she could. The bottle surrendered. The chocolate gushed out…across the front of Brett's shirt.

For one shocked moment, she stared at the dark brown glob.

Brett reacted first. He picked up a spoon and scraped away the top layer. Ginny's brain finally kicked in. She set down the bottle and picked up a dish towel. She dabbed at the gooey mess. "I'm so sorry. I'm only making it worse."

"Don't worry. It's an old work shirt."

Instead of helping, she ended up smearing the chocolate. "Better take your shirt off. I'll soak it before the stain sets."

Ginny never considered the consequences of what she had just asked. She only knew it felt like the right thing to do. Brett unbuttoned and untucked his shirt, along with the T-shirt underneath that had soaked up some of the chocolate.

That big, broad chest encased in a flannel shirt or wool suit had been enticing enough. But there was no way she could have prepared herself for the expanse of skin and muscle and crisp dark hair that lay beneath. Trim and powerful and musky with his own unique scent, this man affected her like no other male ever had.

She put the towel to her lips to hide her gaping mouth and buy a moment to regain her composure. Figuring out how to breathe would be a good place to start. Moving away would be even smarter.

She took the shirts from him, rubbed dish soap into the stains and filled the sink with cold water to let them soak.

Brett moved beside her. The heat from his bare skin singed her arm and lit a wildfire inside her veins. She looked up into the incandescent glint of those irresistible blue eyes.

Ever so gingerly, he touched her. With just his index finger, he traced the corner of her mouth, igniting a new flashpoint of sensation. When he took his finger away she saw it was tipped in chocolate. He put the finger between his lips and licked it off. Ginny's tongue snuck out to lick her own lips, parched by a suddenly consuming heat.

"Speechless?" He taunted her with that sinfully low voice.

Ginny could only nod. She clutched the towel to her chest, trying to muffle the thump of her heart. Trying to hide the tingling sensation in her breasts as they expanded from the heat.

His gaze dropped to the curve of her blouse, and she knew he had seen her reaction to just a look. If he touched her now, she might explode. The unfamiliar flames of such intense desire would completely engulf her.

As if he sensed his power over her, Brett took the towel from her fingers and tossed it aside. "You're so beautiful. So quick to react. How could you ever think you had no passion?"

He dipped his finger to the tip of her breast. Her breath steamed between her teeth as he drew a circle around the pebbled tip. He traced the same finger across the arc of her lower lip. Her tongue darted out toward the pleasurable friction and she tasted chocolate.

"Oh, my." The words croaked through her arid throat. "I seem to have gotten chocolate everywhere."

"I like my sweets as much as you do." Brett's hand moved to the V of her blouse and before she realized his intent, he had the buttons undone and was pulling the tails from her jeans. "But we'd better let this soak before it stains, too."

A sensible enough suggestion. But Ginny's feverish mind refused to understand what was happening to her. To him.

She swayed as cool air hit her naked shoulders. But Brett caught her and pulled her up against his unyielding strength, his abundant heat. Crushed to his chest, she clung to his shoulders as he lifted her. His hands cupped her bottom and roamed her back. His mouth covered hers and sent the room spinning into a fiery maelstrom of sweet tastes and white-hot passion.

With his wicked mouth tracing a torrid path along her jaw to her ear, he set her on the counter in the center of the kitchen. His bold hands pushed her legs apart and he moved even closer, rubbing the front of his jeans against that most tender part of her, transforming her into a combustible powder keg.

"Chocolate, chocolate everywhere." His lips were barely more than a hot brush across the curve of her breast. When his tongue darted out to lap a stray dribble of syrup from the lace of her bra, Ginny squeezed her legs around his hips, drawing herself flush to the evidence of his desire. Matching the pooling heat of her own need against his.

His tongue continued its foray, swirling around the rigid tip of her breast through its sheath of cotton lace. An incoherent sound rumbled in his throat, and then his skillful hands brushed across her shoulders, sliding the straps of her bra down to the crook of her elbows. With a needy tug, he freed her breasts and found them again with his mouth.

His hot, moist tongue feasted on the willing tips as if they were a treat too delectable to resist. Her body reacted to the irresistibly hot sweetness of his seduction more quickly than logical thought. Her breathing could barely keep up with the feverish pounding of her heart. She wound her fingers into the silky fall of his rich, dark hair, and clasped him to one burgeoning peak, demanding his full attention there.

Brett's fingers were never still. They brushed a callused caress over the tip of the abandoned breast, tested the fit of her torso within his grasp, slipped to the front of her jeans and made quick work of the snap and zipper there. And then his big hands traced the elastic waistband of her panties, dipped inside the back of her jeans and lifted her.

Suspended by his strength, she snatched at his shoulders, her aching breasts flattened against the resolute hardness of his chest. He stripped the denim down her legs and cast them aside, leaving nothing between her own damp heat and the bulge in Brett's jeans except a thin layer of cotton. The clench of muscles between her legs was instantaneous and overwhelming.

"Brett?" She pleaded his name in a ragged whisper. Pleading with him to stop? Or pleading with him to ease this needy torment?

He sat her back on the countertop, the cool Formica a jolting contrast to the heat consuming her. He brushed his lips against the shell of her ear. "Angel, I don't know if I can stand much more of this. I don't want to leave you tonight."

Ginny played with a bit of fire herself, dipping her fingers into the waist of his jeans, pressing them into the supple flex of his backside. She smiled against his chest at the power his involuntary response gave her, and tasted a taut, flat male nipple with a blaze of her tongue.

But the heat in her veins soon took her far beyond conscious thought. "Then don't go."

He caught her by the chin and demanded that she look up into the lambent flame of those beautiful blue eyes. "Look into that rational mind of yours and tell me you know exactly where this is leading."

She traced her fingers along that strong jaw and framed his handsome face. "I want you to stay." Murders and threats and heartbreak seemed miles away with this man in her arms. He made her feel safe. He made her feel special. He made her feel whole. "I know this is real, Brett. I want you to stay."

Content with her promise, he scooped her up in his arms and carried her to her bed. He laid her down gently on top of the cool sheets and quickly removed their remaining clothes. She watched with fascination and admiration as every bit of his magnificent body was revealed to her.

He'd be a beautiful man to paint, she thought, without consciously thinking it.

And that's when the first fist of doubt took grip of her heart.

When he lay down beside her, his big, strong body a powerful temptation in itself, she cast aside that doubt. He was twice her size, and took up more than his share of the bed. And when he slid his weight on top of her, propping himself up on his elbows so he wouldn't crush her, the size of the bed didn't matter. They were one. She needed to be one with this man. She needed him.

Brett stretched above her, reaching for the lamp beside her bed. An instinctive panic, borne of too many years of hurt and regret, made her snatch at his arm. "No. Leave the lights on. Please."

The curious expression on his face gave way to a mischievous grin. Not making light of her fears, she guessed, but putting her at ease.

"I don't mind."

His teasing smile anchored her in the moment. She focused on the incredibly deep blue of his admiring eyes. Focused on the erotic discovery of nerve-endings along the length of her arm as he slowly drew his fingertips across her skin.

"I love looking at you," he whispered. "I love seeing how you react to my touch."

In a heartbeat, he brought her to that feverish pitch once more. And when his mouth and body claimed hers, the flames of pent-up passion consumed her. Searing her body with the rough, tender need of his. Branding her heart with one indelible truth.

She loved Brett.

Despite experience, despite wisdom, despite the threats to their future and her very life, for this one night, she allowed herself the joy of loving him.

Chapter Twelve

Had he been dreaming?

Brett's first thought when he awoke alone in Ginny's bed was that he had only imagined the incendiary passion of his cool blond detective. He knew she had been terrified by the break-in last night. Her instant burst of temper had clearly told him that.

He knew she was strong enough and smart enough to handle whatever threats the killer threw her way. But she shouldn't have to handle them alone. He hadn't been able to stand the thought of her being all alone.

And so he ignored her command and came back. Under the very real excuse of securing her apartment.

But then she invited him to stay.

He'd only had glimpses of the real Ginny. Passionate. Smart. Vulnerable. Caring. But last night, the crisp, cool, professional walls that she always tried to hide behind had crumbled into dust.

His body was sated, his mind heady with the memory of shy, sexy Ginny coming alive in his arms, destroying his own control.

He rolled over into the sunshine streaming through the window and caught a whiff of Ginny's fresh, flowery smell lingering on the sheets.

He hadn't been dreaming.

His smile stayed with him while he pulled on his jeans and freshened up in the bathroom. He went in search of coffee, found a half-empty pot in the kitchen and poured himself a cup. The main room and kitchen were spotless. And empty.

That was the first clue that his good mood would only be temporary. He got the second clue when he found Ginny, fully showered and dressed, working in her art room. She'd filled three garbage sacks with broken bits of frame and canvas. She was taping the back of a torn canvas when he entered.

"Good morning." A safe enough way to start a conversation, he thought.

"When you found Mark Bishop at the Ludlow Arms, he was in the basement, right?"

Clue number three.

So she didn't drop what she was doing and throw herself into his arms. He would have settled for a *good morning* instead of this topic.

Ginny propped the painting up on the easel and stood back to study it. Brett hooked one hand over the top of the easel and leaned in, forcing himself into her line of vision. "We need to talk about last night."

"Zeke and Alvin were both found in the subbasement." She sifted through her paintbrushes, but they'd all been matted or broken. She pulled a pencil from a drawer and came back to draw two X's at the bottom of the painting.

Brett looked down at the oil painting beside him and immediately recognized the Ludlow Arms. "You did this?" he asked, impressed by the precision and energy in her work, though not particularly thrilled with the subject matter.

Instead of answering his question, she stood back and tapped her index finger against her bottom lip. Though he recognized the sign of deep thought, his body tightened with the memory of tasting that lip, and of the delightfully daring things that lip had done to him.

"There was an X on the fourth floor, but no body was found there. And the fifth X...what do the other two X's mean?"

Finally, he stepped in front of the painting, forcing her to acknowledge him. "What are you talking about?"

She tipped her chin up, her blank eyes giving no indication that she had been affected by last night the way he had. "The blueprints I wanted to show you. I'll have to pick them up at the station."

She zipped past him to the door. "Sorry I don't have any breakfast. I need to get to the office. Be sure to lock things up when you leave."

He snagged her by the elbow, forcing her to turn and face him. "Ginny, last night—"

Her gaze dropped to his chest. Did she find it as diverting as she did last night? Or was she searching for the right lie to tell? "Last night was a wonderful experience. I'm glad you were here. I wasn't as scared as I might have been. Thank you."

"Thank you?"

Her hands flattened on his chest and pushed, a sure sign that this cool detachment was all an act. "Brett, I have work to do."

"Just like that you shut off your personal life?" He called her on it. He set his coffee on the dresser and lifted her by the waist. Balanced between his hip and arm, he easily tipped her back and pulled her badge from its belt clip. He held the badge between them. "You don't wear this thing twenty-four hours a day, angel."

She snatched it from his fingers and twisted to free herself. He held on until she stilled. "What do you want from me?"

He buried his fingers in the soft curls beside her ear and tipped her face up, asking her to look at him and nothing else. "How about some honesty? How about that warm, real woman who knew how to laugh and love last night?"

"Put me down." It was a plea, not a demand. Brett released her.

Ginny adjusted her blouse and clipped on her badge before saying another word. "When I was nineteen years old, I had an affair with one of my teachers in Paris. He swept me off my feet, made me forget everything but him and me being together. I thought I loved him."

"Is this what you wanted to tell me yesterday? This is the experience you think can keep us apart?"

"Just let me talk. Please."

Those cheeks that blushed so easily flamed with whatever emotion she was feeling. She'd come so far in giving in to those emotions since this engagement first started. But they still frightened her. He leaned his shoulder against the door-jamb, keeping her from running away, but allowing her the distance she needed to pace the room and tell her story.

"Jean-Pierre convinced me to meet him at his studio one night. Said that's where he felt 'inspired.' He seduced me. Made wild, passionate love to me right on the dais where the models would sit when we painted portraits."

Brett's stomach twisted into knots. Maybe this wasn't such a good idea. He didn't want to hear about her wild passion with another man, but he suspected the worst of this story was yet to come.

"It was dark. Completely dark when we made love. We used touch and sound to find each other."

"Is that why you're afraid of the dark?"

She turned and offered him a weak smile. "It's not the dark. It's what lurks in the dark. The horrible things waiting in the dark to destroy you."

"What happened?"

She hugged her arms around herself. Brett curled his toes into the floor to keep himself from going to her. "When we

were done, the lights came on, blinding me. I heard applause.''

Brett swore. Once. Twice. He steeled himself for the rest
of her confession.

''Jean-Pierre said I had that marvelous blush of new love
and that he wanted to paint me that way. That he wanted
his students to paint me.''

He couldn't take much more of this. He couldn't stand
the thought of his strong, sweet Ginny being used so cal-
lously. ''Tell me you smashed his face and walked out of
there.''

''I was in shock. Humiliated. Someone was snapping pictures. I wrapped myself in a sheet, grabbed my clothes and
hid out in my apartment for a week.''

''Ginny...''

Now her anger started to kick in. But he could see it was
mistakenly aimed at herself. ''The same week, my sister
planned to elope with Mark. She sent me three letters. She
called me. But I didn't read them, I didn't answer her. I was
so consumed with my own mistake that I ignored her—until
it was too late.''

He went to her at last, catching her by the shoulders, shaking some sense into her. ''It was *his* mistake. You were
young.''

Her hands lighted on his chest but didn't push him away.
''I was stupid. Stupid to trust him. Stupid to feel sorry for
myself. I can't let my emotions get in the way of doing
what's right.''

''They aren't mutually exclusive.''

Now her hands were clinging to him, desperate for him
to understand. ''I didn't do my job. I will never make that
mistake again.'' Her fingers brushed a tremulous path down
the center of his chest, petting him, soothing him, begging
something from him. ''I can't love you, Brett. I can't.''

Tears pooled in her eyes when she looked up. "You deserve a woman who can."

He let her go when she moved away. She'd put on a blazer and picked up her purse before he finally conquered enough of his anger to say something civil to her.

She was on her way out the front door before he stepped into the hallway and asked, "Does Jean-Pierre still live in Paris?"

"I don't know." She tucked a curl behind her ear. At least she could still feign sarcasm. "I didn't keep in touch."

He hoped the bastard had stayed on his own continent. If JP ever dared to cross the ocean, Brett swore he'd be a dead man.

He managed to set his anger aside for the moment. "I'll pick you up tonight for the fund-raiser ball. Anyone who stayed at the Ludlow Arms and lived to tell about it has been invited. Maybe it'll give you some ideas on what those X's mean."

"I don't know if keeping up this engagement is a good idea anymore—"

"We're still a team until these murders are solved." He'd appeal to her sense of duty if he couldn't reach her any other way. "I'll pick you up at seven."

She caught her lip on whatever protest she'd been ready to give and simply nodded.

When the door closed behind her, a bigger door closed on his heart. He'd failed once again.

Maybe it was better that he let her run away. He'd failed to make her understand that he loved her. He'd failed to keep her safe or find her sister's killer. He'd failed to make Ginny understand that they could build a life together, brick by brick.

She knew how to love. She treated his friends in the neighborhood with respect and compassion. She fought for the truth. She made his father laugh and she stood by his side when he needed her most.

But because of this Jean-Pierre and the rotten timing of losing her sister, she'd lost her faith in those strengths. She'd lost her faith in every aspect of her life except her work.

She needed his love and patience and support, now more than ever.

He'd be damned if he'd fail her again.

GINNY PULLED the flashlight from the glove compartment of her car and climbed out to face off against her haunting adversary, the Ludlow Arms. Tall and imposing, the bright light of early afternoon did nothing to soften its unforgiving lines.

Brett's demolition crew had parked their bulldozers and a giant crane in front. But the place was deserted. "Maybe the boss gave them the afternoon off for tonight's party."

As soon as she said it, she couldn't help but form a mental picture of the *boss*. Tall and broad. Full of laughter and kindness. Powerful kisses and a sinfully deep voice that turned her staunchest resolve into putty.

She'd forgotten herself last night. She'd given in to need and wants and led with her heart. Not the brightest move for a woman considered to be so smart. This morning she tried to explain to Brett why she could never truly be his woman.

How could she ever ask him to put up with her fears and doubts? She was just now learning to believe in a few friendships. Merle. Captain Taylor. John McBride. She could never ask Brett to be patient enough while she learned to believe in love again.

"Stop it, Rafferty."

She'd tortured herself with this conversation a hundred times already today. It was time she did something useful. Like make an arrest on this case.

She hooked her purse over her shoulder and pulled out the sketch she had drawn from the blueprints. The X on the fourth floor marked the Bishop apartment, and could simply point out where Mark had first been beaten. Then he'd crawled down to his hiding place in the basement to meet Brett. But he died instead.

The fifth X was the mystery she couldn't figure out. After studying the blueprints from every different direction, she decided to check the subbasement. She only prayed she didn't discover another dead body.

Climbing up the steps and closing the front door behind her felt a lot like Jonah getting swallowed up by the whale. She tried to keep in mind that Jonah had been saved while she picked her way down the broken basement stairs and lowered the ladder through the trapdoor into the subbasement.

She turned on the flashlight when she reached the bottom and let her eyes adjust to the dim light. She pointed the beam and identified the first two locations from the blueprints. Alvin Bishop's burial chamber and the base of the stairwell where Zeke had died.

Shining the light on her drawing, she aligned herself with the layout of the room and stepped off the approximate distance to that mysterious fifth X. She hit a brick wall first, but like that false wall that had buried Alvin alive, this one easily crumbled beneath her fingers.

Stuffing the sketch into her purse and propping the flashlight under her arm, she used both hands to lift out bricks and set them on the dirt beside her. When she'd carved out a hole wide enough to climb through, she squeezed her eyes shut, held her breath and stuck her head in. A rat scurried across the wooden floor above her, sending down a cascade of miniature dirt clods on top of her head.

Startled, Ginny opened her eyes. She coughed the dust from her nose and throat. Then she smiled.

Reflecting the beam of her flashlight like bright, shiny silver, a string of small stainless-steel bells hung from an iron ring bolted into the wall. "What have we here?"

When she picked up the bells, they jingled with a tinny sound, not quite melodic, but certainly loud enough to be heard from a balcony on the floor above, or through a brick wall. Ginny counted four bells and noted the empty knot on the string where a fifth bell had once been tied.

"Think, Ginny." She spoke aloud as she knelt down to go through the rest of the contents of the hidden cubbyhole. A Purple Heart medal. Could that have been Zeke's? A cracked and moldy bottle of whiskey. Enough to pour into a coffee cup to keep Alvin drunk while he was being buried alive. A letter. In a man's scrawled handwriting.

Dearest Amy,

Ginny flinched as if she'd been struck. Dated twelve years ago. Signed, *Mark.*

She dropped the letter and reached into her purse. The killer had taken everything that had once been Amy's from Ginny's apartment. Everything but the last letter she'd stuffed into her purse before dashing to the hospital to be with Brett.

The dampness of the dirt bled into her pants as she knelt beneath the beam of her flashlight to read Amy's last letter. A final plea. A pledge of love. Forgiveness.

Ginny's eyes teared up. She swiped the moisture away with the back of her hand and read on.

...In case something happens to us, I want you to have my silver bracelet. You're the only one who knows how much I love Mark. So I want you to have it. I want you to remember how much we loved each other. I hope you've found this kind of love.

                                                                    Amy

Ginny sat back on her heels. When her sister's body had been brought to the mortuary, her mother had taken all of her personal items—clothes, earrings, her birthstone ring. After her mother's death, her father had passed Amy's things on to her.

"But there was no bracelet." She pressed her finger to her lip, racking her brain for the missing answer. "I never got your silver bracelet."

But she'd seen one.

Ginny closed her eyes and tried to remember. Black suits. Panic. Death. Brett.

Putting on a show to gain Brett's attention.

Her eyelids popped open.

"Sophie."

Sophie had worn a silver bracelet at Alvin's memorial service. Could it be a coincidence? Or had Amy's bracelet wound up on Sophie's wrist? Frank Rascone could check his records at the jewelry shop to see if the bracelets matched.

A frisson of excitement coursed through her at the possible connection. But she was too thorough an investigator to celebrate a victory yet.

While she gathered the hidden items and stuffed them into her pockets and purse, she ran through all the evidence one more time. Somehow, this had to add up to Eric Chamberlain. He could have taken that bracelet from Amy's arm and given it to Sophie. As a gift, or proof of Amy's death, she didn't yet know.

Feeling as if her time was running out, the Ludlow groaned and shifted above her. She heard the clunk of a falling beam. The patter of molding and masonry crumbling above her.

She scrambled to her feet and hurried toward the ladder. Her brain moved even quicker, categorizing clues and narrowing her way toward identifying the killer.

Ruby Jenkins had dated Mark Bishop and been warned away. Lydia Fitzgerald had had an inexplicable accident after seeing Mark. Amy had had her head bashed in for daring to elope with him.

Alvin wanted Mark to stay. He stopped him with a vicious beating. When Alvin wanted something done, he used his fists and his threats. Nothing fancier than that. No planning, no notes, no moving of bodies. All his victims were at the Ludlow Arms.

Amy died at the riverfront.

Alvin didn't kill Amy.

Who else wanted to keep Mark from leaving with Amy?

"Sophie."

Ginny paused on the first rung as she tried to grasp the possibility of a new suspect.

Sophie was tall enough to kiss Brett without standing on tiptoe.

A woman made the 911 call to help Mark Bishop.

Sophie wore a silver bracelet.

Maybe Eric Chamberlain hadn't done all he could to protect Sophie twelve years ago. Maybe Sophie had protected herself.

"Idiot!" Ginny chastised herself for not seeing it sooner. Sophie wasn't jealous of her engagement to Brett. She didn't want Amy's big sister poking her nose into the old neighborhood and finding out the truth.

Ginny stuffed her flashlight into her pocket and climbed the ladder. Crawling through the trapdoor, she saw the shadow of the two-by-four swinging toward her. She ducked, but it was too late.

A million stars exploded in her head and she was spinning, falling. Her chest burned with fire at the second jolt. She turned her cheek into a cool pillow and swallowed dirt.

Four deaths. Mark. Alvin. Zeke. Amy. Four X's.

As her mind swirled into blackness, Ginny realized that *she* was the fifth X.

GINNY BLINKED her eyes open, but saw nothing. Fighting through the cotton stuffing in her head, she opened her eyes again. This time she saw a faint light and reached for it. Her fingers butted against cold metal and she woke to the next level of consciousness. Her flashlight. The batteries had run down and the power was fading.

She rolled over, then cried out at the sharp pain at the base of her skull. The throbbing headache that followed woke her enough to feel the dead weight of her left arm. Maybe the building had collapsed on top of her and she was trapped beneath a pile of bricks.

She tugged on her arm and a white-hot bolt of pain shot through her wrist. "Broken?" She picked up the flashlight and aimed its sickly beam at her left side. She followed the dusty blue length of her sleeve up to her wrist.

A panicked jump cleared her mind completely. She'd been handcuffed. Her left arm dangled above her, connected by her own handcuffs to the iron ring bolted into the wall.

Ignoring the jagged shards of pain radiating through her head, she sat up. A bell jingled and she looked down. A stainless-steel chime had been tied around her neck.

With what was left of her light she quickly scanned her surroundings. Buried alive in the subbasement of the Ludlow Arms was every dark nightmare she'd ever feared come to life.

Ginny breathed deeply, keeping the mind-numbing panic at bay. Someone would come looking for her, right? But she hadn't told Merle or Maggie or anyone else at the precinct where she was headed. Not on this unsanctioned mission to find Amy's killer. She'd been obsessed with finding out the truth. So obsessed, she walked right into Sophie's trap.

How long would it take for anyone to find her?

No one had found Alvin Bishop for twelve years.

Her heart fluttered at her mistake.

The darkness crowded in, attacking her from all sides with its cold, clammy talons. She hated being scared like this.

You're not mad at me. The memory of Brett's voice, darker than the shadows around her, nagged at her subconscious. *You're scared.*

"Of course, I'm scared! Damn you, Taylor. You can't just leave things alone." Her anger brimmed inside her. "You always have to be right. You always have to..."

She stopped talking, stopped berating the man who wasn't there to defend himself. She started cheering the message he'd been trying to share. It was okay to be scared. It was smart to be scared right now. It was smarter to get angry.

And Ginny Rafferty was a smart woman.

Brett would come looking for her. He said he'd pick her up at seven o'clock for that damned ball that neither one of them wanted to go to. And if she wasn't at her apartment at seven... Ginny took control of her breathing. She listened to the thumping in her chest slow to a steadier beat.

If nothing else, Brett's ego would send him looking for her. She doubted he would tolerate being stood up. He'd go storming through the neighborhood to find her and make her live up to her promise.

Thank God for old-fashioned Neanderthals.

But she intended to meet him halfway.

If she could find her way out of this hellhole.

Ginny concentrated on thinking like a detective, and reassessed her situation. She'd been here for several hours. The tingling paralysis of her left arm and the bricked-up wall behind her proved that.

No gun. Little light. Limited oxygen. No broken bones. And, despite the goose egg on her scalp, no brain cells were damaged. She nearly smiled at the memory of Brett telling her she did too much thinking. She'd show him.

With supreme effort, Ginny shut down the last of her doubts and fears and concentrated on thinking her way out of this deathtrap. She had vowed long ago that she would use every skill she possessed to bring her sister's killer to justice.

Being buried alive was no reason to give up now.

Ginny curled her legs under her and pushed to her feet. The brickwork the hook was anchored to was a hundred years old. She jiggled the bolt and ring, and knocked loose a few bits of ancient plaster. "That's what I want to see."

She braced her right foot against the wall and grabbed the cuffs with both hands. Pain shot up her left arm as feeling returned. She tugged on the ring. A chunk of mortar broke and the bolt slipped a fraction of an inch. With that minor success she pushed with her foot and pulled with all her might.

When the masonry started to give, she jerked even harder. The Ludlow's mortar surrendered, shattered into bits. Ginny flew back, hitting the newly built wall behind her. With the mortar still wet, the bricks bowed out. She sat a moment to catch her breath and admire her new bracelet with the ring-and-bolt charms.

Then she turned her attention to the sagging bricks. Putting all one hundred and ten pounds of herself behind it, she turned her shoulder into the wall and shoved. It collapsed and she tumbled with the falling bricks into the dirt.

She was bruised and battered and breathing hard. But she was victorious. She crawled to her feet. "Yes!"

Her shout echoed among the groans and shrieks of the cavernous beast above her. The settling of the building rattled the closed trapdoor. The escape ladder had been removed, but she didn't panic.

Ginny yanked the bell from around her neck and crushed it beneath her shoe in the dirt, stilling its harsh sound. She knew a secret to survival that Alvin had not.

Her killer would come back to see if she was really dead.

Sophie would come looking for her, but so would Brett.

Sinking back into the shadows, Ginny waited to see who would find her first.

BRETT DROVE his truck up onto the curb at Union Station and slammed it into Park. He pushed past the startled valet and strode through the spinning glass door, oblivious of the ticket taker who tried to chase him down, deaf to the friendly greetings shouted his way.

He stopped in the center of the Olympian-sized concourse and looked to the left, then to the right, scanning the crowd for a particular familiar face. He didn't bother looking for Ginny. She wouldn't be there.

He'd pounded on her apartment door until seven-fifteen, hopefully ignoring Dennis Fitzgerald's claim that she hadn't been home all day. He'd called the precinct office. She hadn't checked in since early that morning. Her partner had gone for the day. The shifts had changed and no one there had heard a thing. He called his brother Gideon at the hospital, on the off chance she had stopped by to visit Sid. No luck there, either.

Brett didn't waste another moment. He had connections. He'd pull in every favor he owed, he'd go into debt to get answers this time. "Mitch!"

His voice boomed in the cavernous expanse of the historic train station that had been remodeled into a science center, a theater and several restaurants. Normally, he would have taken time to appreciate the workmanship that went into such a task.

But he had a mission. He had somebody counting on him. Even if she didn't know it yet.

He hurried over to the cousin who was nearly a mirror image of himself. "Mitch, I need some back-up."

Mitch separated himself from the group of bigwigs he'd

been chatting with, and guided Brett a few steps away, affording them some privacy. "What's going on? Where's Ginny?"

Brett's shoulders lifted and sank with a frustrated sigh. "I was hoping you could tell me."

His brother Mac appeared at Brett's elbow, looking as uncomfortable in his tux as Brett felt in his. "Is there a problem?"

"I can't find Ginny. No one's seen or heard from her all day."

Baby brother Josh cast his shadow over the group. "She's a cop. Maybe she got a break on a case."

That was exactly what scared Brett.

Mitch pulled his cell phone from inside his dinner jacket. "I'll call the precinct."

"I tried that already. Nobody's seen her. Couldn't get a hold of Merle Banning, either."

"I'll call, anyway."

Brett raked his fingers through his hair, shaking it free of his starched white collar while Mitch turned away. He scanned the crowd again. "You guys see Sophie? I can't make nice with these people tonight. I've got to tell her I'm leaving."

Josh checked out the people milling about them. "She said hi when I came in, but that was what, twenty, thirty minutes ago?"

Brett latched onto that little piece of information. "Was Eric Chamberlain with her?"

"Nope. She was holding court all on her own."

Mac nodded across the room. "He's over there, talking to Mayor Benjamin."

Brett followed his gaze. No Sophie. Hadn't Eric given the impression that he was Sophie's champion? Or maybe trained watchdog was a better description. Brett crossed the room and interrupted the conversation.

"Where's Sophie?"

Eric excused himself from the mayor and graced Brett with an indulgent expression that grated along the rim of every cell in his body. "She had business to attend to. Don't worry. You'll get your moment in the spotlight."

"Want me to deck him for you?" Josh made a tempting offer.

Brett appreciated the support, but declined the idea. "What kind of business? This is her big show tonight."

"She's not your concern, Taylor."

Josh bounced on the balls of his feet. "Oh please, just one little punch."

Brett's own fingers curled into a fist. "Where did she go?"

Eric sized up the wall of Taylors—Brett, flanked by Mac and Josh—and re-thought his tactics. "Sophie went home. She said she forgot something, and went to get it. She'll be back soon."

Mitch completed the wall when he rejoined them. The stiff set of his jaw caught his full attention, and Eric Chamberlain became a useless party decoration.

"What?" Brett asked.

"Merle says he hasn't seen Gin since she left this morning with a sketch of those blueprints."

"The Ludlow Arms blueprints?"

Sophie went home.

Brett's lungs constricted in his chest. Eric's words had to be a coincidence.

"Anything you want to tell me?" Mitch pushed for an answer. Clearly, his instincts had picked up on Brett's suspicions.

But Brett was already backing toward the door, asking those favors, making demands as he lengthened his stride. "I need you to put out an APB, or whatever it is you call it—"

"You think Ginny's in danger?"

Mitch, Mac and Josh fell into step beside him by the time he hit the row of glass doors and the front sidewalk. "Sophie's gone after Ginny."

"Whoa, Brett. That's a serious accusation."

"Motive. Means. Opportunity. Those are the big three the cops have to prove, right?"

"Yeah?"

Brett counted the proof off on his fingers as his hurried stride turned into a jog toward his truck. "Motive. Abusive father. Mark's not around to protect her anymore."

Josh swung up into the bed of Brett's truck. "Are you talking about old man Bishop's murder?"

"Means. She grew up at the Ludlow and knows every crook and cranny there. How else do you hide from Alvin?"

Mac climbed into the truck cab. "She killed her own father?"

"Opportunity." Brett swallowed hard on this one, before turning the key in the ignition. "She's off disposing of her brother's girlfriend. But Dad's already lost his temper and taken it out on Mark. She comes home and finds Mark dead. So she gets Dad drunk—"

Mac caught on to the story. "Lures him down to the sub-basement—"

"—and buries him alive."

Mitch, the voice of reason and authority, closed the door behind him and asked, "Can you prove that?"

"No." Brett's silence revealed everything he feared. "But I'll bet Ginny can."

Chapter Thirteen

Ginny's visitor arrived shortly after the batteries in her flash-light went dead. The terrors of the pitch-black darkness had tried to sneak into her mind, but thoughts of Brett kept them at bay. The darkness was the chocolate on his tongue when he kissed her. It was the silky length of his hair curling against his collar.

The darkness was his voice, whispering loving little praises to her in the middle of the night.

She twisted the ring on the third finger of her left hand.

With Brett's help, she could do this.

With Brett as her partner, she could do anything.

A shower of dirt hit her in the face as footsteps fell on the floor above her. She backed against the farthest brick wall to avoid detection by any light from above. She breathed silently as the ladder was lowered through the trap-door.

Rescue? Or death?

Of all things, the red silk pumps descending the ladder surprised her. But she held her breath until Sophie touched the dirt floor. When Sophie swung her flashlight around to the broken wall, Ginny leaped from the shadows and wrapped the handcuffs around her neck.

With her knee in the back of Sophie's sequined red gown,

she jerked back on the cuffs, choking the air from the woman's throat.

"Why the hell did you kill my sister?" Ginny's grip tightened like a tourniquet as the anger poured strength into her arms. "Why did you kill Amy?"

But Sophie was the daughter of Alvin Bishop. She'd survived growing up in the Ludlow Arms.

With a vicious twist of her elbow, she caught Ginny in the gut, loosening her hold. Those perfect, painted nails scratched gashes in her weak wrist. Losing her advantage, Ginny planted her feet and charged, knocking them both to the floor. The flashlight careened out of Sophie's hands. Ginny picked up a brick. Tangled in her slim-fitting gown, Sophie could only roll, dodging the attack. Ginny scrambled after her, raised the brick again.

"Drop it!"

She froze as Sophie sat up and pointed Ginny's own 9 mm sidearm at her.

Tossing the brick aside, Ginny stood. Both women were breathing hard, neither woman blinked. She waited until Sophie motioned her toward the ladder with the gun before she spoke.

"This isn't your usual style, is it, Soph? You prefer your victims to be unconscious before you dispose of them, don't you?"

"You're the one who insists on doing things the hard way. Now climb."

"Gonna push me down the stairs, too?" Ginny toyed with the idea of kicking the gun from Sophie's hand, but Sophie timed her climb just right, too slow to be within reach, too quick to be left behind on the ladder.

The basement stairs came next. "Was my sister really such a threat to you?"

Sophie jabbed the gun into Ginny's back and forced her to climb. "She was going to take Mark away from us. He told me they were going to elope. He was going to leave me behind. I met her at the City Market and told her Mark had changed their plans, to meet him by the river. A rock was all I needed to get rid of her.''

Bile churned in Ginny's stomach, threatening to choke her. ''You helped Alvin get rid of all the women in Mark's life, didn't you?''

''Shut up and walk.'' Sophie guided her to the hidden servant stairs. As they made new tracks in the dust, Ginny swallowed the bitter taste. ''Why did you take her silver bracelet?''

''To prove to Daddy that I killed her. To make him happy. To keep him from hurting me anymore.''

Ginny stepped across a missing stair and glanced over her shoulder to see if Sophie could make the same move in that ridiculous dress. By the time they'd reached the third floor, she'd hatched an idea. Time to disrupt Sophie's concentration.

''But Daddy had already taken his anger out on Mark, hadn't he. When you brought that bracelet back, Mark was already dying.''

''Shut up!'' The shrill warning curved Ginny's lips into a satisfied smile. ''I loved Mark. I tried to help him. I called the ambulance.''

Sophie's long heel poked through the thin wood on the landing and she stumbled. Ginny turned, but the gun held steady. The cool sophistication that had taken Sophie to the top of her profession was marred by a contorted grimace of anger. ''Keep moving. All the way to the roof.''

''It was too late then, wasn't it.'' Ginny tested a weak riser. The wood shattered and fell into the abyss below them. Swallowing back her fear, she skipped the step and moved on. ''Is that when you devised your plan? You took American lit in high school, I'll bet. You were probably a big fan of Edgar Allan Poe.''

Sophie hiked her skirt to avoid the broken stair, but kept the gun trained on Ginny. "I poured him his usual Irish coffee and told him your sister was hiding out in the sub-basement. He was too drunk to figure out what was really going on. After the ambulance took Mark away, I went to the library to study."

"Did you really love your brother?" Ginny taunted. "Or did you just use him the way you use everybody else around you."

"Yes, dammit! I loved him. He was all I had in the world. He took care of me. He kept me safe. I didn't want him to die."

When the angry tears started to flow, Ginny kicked out. The gun fired and flew from Sophie's hand. Ginny lunged and the two women rolled and crashed down a flight of stairs. Boards cracked and fell away. The last two steps smashed into bits and disappeared. Dazed by the fall, Sophie tried to stand, but her heel slipped and she fell through the gap.

Ginny snagged the sleeve of her gown and held on. Sophie swung back and forth like a pendulum, each to-and-fro motion working with gravity to pull Ginny inches closer to the chasm below. She hooked her toes over the edge of the landing and anchored herself in place.

But an unmistakable chain of events had been set into motion. A support beam fell and crashed at Ginny's feet. As the floor slowly buckled beneath the extra weight, the walls of the stairwell creeped in. The Ludlow was caving in on itself, crushing its awful secrets floor by floor.

"Help me." Sophie snatched at Ginny's wrist, hooking her fingers through the locked handcuff. If Sophie fell, Ginny would plunge down with her. The bitch had killed her sister. She wouldn't let Sophie take her life, too.

"Can you brace your foot on anything?"

An awful clamor of compressed stairs snapping in two

rushed toward them. Bricks popped free of their mortar and joined the gathering downpour of wood and plaster and metal.

"Ginny!" A deep voice from her subconscious mind shouted her name, dared her to be strong.

Memories of the fourth-floor collapse were playing tricks with her brain now. The floor beneath her stomach tilted and Ginny slipped an inch closer to the edge of the broken stair.

"Hold on to one arm with both your hands," she ordered.

"I can't."

"Do it!"

"Ginny!"

She ignored the familiar, masculine voice and stretched her fingers out to reach the neckline of Sophie's dress. A chip of wood splintered off the edge of the stair and they dropped another inch. Crushing a handful of silk and sequins in her fist, Ginny heaved.

Glass shattered like an explosion somewhere below them. The muscles in her arms and back burned with the stress of holding on to Sophie. She was going to die in the building that had already claimed so many lives.

But at the very last, Ginny would have her justice.

"Did you kill Zeke, too?"

"Yes!"

"You sent me those threats?"

"Yes! All of them. Your sister ruined my life. You were going to ruin it all over again."

Ginny closed her eyes against the pain and prayed. "Peace, Amy."

"Ginny! Dammit, angel, answer me!"

That's when she heard the distinct sound of sure footsteps amid the crumbling dust of the building around them.

With nothing left to lose and everything still to gain, she braced her feet and pulled again. Sophie grabbed on to a broken railing. Then the landing itself. And then Ginny pulled her up over the edge and the two women collapsed.

Their respite was brief. The floor jerked and dropped half a foot. The landing split, with Ginny on one side and Sophie on the other. The floor sank like the letter V, and they slid toward the widening gap.

"Climb, Ginny! Climb! Get off the stairs!"

The voice shouted from above. Not a memory. Not her mind playing tricks on her.

"Brett?"

He leaned through an archway to the floor above them. "Right here, angel. Climb up to me. Hurry."

On their hands and knees, Sophie and Ginny climbed. Like an evil spirit hunting them down, the stairs seemed to fall away beneath their feet. Arms reached out and pulled Sophie through the doorway.

But the final step broke before Ginny could reach it. She leaped for the door, raked splinters into her hand as she slid past it. "Brett!"

Her shoulder jerked in its socket as something caught hold of her. She dangled six stories above the crashing, crushing vengeance of the Ludlow Arms.

"I've got you, angel."

She watched the blank air beneath her feet fill with a rising mushroom cloud of dust and debris. But it never reached her.

Strong, loving arms lifted her to safety.

She was only vaguely aware of the surrounding warmth, the resolute strength, the needy grasp of the man who carried her with unerring balance and expertise through the collapsing fury of the Ludlow Arms. Another man led Sophie by the arm. An angry roar chased them through the foyer, spat dust and debris into her eyes and ears and nose.

And then she breathed fresh air.

The familiar blink of red, white and blue lights made her

realize she was outside. Someone was shouting. People were running back and forth. The adrenaline faded, and shock gave way to confusion. Only the comforting, blessed awareness of being carried in Brett's arms made any sense.

"Dammit, Brett. Don't let them do this to me."

Ginny turned her head at Sophie's plea. The woman in red got her own set of handcuff bracelets and was stuffed into a patrol car.

Brett's low-pitched anger rumbled beneath her ear as he unleashed his anger at Sophie. "I tried to take care of you. All the guilt, all the anger—all these years. I loved Mark like a brother. That made you family."

"Then take care of me," Sophie pleaded.

"Take care of yourself."

Ginny stirred from her secure haven and tried to see his face. She wanted to soothe the hurt she heard in his voice.

Brett turned and Ginny clutched at his jacket, holding on against the dizziness pounding inside her skull. "Shh, angel. I've got you. I'm not letting you go."

She surrendered to the comfort of his voice and turned her cheek into the black wool of his jacket and pressed her ear to his strong, steady heartbeat, taking strength from his strength.

Learning love through his love.

Another man in a tuxedo got into the front seat of the car where they sat. When did Captain Taylor start wearing tuxedos to work? "I'll drive you straight to the hospital."

The fact that everyone was so dressed up made her curious. She murmured against Brett's nubby label. "Did I miss the party? You all look like somebody died."

His arms tightened around her. His shaky voice rumbled inside his chest. "No, angel. Not this time. I didn't fail you this time."

GINNY KNELT IN FRONT of the rose-colored marble marker and traced her fingertips over the Rafferty name.

"I did it," she whispered. The early-morning chill of spring blew a gentle breeze across her cheeks. "Amy's killer is in jail and she'll stand trial for three counts of murder and one attempted murder."

She brushed a fallen leaf away from the base and laughed, talking to the stone the way she would an old friend. "Once we put Captain Taylor on the case, we found Charlie Adkins hiding out in an alley over in Independence. Our old man knows how to get things done, that's for sure. Charlie still won't talk, but he's willing to write a deposition for our case."

She breathed in deeply. She clutched at her chest and cringed against the protest of sore muscles. For twelve years, she'd made this vigil to her family's graves each time she took on a new case, each time another life was lost. Promising with each visit to bring justice to the world.

Now that Amy and her parents had been vindicated, the visit took a more personal turn.

"So many people got hurt along the way. So many innocent people paid a terrible price. But I'm trying to make it right. I'm trying to understand the gift you gave me, Amy."

She fingered the silver bracelet adorning her left wrist beside the plastic hospital band from her release less than an hour ago. Ginny closed her eyes and pictured a clear image of her young, beautiful sister. The remembered laughter made her smile.

"You led with your heart to the very end." She opened her eyes and looked at Amy's name. "Somewhere along the way I forgot how to use mine. I got hurt, and then I lost so much, and it just didn't seem like I could find my way back anymore."

The tears started then, and Ginny let them come. She cried

for her family and sweet old Zeke Jones. She cried for Mark Bishop and all the pain his family had endured. She cried for the families who had lived and suffered at the Ludlow Arms.

She cried for Brett. For the guilt he hadn't deserved. For the hero she knew him to be.

She cried for herself. For the trusting young girl she'd once been, for the frightened woman she'd become.

The roar of a truck engine echoed through the hills of Mt. Washington. Ginny smiled and dried her tears.

The truck careened around the hairpin turns of the cemetery road. The high screech of brakes scattered birds from the trees. She stood and watched a robin fly back to its nest. The sound of a slamming door startled her, but she didn't turn around.

She waited for the deep, dark voice to find her first.

"I stayed with you all night at the hospital while they stitched you up and made sure you weren't seeing double. This morning, my brother convinces me to get a cup of coffee. I go back to your room, and you're gone. Damn lucky I know a few cops who can find out where cab companies drop their fares."

Brett splayed his hands on his hips and leaned over her in that arrogantly masculine stance that she found so blatantly sexy. His rumpled tux with the tie long gone and the collar unbuttoned added a boyish touch that endeared him all the more.

She looked up and smiled. "I had something I needed to do."

"I would have brought you here."

"I know." She reached out and spread her palm in the middle of his chest, absorbing his heat, his strength and the steady beat of his heart deep into her soul. "I had some thinking to do, and I don't always think clearly when you're around."

The gruff line of his mouth softened. "Is that so?"

"Yeah."

"Ooh. Snappy comeback." He smiled and her courage doubled.

"Thank you for saving my life."

He covered her hand with his and held it over his heart. "I wasn't about to let you stand me up on our date. When I saw that burial chamber at the Ludlow Arms, I..." Her hero faltered. Ginny reached up and cupped his cheek in her hand. "I didn't think I could get to you in time."

"But you did." She tunneled her fingers into his hair and held his gaze. "You didn't fail me, Brett."

It took a while for her words to sink in. When he finally accepted them as the truth, he asked, "So where does that leave us?"

"Back where we started."

Her gaze dropped to his chest. She'd rehearsed this on the cab ride over, but now, with Brett here in person, standing chest and shoulders above her, the words escaped her.

"Uh-uh, none of that." He captured her chin between his thumb and forefinger and lifted her face. "You don't look me in the eye when you're getting ready to tell a lie. If you're trying to tell me we don't mean anything to each other, that the engagement is off, forget it. I love you. Whether you want to hear that or not, I still do. You're not getting rid of me that easily."

"I don't want to get rid of you."

"You seemed anxious enough to leave me when you ran away from the hospital."

The accusation stung. He loved her. And yet...Ginny tucked that wayward curl behind her ear and stepped away. She clearly had a lot left to learn about leading with her heart.

"Dammit, Brett, I love you, too. But I don't know how to tell you. I don't know how to make you believe it's not part of this stupid charade. How do I make you believe me?''

Her plea for help met with stony silence. At least there was no applause for her mistake this time.

''I think you did fine just now.'' That rich, deep voice shivered along her spine. It warmed her enough so that she found the courage to turn and face him. ''The only thing that could make your profession of love more convincing is for you to come over here and kiss me.''

''That's it? It's that easy?''

Those blue eyes sparkled with a perennial challenge. ''You haven't kissed me yet.''

''Brett—''

She'd only taken half a step toward him when he scooped her up off the ground and crushed her against his chest. Ginny looped her arms around his neck, tangled her fingers in his hair, and kissed him with every ounce of feeling she possessed.

Minutes later, breathless and rumpled and achy with the passion he stirred in her, Ginny touched her feet to the ground. She wrapped her arms around Brett's waist and pressed a kiss to his chest.

''I have a proposition for you.''

His arms encircled her, sheltering her near the heat of his big heart. She felt the laughter in his chest and snuggled closer. ''Is it as crazy as when you marched into my construction site and asked me to marry you?''

''Crazier.''

''You worry me when you start thinking like that.''

Ginny tilted her neck all the way back and looked straight into his eyes so he'd know she meant what she said.

''Will you marry me, Brett? For real?''

He pulled her left hand from his waist and held it up between them. The sun caught in the sapphire and sparkled almost as bright as the love in Brett's eyes. He pulled her hand to his lips and kissed the ring. The scruff of his beard danced across her knuckles and her knees felt weak.

"If you marry me, it'll be a big affair," he warned her with a smile. "Lots of family, food, friends, fun."

"I can handle it. I have new friends I want to get to know better, friends I've yet to meet. I love your family." Because of Brett, she'd opened up her heart to life, to friends, to love. She wondered if he understood the miracle he had brought into her world. "I owe all that to you. I gave up my faith in love. But you proved me wrong. I believe in love now because I believe in you. Because you love me."

He lowered his head and claimed her lips, taking his time to show her just how much he loved her.

When he lifted his mouth, he grinned. Ginny knew she was in trouble. "Wait a minute. You just said I proved you wrong. Are you saying I was right?"

She swatted his shoulder in a playful shove. "Don't let it go to your head, Taylor."

"You're the only thing that goes to my head, Detective."

Brett Taylor was a man of action. He proceeded to demonstrate exactly what he meant.

* * * * *

In December 2001, look for
SECRET AGENT HEIRESS
by Julie Miller.

This exciting story will be
included in Harlequin Intrigue's
new in-line continuity,
MONTANA CONFIDENTIAL.

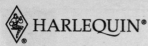

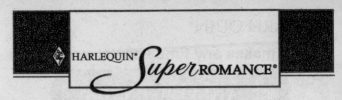

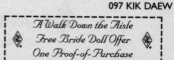

In a place that had been named for
paradise, evil had come to call....

HARLEQUIN®

INTRIGUE®

presents a brand-new trilogy
from bestselling author

AMANDA STEVENS

The sinister small-town shadows of Eden, Mississippi,
cast a community in the chilling grip of fear when
children go missing. Find out how together
they slay the beast in

EDEN'S
CHILDREN

THE INNOCENT
July 2001

THE TEMPTED
August 2001

THE FORGIVEN
September 2001

Available at your favorite retail outlet.

HARLEQUIN®
Makes any time special ®